PARADISE VALLEY

C.J. BOX is the winner of the Anthony Award, Prix Calibre 38 (France), the Macavity Award, the Gumshoe Award, the Barry Award, and the Edgar Award. He is also a *New York Times* bestseller. He lives in Wyoming.

ALSO BY C. J. BOX

PARADISE VALLEY

C. J. BOX

HEAD
of ZEUS

First published in the UK by Head of Zeus in 2017

Published by arrangement with St Martin's Press

Copyright © 2017 by C.J. Box

The moral right of C.J. Box to be identified
as the author of this work has been asserted in accordance with
the Copyright, Designs and Patents Act of 1988.

9 7 5 3 1 2 4 6 8

A catalogue record for this book is available from the British Library

ISBN (HB): 9781786693181
ISBN (TPB): 9781786693198
ISBN (E): 9781786693174

Printed and bound by CPI Group (UK) Ltd, Croydon, CR0 4YY

Head of Zeus Ltd
First Floor East
5–8 Hardwick Street
London EC1R 4RG

WWW.HEADOFZEUS.COM

For boys who dream . . .
and Laurie, always

And much of Madness, and more of Sin,
And Horror the soul of the plot.
—EDGAR ALLAN POE, "THE CONQUEROR WORM"

There's a killer on the road
His brain is squirming like a toad. . . .
—JIM MORRISON

PART ONE

GRIMSTAD,
NORTH DAKOTA
2017

ONE

"THE TRAP IS SET and he's on his way," Cassie Dewell said to Sheriff Jon Kirkbride. She was out of breath from mounting the stairs to the third floor instead of waiting for the elevator.

Kirkbride leaned back from his desk and cocked an eyebrow. His thick gunfighter's mustache obscured the expression on his lips, but his eyes narrowed. "The Lizard King?"

Cassie nodded her head furiously. She was both excited and scared. She was also hot and she peeled off her Bakken County Sheriff's Department fleece.

"You're sure it's him?"

She said, "I sent you a video link in an e-mail five minutes ago."

He frowned. The sheriff disliked communicating by e-mail. "What's in it?" he asked.

"Let me show you," she said. She shed the fleece in a chair and quickly advanced around the desk, and he rolled his chair back to accommodate her. She reached across him to toggle the space key on the keyboard to wake his computer up. She was aware that her hip was pressed against his right shoulder but she didn't care. Not now.

———

IT WAS TUESDAY, September fifteenth. Cassie had left the first set of footprints in the frost across the still-green grass of the Law Enforcement Center that morning. She hadn't even heard the loud honking from a V of geese descending through the river cottonwoods to the Missouri River. All indications were of an early winter.

Thirty-nine-year-old Cassandra "Cassie" Dewell was the Chief Investigator for the BCSD, and she knew the sheriff would be in his office early. He always was. Even though he had horses to feed and stalls to clean out, he was at his desk hours before the morning shift showed up. Judy Banister, Kirkbride's office administrator and the only other female within the agency, hovered just outside the door.

Cassie had been three years on the job. The apartment unit she'd first moved into when she arrived was in view outside Kirkbride's window, although it was now occupied by a deputy hired straight out of the law enforcement academy in Minnesota.

Kirkbride had been the sheriff when Grimstad had 8,000 residents and was losing population every year. The demographics of western North Dakota at that time were a mix of German and Scandinavian farmers and a few Scot ranchers. That was before hydraulic fracturing in the Bakken Formation produced twenty percent of the nation's oil and the county boomed beyond anyone's imagination. He was still the sheriff when the unofficial census swelled to 45,000 in town and 80,000 in the county, and his department had grown from four deputies to forty.

The sheriff had hired Cassie away from the Lewis and Clark County Sheriff's Department in Helena, Montana, and had made her promise she would stay with him until his official retirement at the end of the year—three and a half months away. Since his announcement, he'd made it clear to anyone who would listen that he wanted her to be his hand-picked successor. What he'd not done was ask Cassie what she thought about that.

Recently, she'd let her short brown hair grow to her shoulders and was debating with herself whether to color it to hide the gray strands that seemed to have shown up overnight. That, along with fifteen pounds that strained at her underwear and once-tailored uniform. Her own body, she thought, had recently conspired to make her unattractive and uncomfortable. Just in time for her wedding.

That's why she had sat down at her home computer that morning: to compose an e-mail to the dress shop in Bismarck asking them to delay sending her wedding dress until she could get up there and get re-measured. It was a miserable admission to make. But before she keyed in the request an incoming e-mail arrived.

It was from Wilson, North Carolina.

When she opened it an electrical charge shot through her.

Then her cell phone lit up. The call was from Wilson County Prosecutor Leslie Behaunek.

"It's him," Behaunek said. She was calling from her cell phone and Cassie imagined her walking fast down the courthouse hallway. "We've *got* him this time . . ."

Cassie forwarded the e-mail to her address at work as well as to Kirkbride.

THE SHERIFF HAD 198 unopened e-mails on his computer. Cassie guessed that was fewer than usual. She scrolled to the top of the list until she found her own address as sender. She clicked on the file.

It took a few seconds to load.

"I really need to get Judy to weed through those e-mails," Kirkbride grumbled. Then, "Okay, what are we looking at?"

The view was of dozens of tractor-trailers parked shoulder-to-shoulder in a lot. It was obviously nighttime. The viewing angle was from above the vehicles. The video feed was dark and grainy, and it appeared at first to be a still photograph. After watching it for a few seconds, though, exhaust from the stacks of the trucks curled up into the night air and occasionally a curtain would part from one of the sleeper cabs. There was no audio. The timestamp in the bottom right-hand corner said 10:53 PM.

She said, "This is from a closed-circuit security camera at a truck stop outside of Eau Claire, Wisconsin, last night."

Kirkbride was still. He was concentrating on the monitor.

"Watch the top left," Cassie said, pressing the tip of her index finger on the screen on a distant truck cab. Beneath her finger the passenger door opened and there were a few seconds of illumination from the inside dome lights as a thin woman appeared, framed by the door. She wore a short skirt that hiked up her thighs as she climbed down from the cab. In the harsh half-light her pencil-like legs looked as white as chalk. She vanished in the shadows between the trucks for a moment. A meaty naked arm appeared from the sleeper section of the cab and shut the door behind her.

"She's a truck-stop prostitute," Cassie said.

"I figured."

"They call them lot lizards."

"Got it," Kirkbride said. "That's where the guy gets his name."

"Right," she said. "Now I'm going to speed it up a little."

She clicked on fast-forward and the prostitute appeared to comically teeter from truck to truck on high heels. One by one, she sidled up to the driver's side of each vehicle and apparently knocked on the doors. The driver in the first truck didn't respond. The second driver flashed on his lights, saw who was out there, and turned them off again.

Before the prostitute could approach the side of the third truck someone—either a wife or companion driver—apparently saw the prostitute coming and unfurled a brassiere out the driver's side window and pinned it in place by rolling the window back up.

"That means, *'Beat it, lot lizard, there's a woman at home,'*" Cassie explained.

"Gotcha."

"Three refusals," Cassie said. "But now watch."

The prostitute moved parallel to the front bumper of the truck with the bra in the window and turned and walked between the third and fourth trucks. She was blocked from camera view by the side of the fourth truck.

"We can't see her, but we can assume she's standing between the two trucks negotiating with the driver in the fourth truck. If you watch closely, you can see the curtains rustle in the sleeper cab." Cassie pointed it out. "He's going to invite her in," Cassie said.

There was a glimpse of the prostitute through the passenger window—just a smudge of white—as she entered the cab and turned toward the sleeper cab.

"I couldn't see her very well," Kirkbride said.

"That's because he must have disconnected his dome light so none of the other truckers could see her get in. Why do you suppose he did that?"

Kirkbride didn't answer. He didn't need to.

"Note the time," Cassie said, pointing toward the time stamp. "It reads 10:58 PM."

Kirkbride nodded.

"I'm going to fast-forward again but it doesn't matter. You can see that nothing happens . . . until 11:17."

The only movement in the nineteen minutes was the crazy swirling of exhaust from the stacks of the idling trucks, a cat that seemed to skip across the pavement going left to right, and a vibration in the curtains of the sleeper cab.

Cassie poked the icon to slow the video to normal speed.

At 11:18, the headlights came on from the fourth semi followed by its running lights. The truck slowly pulled out of the slot, turned sharply, and drove out of camera view.

The space left by the departing truck was empty.

"She didn't get out," Kirkbride said. "She's still inside."

"We know his MO," Cassie said. "He's done this dozens of times—maybe hundreds of times. He gets them inside his truck and injects them with a syringe filled with Rohypnol. When she's comatose, he binds her up and drives her away. Either that, or he stashes them in the kill room he's built in his trailer that we discovered in North Carolina. But in this case, he can't risk taking her outside to put her in there . . . So he drives down the highway to a pull-out or rural road and *then* stashes her.

"It's his truck," she said. "Bright yellow Peterbilt 389 with a Unibilt Ultracab pulling a reefer trailer. North Dakota plates. It's him all right."

"Where did you get this clip?"

"Her name is Leslie Behaunek," Cassie said. "She's the county prosecutor in Wilson County, North Carolina. I met her last year when they flew me there to try and identify the Lizard King. Leslie felt guilty that he got away on a technicality and she blamed herself. Since then, Leslie and I made a pact to stay in touch and to finally get this guy. She's made contacts with law enforcement and truck-stop owners across the country. Her contact in Eau Claire sent her this just a couple of hours ago."

Kirkbride shook his head. "Why didn't this contact call the Wisconsin Highway Patrol?"

"Because by the time he saw this clip he knew the Lizard King was likely out of the state and hundreds of miles away. That's the thing—he's always moving. He's five states away by the time anyone realizes a prostitute didn't come home. That's why he's been impossible to catch."

"Do you think she's still alive?"

"I do," Cassie said. "He doesn't kill them right away. He likes to make videos of himself while he does it to watch later. The videos are his trophies. He assaults them, sometimes for weeks. That's his history. *Then* they disappear."

"And he's headed here to Grimstad?"

"Yes, sir."

"What's his ETA?"

She shot out her arm and checked her wristwatch. "Three hours, fifteen minutes. He should be here by eleven this morning."

"How do you know that?"

Cassie spoke fast. "He stopped at the weigh station in Hudson, Wisconsin at 1:10 AM. As you know, weigh stations are the bane of every trucker's existence and every state has to have them to make sure trucks are safe and overweight rigs don't pulverize their highways—and so they can check driver logs to make sure the truckers are in compliance and their log books are up to snuff. The truckers call them 'coops' like 'chicken coops' and the ones in Wisconsin are called 'badger coops.' Anyway, the station is unmanned that time of night but truckers have to drive through it and get weighed. When they're on the scales they get a photo of the DOT number of the truck on the door and the license plate and they go after the driver later if there's a weight issue."

She took a breath and tried to be calm. Kirkbride watched her warily.

"Anyway," she said, "it's ten hours from that weigh station to Grimstad. That puts him here at eleven."

"Assuming he drives the speed limit," the sheriff mused.

"Oh, he does," Cassie said. "And he never misses a weigh station, either. One thing we know about this guy is he's a stickler for rules and regulations because he doesn't want to get pulled over for something trivial. He knows that the only serial killer truck driver ever caught red-handed was when a state trooper in Arkansas pulled a guy over for a busted taillight and saw a human leg inside the cab. So our guy obeys every traffic law and regulation.

When he drove through Hudson his gross vehicle weight was seventy thousand pounds. So he was ten thousand pounds light."

"And you know he's coming here?"

"Yes."

"Cassie, how do you know that?" Kirkbride said, genuinely puzzled. Then: "Oh yeah, I remember now. You set up a scheme to lure him in."

"And he finally bit," Cassie said. "I actually talked to him myself."

"When?"

"Yesterday afternoon. He called from somewhere in Michigan. He said he was headed west. I didn't say anything to you at the time because there was no way to promise he'd follow through. Sometimes he's called—I recognized his voice—but he was shopping rates for the best deal and he never came. He's done the same to Leslie. But this time he texted a confirmation. He's coming. I alerted the highway patrol but told them not to intercede in any way. They're to report his progress only. He'll show up at Dakota Remanufacturing to pick up the load."

Kirkbride stroked his mustache. "If he texted you then we have his cell number. We can track down the location of the phone."

"No we can't," she said. "He uses burner phones he buys in bulk at truck stops. They don't have GPS chips. So when he calls the display reads UNKNOWN CALLER."

"I should have known," the sheriff said. "He's always a few steps ahead of us."

"Until now," she said.

"Have you called Tibbs?"

Avery Tibbs was the new county attorney. They both knew he might be a problem.

"Not yet."

"The FBI?"

"Not yet. I just got that confirmation text from him ten minutes ago and I came straight to you."

Kirkbride thought about that for a moment. Then he reached forward and plucked the handset from his landline. Before he hit the speed dial, he said, "I'll handle Tibbs. You call your Fed."

"Special Agent Craig Rhodine," Cassie added.

"Yeah, him."

"He's got a special team on call. I don't know how long it'll take him to get them geared up and on the plane."

"He's got a *plane?*" Kirkbride scoffed.

"A Boeing 727," Cassie said. "It's reserved for the FBI's Critical Incident Response Group."

His eyebrows rose. Kirkbride was always immediately suspicious of federal law enforcement intervention.

"The what?"

"The Critical Incident Response Group," she said. "From what I understand it's a group made up of a tactical assault squad, snipers, criminal profilers, attack dogs, and crisis managers. They show up in a 727 with blacked-out windows. Plus Rhodine himself, of course."

"Sounds like overkill," the sheriff said, more to himself than to Cassie.

"Don't forget who we're up against," she said.

"I haven't. How many years have you been after him?"

"Four," she said. "Well, three and a half."

"Will they get clearance at Sloukan?"

Sloukan Field Airport had once been located on the northeastern town limits of Grimstad before the growth of the community had overrun it. It was now in the middle of town surrounded by still-to-be-completed subdivisions.

"I don't know," she said, flustered. "I assume they'll take care of that themselves. I'll ask them."

"Don't forget we have commercial flights now," Kirkbride said.

She had no response. She had no idea why he was focusing on the flights that had been introduced to Bakken County by Delta and United to service the traffic generated by the oil boom when the Lizard King—also known as Ronald Pergram and Dale Spradley—was finally on his way directly to them.

"Jon . . ."

"I know, I know," he said, holding up his left hand. "I just worry about logistics. That's a lot of firepower coming into my little town."

As Cassie strode to the door Kirkbride called out to her to stop.

When she paused in the doorway, he said, "I've got a bad feeling about this, Cassie."

"Please don't say that." It hurt that he said it.

"Don't get me wrong," he said. "I'm with you. I trust you. I've got your back all the way. But this is happening fast. You've told me the Lizard King is smart as hell and he's gotten away more than once. He knows the law and he knows how to hire the best defense lawyers to keep him out of jail. I worry about not building a careful box around this guy. We can't screw up. We can't let him escape again."

Cassie turned and narrowed her eyes. "He won't get away this time."

"How do you know that?"

"Because," she said, "we're going to kill him if we have to."

Kirkbride was still. The phone was still in his hand, still poised halfway between the handset and his ear.

"Good thing I didn't hear that," he said.

CHAPTER

TWO

CASSIE LOOPED THROUGH AN EMPTY roundabout in her department Yukon and caromed out of it onto a wide suburban street called Abell Drive, after George T. Abell. She took a right on Erle Halliburton Way up to the driveway of her home, which was the only occupied house in the cul-de-sac. All of the streets in her new subdivision had been named after members of the Petroleum Hall of Fame based in Midland, Texas. One of the city council members had come up with that during the apex of the boom.

She'd purchased the split-level home before the bottom fell out of oil prices. Time had proved that she'd paid too much for it but she was stuck. There were five empty but finished houses on the cul-de-sac and scores of them within the subdivision. She'd wanted Ben to live in a real house with a real yard in a real neighborhood with other kids around, because he'd been the only boy his age in the county housing complex next to the Law Enforcement Center. Not that Ben seemed to mind, though. He liked interacting with the officers he saw in the elevator and hallways— all those uniforms and guns—and they seemed to like him.

Unfortunately, there were no other boys his age in the subdivision and only one other family, and they had a FOR SALE sign in their front yard.

She left the Yukon running and her door open and was about to charge up the steps to the door when she paused. Her heart was racing and she took a deep breath to try and calm herself.

Cassie turned on the porch and looked out at the Missouri Breaks in the valley below her. It was a cool and still fall morning and quite a contrast to the way she felt inside. Thick river cottonwoods fused with yellow and red clogged the banks far below and extended in a multicolor ribbon to the east as far as she could see. In the early mornings or at dusk she often saw white-tailed deer in the meadows beyond the trees, and there were always geese and ducks cruising above the treetops. One of the reasons she'd jumped at the chance to buy the house was because of the view. It reminded her a little of Montana, her home state, but with no mountains or elk. And in the fields beyond the river in every direction, oil wells winked at night, making Grimstad look much bigger from the air than it actually was.

"WHERE DID YOU GO?" her mother Isabel asked as Cassie entered the house. "I heard you talking to someone on your phone early this morning but when I got up and looked around you were already gone."

The *Grimstad Tribune* was opened in front of her on the kitchen table. The kitchen smelled of fresh coffee.

"The office," Cassie said, looking around for signs of Ben.

"He's getting dressed," Isabel said.

Cassie looked at her watch. They usually left for school by this time.

"You'll make it," Isabel said. "Just drive like you normally do."

"*Ben*," Cassie called in the direction of the stairs. "Let's go."

"Coming, mother," Ben responded from his bedroom upstairs. There was exasperation in his tone, plus the word *mother*, which was an unwelcome new addition to his repertoire.

"Coffee?" Isabel asked, not getting up.

"No time."

"Of course not," her mother said. She disapproved of people in a hurry, especially Cassie.

Isabel—she had always insisted Cassie call her by her made-up hippie name from the sixties instead of "mom"—had settled into Grimstad much better than Cassie had anticipated she would. The go-go atmosphere of rampant maleness and naked capitalism had somehow energized Isabel to become even more of a bulwark against both. Rather than throw up her hands in despair, Isabel had founded a small group of disaffected newcomers called "Progressive Grimstad" to agitate for larger budgets for social workers, homeless shelters, and a cooperative grocery store that sold non-GMO organic food. Cassie found herself agreeing with the need for the first two projects but was not enthusiastic about the third. Progressive Grimstad had made the proposals at county commission meetings and suggested that the funding should come from the "bloated" sheriff's department budget. The proposal was shot down although Cassie had hoped it would pass, and Isabel vowed to raise funds to renovate an empty building downtown to house social workers. Still, Sheriff Kirkbride was annoyed about the potential raid on his budget.

Plus—although Isabel wouldn't admit it to her daughter—Cassie suspected Isabel enjoyed the attention she received from oil field and construction workers when she ventured out in public with her flowing robes and waist-length silver hair. Although Isabel had always looked like an individual in Montana, she *really* stood out in North Dakota. And she was surprisingly effective in obtaining funding commitments from area businesses and newly wealthy landowners in the area.

Isabel liked standing out. Cassie often thought that if Isabel wasn't her mother she wouldn't have much to do with her at all. Too much drama, too many sharp opinions, too many high-minded causes that rarely produced any tangible results—until now. Isabel was on a mission.

Isabel had dragged Cassie around with her for eighteen years and when Cassie got her position in Grimstad she felt she needed to return the favor. And Isabel truly loved Ben.

"DID YOU GET BREAKFAST?" Cassie asked Ben when they were in the Yukon. He was wearing his daily uniform: baggy jeans, high-top Nikes, Grimstad Vikings hoodie, unshaped trucker cap. His backpack was on the floor near his feet.

"Not hungry," he said.

"That doesn't matter, Ben. We've talked about this. You *need* breakfast."

"I'm fine."

"I don't care," she said, shaking her head. "Tomorrow, you eat something. No argument."

He shrugged and looked out the window. Then: "So what's going down?"

"What do you mean?" she asked, stalling for time until they got to school.

"I'm not stupid," Ben said. "I know you've got those two cell phones. One is a normal phone and the other is for that trucker. I know you've gotten calls on that trucker phone and I can tell you're all worked up."

"I'm not worked up," she lied.

"So what's going on?" he asked.

She couldn't tell whether he was concerned for her or curious about the law enforcement operation itself. She guessed a little of both. She hoped it was more of the former since Cassie was all Ben had except for Isabel.

Ben's father and Cassie's husband Army Sergeant Jim Dewell had died during the Battle of Wanat in Afghanistan in 2008. Ben had never met his father but he always kept a photo of him in the camo uniform and helmet on his desk. Ben had recently written a paper for his English class entitled "Jim Dewell: Wartime Hero for Our Time." Cassie had read it with tears in her eyes. Ben wanted his father to be heroic in every sense. Cassie saw no reason to correct Ben's hopes, and she'd vowed to never do it although in fact Jim had enlisted in the military the day after he learned she was pregnant.

Jim was by no means a coward, though. He did his duty and he served his country with honor. He just didn't want the responsibility of being a dad.

"It's a big operation," Cassie said as she slid the Yukon into a line of cars nearing the school. "A sting."

Ben nodded because he'd been right. He said, "I wish I could come with you. I'll be sitting in a bunch of boring classes and you'll be out there doing something exciting. Kyle says you can learn more *not* going to school than you can learn *in* school."

"Kyle should keep his opinions to himself," Cassie said.

Kyle Westergaard was Ben's fourteen-year-old friend. Kyle had a mild case of fetal alcohol syndrome that primarily affected his ability to speak. Ben understood every word he said, though, and he looked up to him. Kyle had been involved in a tragic situation two years before when he lost his mother but bravely shot two gangsters, killing one of them. His status after that among boys Ben's age had grown almost mythic. Kyle, to his credit, didn't seem to notice, Cassie had observed.

"I hope he doesn't leave," Ben said to the passenger window as Cassie turned into the drive that took them to the front doors. It was slow going as parents in preceding cars dropped their kids off and reminded them of last-minute instructions.

"*What?*" Cassie asked, surprised.

Ben looked as if he'd been caught. "Nothing."

"Ben, what do you mean Kyle might leave? Is his grandmother moving away?"

"Naw, forget I said anything," Ben said.

They reached the drop-off zone. Cassie checked her mirror to see a dozen cars behind her. All, like her, were running late.

"Ben, are you keeping something from me about Kyle?"

"No," he said, reaching for the door handle. He wouldn't meet her eyes which meant he was lying. Lying was new, too. It started around the same time he started calling her *Mother* in that passive-aggressive tone of voice.

"Ben?"

"Hey, I gotta go."

"We'll talk tonight," she said sternly.

Ben couldn't get out of the Yukon fast enough. Before he closed the door he said, "You don't need to pick me up. I'll walk home after football practice."

"You're sure?"

"Yeah. Hey, good luck with your sting today."

She started to caution him to not say a word about it to anyone but he'd already closed the door, turned away, and joined a group of friends all wearing the same uniform.

Cassie glanced at the clock in the dashboard. Minutes she needed back had burned away.

THREE

WHEN CASSIE ARRIVED five minutes later at the Dakota Remanufacturing building located within an industrial park north of Grimstad there were already four sheriff's department vehicles in the front parking lot and she cursed out loud.

Word was already out about what was about to happen. She could only hope that the deputies had been off-channel and that the Lizard King wasn't monitoring police-band frequencies.

She pulled her department Yukon around the building to the back loading dock. Eight of the ten pallets of reconditioned and shrink-wrapped oil field parts were already there. She could see a forklift operator spearing the ninth pallet inside to move it to the dock as well.

At least that part was going right, she thought.

Cassie killed the engine and mounted the outside steps to the dock. She had her cell phone in one hand and a handheld radio in the other.

As soon as she entered the darkened warehouse she made out a small knot of deputies standing in the center of the vast concrete floor and she turned toward them. They could apparently tell by

the way she strode—her low heels clicked on the concrete floor—
that they were in trouble. Their conversation stopped.

"We got here as soon as we heard," Deputy Ian Davis said. The
former undercover officer was clean-cut and he looked good in
his uniform. He was of medium height and build and he had soft
brown eyes and a baby face that had been obscured by the beard
and long hair he used to wear. He looked ten years younger than
he was.

Standing with him in a scrum in the middle of the warehouse
floor were deputies J. T. Eastwood, Tigg Erger—both new hires—
and Fred Walker. Walker, like Davis, had four years under his
belt at the department. In Bakken County, that meant they were
wily old veterans.

She said, "Guys, you need to get your vehicles out of sight *right
now*. Anybody driving by this place will see them out front and
know there's a situation in progress."

The deputies exchanged guilty glances.

"Move them out one by one," she said. "Don't all of you peel
out at the same time or *that* will draw attention."

"So where do we put them?" Eastwood asked.

"Someplace else," she snapped. "There's at least four empty
buildings within a quarter of a mile. Guys, the Lizard King is
coming and there's a woman's life at stake."

Eastwood, Erger, and Walker slunk and grumbled toward the
front of the building where their vehicles were. Eastwood said
something that included the words "lot lizard" and Erger stifled a
laugh.

Davis stayed.

He said, "Cassie, are you okay?"

Her eyes flashed. "Of course I'm not okay, Ian. What do
you expect? I've been waiting four years for this. I *can't* screw
this up."

"Like I didn't know that," he said and smiled gently. Paternalistically, she thought. Then he reached out with both hands and rubbed the top of her shoulders.

She pulled back and raised the cell phone in her hand like a weapon. "Damn it, Ian. You know better than that. It's hard enough concentrating on what we're here for without you touching me."

"Sorry," he said, not losing the smile. "It's not like they don't know."

"Pretend they don't," she snapped. "Be professional. We're on thin ice as it is."

That stung him and he squared his shoulders. The smile was gone, replaced by guilt.

"You're right," he said. "I just want to watch out for you. I'm sorry."

"Quit saying you're sorry," she said, angry that now he had the ability to make her want to comfort *him*. She resented him for that. "We've got just a few more months of this. I know it's uncomfortable for you. It's uncomfortable for me, too. It's a problem. Then we're married and we have a whole set of new problems."

He nodded. They'd talked about it for months, that married county employees were prohibited from working together in the same department. He said he was eager to move on, maybe to the city, state, or federal law enforcement. He had an interview scheduled in three weeks with the DEA.

"I'll go move my car," he said.

"Please move mine while you're at it," she said, handing him her keys. It was a trivial command, one that he wouldn't have hesitated doing a year before when their roles were cleanly delineated. Before he asked her to marry him for the third time and she accepted.

Now, though, she felt like a dominatrix for asking. And Ian, no doubt, felt a little the same way.

She nodded and watched him walk away. He was a good man

with a good heart and she loved him in a way she didn't think she could ever love a man again. It wasn't the passionate over-the-top love she'd had for Jim Dewell when she was a young woman, but it was a kind of deep appreciation that came from being with a truly decent and kind man. He wasn't aggressively ambitious but she didn't need that. And he wasn't looking for a mother, but a partner. He didn't ask much of her and he was attentive to both Ben and her. Ian spent time with Ben doing boy things and Ben adored him. Even Isabel liked him. And Ian made Cassie laugh, which was perhaps the most important quality of all.

And she'd just sent him away with her keys in his hand.

She fought the urge to chase him down and hug him.

Instead, she called out, "Thanks for being here, Ian. I do appreciate it. But please cut me some slack. I'll try to hold it together. This," she said, gesturing to the warehouse, "might finally be happening."

He mumbled something that sounded conciliatory, but she couldn't make out the words.

CASSIE DUCKED INTO THE OFFICE of Judi Newman, the owner of Dakota Remanufacturing. Cassie still clutched her cell phone and radio.

It was obvious Judi had been watching Ian and her out on the warehouse floor through her window.

"Lucky you," Judi said.

"I probably don't deserve him." She meant it.

"Then send him my way." Judi laughed.

"Ben needs a man around maybe even more than I do."

Judi nodded.

"Thank you for getting those pallets out on the dock for pickup," Cassie said.

Judy leaned back in her chair. "Anything I can do to help. How much time until he gets here?"

"Two and a half hours."

"Wow."

In the last year, Judi Newman had taken over the company from her husband Russ who was in prison in Bismarck for human trafficking. He'd arranged for four underage prostitutes to arrive in Grimstad from Canada to entertain oil field workers and perhaps himself as well. Cassie and Ian Davis had been tipped to their arrival and they caught the girls climbing out of a van to meet Russ Newman in a fast food parking lot in Watson City. They'd arrested Russ and the trafficker from Alberta. The girls, all Asian, were turned over to U.S. Immigration and Customs Enforcement.

When Judi had called the sheriff's department to complain that she'd seen two of the girls giggling and buying makeup at Walmart, Cassie had driven to Dakota Remanufacturing to explain that ICE no longer enforced immigration laws and that it was as frustrating to local law enforcement as it was to her. They struck an instant friendship partly because they were about the only single women their age in Grimstad, which was twenty-to-one men to women. It became clear to Cassie right off that Judi wasn't unhappy at all to be rid of her husband Russ.

Cassie had told Judi about her history with the Lizard King and her scheme to draw him in. When Judi learned of the plan she promptly offered to use her firm as a front. Judi had read about the Lizard King on the Internet and she'd also heard references to him over the truck-dispatching channels she monitored at work.

"Have you been listening all morning?" Cassie asked, gesturing to the radio unit on a credenza behind Judi Newman.

"I have. I haven't heard anything unusual, She-Bear."

Cassie usually chuckled at the name but not now. Judi had been calling her "She-Bear" ever since she'd heard an angry trucker use the term for a female police officer in a rant as he rolled out of

Grimstad in his unit. Cassie had ticketed the driver for exceeding the speed limit on county roads after he blew by her in her civilian car. For a half hour after receiving the citation the driver complained over his radio about the "She-Bear" who had pulled him over. He was especially incensed that she asked to look through his cab and into his sleepover cab. He had no idea what she was looking for or why she was looking.

Cassie didn't mind the name because she liked to think she had the protective qualities of a she-bear when it came to her family and her principles. Nevertheless, she told no one including Ian about the nickname she'd been given by an angry truck driver.

"You'll need to get your people out of the building," Cassie said. "I don't want any of them to get hurt, including you. If we could borrow some uniform shirts for my guys that would be great, too. I'll write you a receipt for them."

"Don't worry about that," Judi said, waving it off.

"I'm sure one of our deputies knows how to drive a forklift. If not, we might need to ask your driver to give us a quick tutorial."

Judi agreed. "Any of the guys can do that. They load and unload about a dozen trucks a day. It used to be that all of the dirty equipment was coming in for us to clean up and retrofit for the Bakken. Now, we're shipping most of the pallets *out*. Things have changed, you know."

Cassie nodded. The boom had come so fast that it was hard for many of those who'd lived through it to grasp the fact that the oil field exploration activity had slowed to almost nothing. Judi Newman, though, had adapted her business to the new reality. She was now an oil field parts exporter rather than an importer.

"I'll call you as soon as it's over," Cassie said. "Will you be at home?"

"I'll be at the Wagon Wheel drinking dirty martinis," Judi said. "Maybe you can join me."

"Maybe," Cassie said, trying to grin. But she was so tense her mouth wouldn't let her.

"Looks like you need one now," Judi said, gathering up her coat.

SHERIFF KIRKBRIDE AND COUNTY ATTORNEY Avery Tibbs had entered the warehouse together and were striding toward the loading dock. Kirkbride was in his department fleece and Stetson. Tibbs wore a long overcoat that was usually open as it was now, Cassie observed. She speculated that Tibbs liked the coat because of the dramatic figure he cut when it flowed behind him as he walked.

It was an odd juxtaposition to see them together, Cassie thought. She knew they didn't get along at all. Kirkbride had vocally supported the old county attorney who'd been challenged by Tibbs in the past election. It had been a nasty campaign that was unusual in Bakken County, where elections had previously been low-key coronations of incumbent politicians. Tibbs had outspent the previous county attorney seven-to-one and had brought in political consultants from Bismarck to help sharpen his attack on the old man. It had worked and Tibbs won the seat by twenty-seven votes.

At his victory party, Tibbs had vowed to continue to "clean up Bakken County," which everyone took to mean that one of his goals was to replace the sheriff who'd been in office over twenty years. Kirkbride had backed the wrong horse.

"There she is," Tibbs said when he saw Cassie come out of Judi Newman's office. He turned on his heel toward her and the sheriff reluctantly followed.

Tibbs wore a dark gray suit and a lime-green tie. He had close-cropped hair, a thin face, tiny dark eyes that were usually in a squint, and a downturned mouth without visible lips. It was no secret that Tibbs planned to run for North Dakota's single U.S. Congressional seat within a year as a law-and-order candidate.

"Chief Investigator Dewell," Tibbs said as he approached Cassie, "you've got some serious explaining to do or I'll shut this whole thing down right now."

Cassie looked to Kirkbride who was a few steps behind Tibbs. Kirkbride rolled his eyes. He'd been trying to get along with the new county attorney but he wasn't very good about disguising his true feelings toward him.

Tibbs said, "I'm not real fond of the idea that I've got a cop who has been conducting a one-man vendetta against a target without ever once informing the County Attorney's office. I don't like finding out about it with *two hours' notice and the FBI on the way.*"

He stopped so close to Cassie she could smell his bodywash. It smelled pretty good, she thought. Maybe she could get Ian to . . .

"I don't like it either," she said. "I'd just about given up on the chance that it would *ever* happen, much less this quickly. This is the first time everything finally fell into place."

Tibbs took a deep breath and when he did his narrow eyes squeezed together so tightly Cassie couldn't tell if the man could see her.

He said, "The sheriff said you've been baiting this trap for quite some time."

"Four years," Cassie said. "I briefed the former CA on it when we began. I assumed . . ."

"Never assume," Tibbs interrupted. "When you assume you make an 'ass' out of 'u' and 'me.' If you didn't get that, I just spelled 'assume.'"

Behind him, Kirkbride rolled his eyes again.

Cassie said, "I've got to get our team in place and we've got a lot of work to do here. I'm going to run out of time explaining everything. What do you want to know?"

Tibbs jabbed a single finger at Cassie. "Do not use that tone with me."

"What. Do. You. Want. To. Know?" she said. She wanted to reach up and bend his finger back.

Tibbs said, "I know about the Lizard King or whatever he's called. The sheriff told me all about him on the way over and he told me you had a traumatic experience with him back in Montana. He told me you killed a dirty Montana State Trooper in a shoot-out but the Lizard King got away. And he told me that you were flown to North Carolina two years ago when they had a suspect in custody they thought was your guy, but the case against him was botched from the start.

"What I need to know," Tibbs said, "is if that's going to happen again here. Are we going to bring this guy in under false pretenses only to have him released again? You know who will be on the hook if that happens, don't you?"

"I do," Cassie said.

"That's right—me. You're handing me a case that could make or break me in the eyes of the voters."

She nodded.

He paused. Behind him, Kirkbride looked away.

"Tell me how you got him to agree to come here," Tibbs said.

"He's an independent trucker," Cassie said. "That means he doesn't work for a long-haul firm and he doesn't even contract with a dispatching service that takes a cut of every load he delivers. There are reasons for that beyond the fact that he likes to be his own boss. He is an Indy because there's nobody out there tracking his movements through GPS or the other devices trucking companies use. That means he can travel across the country and stay off the grid. He's on nobody's clock but his own. That gives him the space he wants to abduct, torture, and dispose of the women he picks up.

"Independent truckers have to survive by their wits," she said.

"They get their freight jobs from log-board monitors found in just about every truck stop in the country or on the Internet. It's all about keeping that trailer full at all times to maximize income. If they're lucky, they find a job close to where they unloaded their last freight so they aren't deadheading anywhere."

When Tibbs cocked his head to indicate he was puzzled, she said, "Deadhead means driving with an empty trailer. It's a money-suck for a driver."

"How do you know so much about truckers?" Tibbs asked.

"My dad was a trucker," she said. "I used to go on runs with him. Anyway, an Indy always hopes he can fill his trailer with a full load from one place. That way, he doesn't have to travel LTL— less than a load—for very long. But it doesn't happen very often. Indies have to constantly look for freight that will fill them up along the way."

She gave the example of a Washington State farmer who had fifteen pallets—truckers called them "skids," she said—to deliver to a small grocery chain in Boston. Most trailers could handle twenty-three skids before they were full. Rather than contract with a large trucking firm for a once-a-year job the big firm wouldn't be enthusiastic about because of the "short" load, the farmer posted the information on a log board specifying the quantity of apples, the number of skids, where the apples were to be picked up, and when they had to be delivered. If an independent trucker was in the Pacific Northwest and saw the post he could call the farmer and negotiate a rate. If both parties agreed, the trucker would load the apples into his refrigerated truck first and start driving cross-country.

"But the trucker only has fifteen skids," she said to Tibbs. "He won't make much money on the run unless he can supplement that load with eight skids of something to fill his truck. Let's say he sees that a sugar beet processor in Wyoming has eight pallets of pulp to deliver to a warehouse in New Bedford, Mass., fifty-nine miles from Boston. The Indy does the math: If he drives south into Wyoming en route to Boston and picks up the pulp he can drop it off in New Bedford and get paid on the way to Boston. That's the kind of situation an independent trucker is in every single day on the road and the good ones can make a lot of money by avoiding LTL situations."

"Okay . . ." Tibbs said impatiently.

She said, "Our target is independent—we know that. He doesn't have a home and he's constantly on the move. He's scouring the log board every single day. Our plan was to put a small but profitable offer out there: ten skids of remanufactured oil field parts to be picked up in Grimstad for delivery in Portland, Oregon. It's an easy run especially for a trucker already going east to west. We were banking on the possibility that he'd be coming through with room in his trailer one of these days."

"But that's crazy," Tibbs said. "How did you know this particular trucker would bite?"

Cassie shrugged. "We just played the odds. There aren't that many purely independent truckers out there anymore. It's too tough a business on your own unless you just aren't capable of working for anyone or you have another agenda. So every few days my friend Leslie in North Carolina would bait the trap on the log board. The number to call was this dedicated cell phone," she said, showing him the phone. "I got hundreds of calls I had to turn down at all hours of the night. We hoped that he'd call eventually."

Tibbs shook his head. "How did you know it was him?"

Cassie and Kirkbride exchanged a look, and Cassie said, "I'm probably the only woman who has ever heard his voice who is still alive to identify him."

Tibbs turned to Kirkbride for affirmation. Kirkbride nodded.

"This is the first time everything has fallen into place," Cassie said. "After he called we got the video clip from Eau Claire, so we know he's got a victim. Then we tracked his truck in Hudson so we know he's on his way. I was always worried that he'd finally show up here and the FBI would search his truck for trace evidence and find nothing again. But this time we know he's got a girl with him."

"What if he already dumped her?" Tibbs asked. "Then what?"

"It's possible," Cassie said, "although the timeline works against him if he's on his way here. The Lizard King steam cleans his kill room in his trailer and power washes his cab so there's no evidence. That's why we couldn't nail him when we had him the first time. But he hasn't had time to do that since last night and still get here when he agreed to show up. Even if he killed her and dumped the body along the highway, the FBI will find traces of her in his rig. And we'll nail him.

"Now, if you don't mind," she said, backing away, "we have a lot of work to do before he gets here."

"Hold it," Tibbs said. "How sure are you it's him? All you have to go on is his voice."

She thought about it. "Ninety-eight percent." She thought, *I'll never forget that voice.*

The Lizard King—aka Ronald Pergram aka Dale Spradley—had a naturally high-pitched prairie voice he tried to disguise by lowering it to guttural level and speaking slowly and deliberately with an indecipherable drawl. He'd gotten quite good at it over the years, and only when she confronted him in North Carolina did he let it slip. He, like Cassie, was from Montana. He had a flatness to his words and a cadence while speaking she was familiar with from growing up around it.

"And if you're wrong?" Tibbs asked. "Then we arrest an innocent trucker in a huge display of force and find out there's no evidence in his truck to prove he did anything wrong. At best it's a public embarrassment and at worst we're talking about a civil suit for assault, battery, and false arrest or a Section 1983 claim."

"I'll take that chance," Cassie said.

Tibbs jabbed his finger at Cassie. He said, "If I go down I'm taking you down with me."

"Understood."

Tibbs wheeled around and faced Kirkbride. "You too," he said.

CASSIE'S PERSONAL CELL PHONE BURRED and she looked at it. Both Tibbs and Kirkbride observed her carefully.

She took the call, listened, and punched off.

She said, "A state trooper east of Dickinson just ID'd his truck. He should be here in two hours."

"Oh, man," Tibbs said. "We're really going to do this, aren't we?"

"You bet we are," Kirkbride said.

FOUR

"SO WHERE IN THE HELL is he?" Tibbs asked impatiently from the backseat of Sheriff Kirkbride's unmarked Yukon. "He's a fucking hour late."

"I know," Cassie said, checking her watch.

They were parked tightly alongside an abandoned pipeline distributor building a hundred yards from Dakota Remanufacturing. The location gave them a good view through the windshield of the loading dock but they'd be out of sight to an approaching semi. Kirkbride had checked out two other locations before deciding this one was the best. The sheriff was behind the wheel, Cassie next to him in the passenger seat.

"Maybe he stopped for lunch or fuel," Kirkbride offered.

"Or maybe he got wise to us," Tibbs said. "Maybe he got scared off? Or maybe he was *never even coming in the first place?*"

"Please," Cassie said. She glanced at her second cell phone—the one she thought of as her "trucker phone"—to see if the Lizard King had called or sent a text about being late. Nothing.

"Maybe I should text him and ask him for his ETA?" she said. "I mean, it would be normal to do that, right?"

Kirkbride shrugged. He didn't know. He said, "Give him an-other ten minutes. We don't want him to think we're too anxious."

She agreed with that and raised binoculars to her eyes. She wished she could also raise something to her ears to block out the running commentary from the county attorney in the backseat.

CASSIE WAS FEELING the heat.

Because all communication was off-channel to avoid the risk of the Lizard King picking them up over the radio, the last hour and a half had been a blizzard of cell-phone calls between all the principals involved in the sting. At one point she was receiving three calls at once.

The editor of the *Grimstad Tribune* had left two messages say-ing he'd heard rumors of a major bust about to occur. Cassie ig-nored him.

The FBI's 727 was due to land in fifteen minutes. Special Agent Rhodine wanted to know who would meet him at the airport and how many vehicles would be available after landing to ferry men and equipment to the industrial park. The answer to that was: *None. He'd just have to wait.*

Ian Davis had called to ask how many times he was supposed to pretend he was delivering the tenth pallet to the loading dock after he'd done it twelve times. The idea was to have what looked like normal industrial activity going on when the Lizard King ar-rived. Cassie had hidden her distress when she learned Ian was posing as the forklift operator since he'd be exposed, but she held her tongue. Pulling him off the detail and replacing him with another officer would result in a hellstorm of controversy and second-guessing about preferential treatment of her fiancé.

The answer to Ian's question was: *Just keep taking that pallet out over and over like you're doing it for the first time.*

The remaining six deputies on-site needed to know who was

playing the dock foreman, clipboard in hand, who would actually approach the Lizard King in his cab. The other five would disperse with two men hiding within the warehouse on the left side of the loading dock door and three men on the right. All would be armed with shotguns or AR-15s. No one was to fire unless someone saw a threatening move by the driver.

Answer: *Fred Walker was to play the foreman, J. T. Eastwood and Tigg Erger would be on the left, and deputies Jim Klug, Tom Melvin, and Shaun McKnight would be on the right.*

Cassie had briefed all the deputies before leaving with Kirkbride and Tibbs, reiterating that the Lizard King was armed and dangerous. He was known to pack a Taurus .380 ACP semi-automatic pistol as well as tools that included a Taser, hypodermic syringes filled with Rohypnol, an array of knives and bone saws. And who knew what other weapons he may have added recently, she said.

She'd gone over their roles and asked them all to repeat back to her what she'd said. Walker would ask the driver to climb out of his cab under the pretext there were bills of lading and other paperwork to sign. That act alone might trigger a suspicion in the Lizard King, she explained, because often drivers never even left their vehicle as they were loaded.

If the driver *did* get out, the deputies were to rush him from two sides with weapons drawn. Cassie said she wanted their target facedown on the asphalt, searched, and cuffed. No one was to play cowboy. No one was to play hero.

If for some reason the Lizard King caught on to what was happening and decided to drive away, Kirkbride was to roar out from the side of the abandoned building and block the exit out of the yard. Four deputies in SUVs and two state troopers were on call, ready to flood the yard with vehicles and weapons as needed. Spike strips were unpacked and ready to deploy on the roads leading out of town if it came to that.

While they waited and minutes passed, she asked her team to repeat the plan back to her one more time.

"AN HOUR AND A HALF," Tibbs fumed. "Call the guy or we'll abort this whole charade."

Cassie's chest hurt and there was a slow rolling boil in her stomach. Her cell phone vibrated across the dashboard of the Yukon—another call from Rhodine, who was incensed that no one had been at the airport to meet him.

As she reached for the phone Kirkbride quietly said, "Ignore it. Here he comes."

She looked up to catch a one-second snapshot of the yellow Peterbilt 389 as it sliced between the space of two buildings a block away. The truck was driving from right to left and was now blocked by the structure they were hiding next to.

"That looks like him," she whispered.

She wanted to grab the radio mike and alert everyone, but she couldn't risk it. Instead, she hoped her team hadn't lost focus because of the delay and would get ready the second they saw the big rig.

"Don't forget to breathe," Kirkbride said to her while they waited.

For once, Tibbs was quiet in the backseat.

CASSIE REFUSED THE CALL from Rhodine so she could clear her line and speed-dialed Walker who was inside the warehouse. She activated the speaker on her phone so Kirkbride could hear the entire conversation. She appreciated how much the sheriff trusted her to lead the operation without stepping in.

"Do you see him?" Cassie asked Walker.

"I've got eyes on him," Walker said. "He's coming down Maple right in front of us on the other side of the fence. He's about a hundred feet from the gate."

"Can you see the driver?"

"No. The windows are dark."

"Do the guys know it's on?" she asked.

"Affirmative. They're locked, loaded, and ready to rumble."

On cue, she saw Ian wheel out of the darkness of the warehouse with the tenth pallet on the forks of his machine. He didn't look tense or jumpy, and she wondered how he was capable of that. He hadn't even glanced toward the yellow Peterbilt.

"He's slowing down in the yard," Walker said.

"Why is he slowing down?" Tibbs demanded from the backseat. There was panic in his voice.

"Doing a three-point turn," Walker said. "So he can back up to the dock like he's supposed to."

Cassie could hear the grinding of the gears of the Peterbilt although she couldn't yet see the truck.

"Back her on in here, big boy," Walker said to no one in particular.

The big silver trailer behind the yellow tractor aimed at the open dock door and moved into view just as Ian Davis lowered his pallet near the rest of the load. Hydraulic brakes wheezed as the rear of the trailer pulled within inches of the dock.

Cassie could hear the rumble of the huge diesel engine as it idled. From the angle they were sitting at she could see just the back half of the sleeper cab but not the front of the cab where the Lizard King sat.

Kirkbride, on her left, had a better view.

"Is it him?" she asked.

"Can't tell," he said. "I can see there's a profile but I can't see his face."

Then Walker said, "Okay, I'm going to go get the man himself to sign my paperwork."

Walker punched off.

"Damn it," she cursed. "He turned his phone off. I wanted him to keep it on so we can hear his conversation with the driver."

"Call him," Tibbs said.

"Not now," she said. "Not with him this close to the cab."

Walker emerged from the warehouse and walked across the dock to the stairs on the side. He carried his clipboard and looked natural, she thought. His Dakota Remanufacturing coveralls were a little baggy and open in front. She guessed he'd done that so he could reach inside easily for his weapon if need be.

She couldn't see the deputies on either side of the opening. That was good.

Cassie leaned into Kirkbride so she could see better and the sheriff squished himself into his door so she could.

Walker strode the length of the big truck and knocked on the driver's side door and stepped back.

"Be careful," she whispered.

The massive flash was followed a quarter-second later by the boom as the cab of the truck blew out and up. The ground shook with the explosion and rocked the Yukon back on its springs.

Then shards of metal and grass rained down. A football-sized piece of steel bounced off the windshield and shattered it.

There was a beat before the fire in the cab ignited the dual 125-gallon fuel tanks on each side of the rig.

It was later reported that the resulting fireball could be seen as far as Watson City, twenty miles away.

CASSIE FELT HEAT on her face from the fire as she jogged toward the burning truck. Curls of black smoke roiled into the sky and small flakes of gray ash fell around her like snow.

Walker's body was splayed out on its back twenty feet from

where he'd stood to receive the driver. His arms and legs were bent in grotesque angles, and his coveralls were on fire.

She stopped and raised her arm to her face to protect it from the blistering heat.

The trailer behind the cab was now on fire as well, and she thought about the prostitute from Wisconsin who was likely in the tiny kill room directly behind the cab.

Behind her, Tibbs shouted, "Oh my God, oh my God, what just happened?"

She turned around to see if the county attorney was right behind her, but he wasn't. He was still in the Yukon.

Sheriff Kirkbride was out, though. But instead of standing behind her he was down on his knees, his hat knocked off, holding his face in his hands. Blood poured through his fingers.

Then she thought of Ian.

The forklift on the dock had been blown over on its side. There was no sign of him in the cage of the equipment or on the dock itself.

There was panicked shouting and cursing from inside the warehouse.

Someone yelled, *Officer down, officer down* . . .

FIVE

"WHAT WAS *that*?" Raheem Johnson asked Kyle Westergaard after the ground shook with two explosions. "It was like *bang* and then *BOOM*. Something really blew up, bro."

Kyle nodded and looked over his shoulder in the direction the sounds had come from. The concussions had quieted the ducks preening themselves on the river and squelched the squirrels in the trees, and for the moment, the silence was awesome. Dried leaves floated down from river cottonwoods as if shaken loose. He'd felt the impact through the soles of his worn Nikes.

Kyle said he didn't know what had blown up but that it sounded like it'd come from Grimstad.

"No shit," Raheem said. Then: "This might be good. It might work for us."

Kyle was thinking the same thing. "Let's get the boat packed and get it in the water."

THE TWO FOURTEEN-YEAR-OLDS HAD BRIBED a neighbor of Raheem's named Burt with a twelve-pack of Busch

Light beer to load the fourteen-foot wooden flat-bottomed john-boat into the back of his pickup and take it down to the timbered bank of the Missouri River two days before. Burt was fat and un-shaven and he apparently lived on disability paychecks from the oil company he'd been employed by at one time. He lived next door to Raheem and he was always at home with his television set on. Burt liked game shows and baseball games at high volume. And he liked the Busch Light that Raheem had stolen from his father's stash in the garage.

The boat was much heavier than Kyle had suspected and it took the three of them to lift it into the bed where they secured it with rope and bungee cords. The two boys rode in the open boat in the back of the truck and directed Burt down to the river.

After unloading the craft, Burt left with his beer and the boys piled branches and debris on it so it wouldn't be spotted easily from the two-track that paralleled the river. For the next two days they'd used their bikes and a four-wheel ATV to ferry gear they'd need from town to where the boat was cached. It took fourteen trips back and forth before they had everything down there that matched Kyle's checklist.

The river bottom itself fascinated Kyle. It was a different, wilder world than he was used to. While the prairie in all direc-tions was flat and treeless and marked only by old farmhouses and silos and new directional oil rigs, the river bottom was an impen-etrable jungle of thick cottonwoods, dense brush, and the hushed flow of the river. White-tailed deer ghosted through the trunks of the trees at dawn and dusk, then vanished within the undergrowth.

Both Kyle and Raheem lived in fear they'd be discovered be-fore they could push off. So many things could go wrong. Some-one could see them taking duffel bags and equipment down to the river and call them out. Someone could be driving down there along the bank and find the boat and steal it or vandalize it.

Raheem's dad could discover his missing twelve-pack, the $600 gone from the shoebox on the top shelf of the closet, or realize the johnboat that had been on the side of his house when he bought it three years before was now gone. Or Ben Dewell, Kyle's twelve-year-old friend, could squeal on the two of them to his own mother or Kyle's Grandma Lottie.

Kyle was still stinging from telling Ben *no*. Ben had been upset and asked why.

"Twelve is too young," Kyle said.

"When you were the same age you shot two men," Ben said.

Kyle had no good response for that but explained that there truly wasn't enough room in the fourteen-foot boat for three bodies plus all the gear.

Ben complained and threatened to blow the whistle on Kyle and Raheem.

But it hadn't happened.

Kyle felt blessed. He felt like the explosions they'd heard in town would distract attention away from them. Especially when sirens filled the air a few minutes later.

"LET'S HURRY," KYLE SAID.

Raheem nodded and bounced up and down on the balls of his feet. He did that when he had nervous energy. Raheem had a lot of nervous energy. He let Kyle do the thinking most of the time, though. When it came to the great adventure the two boys planned to take on the Missouri River, Raheem deferred completely to Kyle because it had been Kyle's obsession in the first place.

For over three years, ever since he'd seen the old black-and-white photo of Theodore Roosevelt chasing down a pair of boat thieves on the Missouri, Kyle had wanted to set off on the river. He'd started a list of things he would need and kept the list, and

the gear he could find, hidden in his bedroom and in a part of
Grandma Lottie's garage she never checked out.

The list started with:

Sleeping bags
Food (jerkie jerky, crackers, things like that)
Fishing poles and tackel tackle
Rain coats
~~Binokulars~~ Binoculars
Pistol or rifle (animals, hoboes)
Journal for writing
Map
Knife
X-tra clothes
Swimming trunks
Rope
Tent
Plates and utensuls utensils
Matches
Oars (get B4 summer)
Cell phone
Money

And went on to include a camp stove, sleeping mats, freeze-
dried stew, a pump water purifier, cooler, books (including a paperback of *The Adventures of Huckleberry Finn* he'd struggled with
and hoped would make more sense once he was on the river), an
iPod for music (which Raheem had been loading with hip-hop
and country), and dozens of other items. Kyle had started the list
years before and had corrected a few words he'd misspelled earlier
but he was still a poor speller.

The discovery of a beat-up Marlin .22 bolt-action rifle with a
seven shot magazine was like discovering a pirate's buried trea-

sure for Kyle. It had been propped in the corner of a garage of an abandoned house along with a hundred rounds of ammunition.

The load got so big that Kyle added a new item: *supply raft*. They'd lash a gear-laden raft to the boat itself and tow it down the river.

Kyle had located nearly every item on his checklist in garbage cans and Dumpsters that he'd looted in the alleys of Grimstad during the summer and before and after school. He was always astonished at the value and importance of things people threw away. The pickings were the best when the price of oil dropped and people moved away. Often, they simply piled perfectly good stuff on their driveways just before they drove out of town.

Like the brass sextant Kyle found in one pile. He couldn't believe it. Although Kyle didn't know how it worked, he knew a sextant could be valuable for on-the-water navigation.

Still, though, Kyle felt uprepared. He'd never actually spent time on a boat or gone overnight camping except in Grandma Lottie's backyard. He knew there would be dams and other obstacles to be negotiated somehow, and he had little knowledge and less experience to deal with them. But he recalled Ben's mom Cassie saying to him that he'd "been dealt a bad hand since Day One but that never seemed to hold him back." He liked that.

And he hoped she was right.

RAHEEM HAD BEEN THRILLED that morning when Kyle peddled his bike to his house on the way to school and said, "Today is the day."

Raheem surprised his father by going back inside and hugging him and saying goodbye. Apparently, he hadn't done that for a while.

For his part, Kyle had left a short letter on Grandma Lottie's kitchen table. Monday morning was when she left for her weekly appointment to get her hair done.

It read:

>*Grandma Lottie:*
>
>*I won't be home after school because today I am going on a great adventure. I want to see more of the country than North Dakota but don't think I don't like North Dakota because I do. I want to see what's out there in the world on my own.*
>
>*It has nothing to do with you. I love you and you're great. Please don't be sad.*
>
>*I can't tell you where I'm going or you'll try to get me back. I'll come back but not for a while.*
>
>*I borrowed $120 from your drawer. I'm sorry and I'll pay you back twice that when I can. I'll send you the money when I can. We needed to get going before it got too cold and icy.*
>
>*This was nobody's idea but mine.*
>
>*Love,*
>
>*Kyle*

AS THEY TIED the supply raft to the stern of the johnboat, Kyle looked up. A dark curl of smoke from town was rising above the tops of the dense cottonwood trees near the river. The sirens howled so relentlessly he had to shout.

"Did you get my map?"

Raheem pointed to his ear indicating he couldn't hear.

"*My river map.*"

His friend understood and gestured to a thick flat Ziploc bag pressed down by a strap to the top of a duffel bag. Kyle nodded his approval.

The map consisted of pages he'd ripped out of an atlas from

the school library. It looked like a pretty good map and Kyle wanted it handy even though he had the route memorized.

They'd float downriver to Lake Sakakawea and on to Bismarck. Then they'd exit North Dakota into South Dakota: Mobridge, the Cheyenne Indian Reservation, Pierre, the Lower Brule Indian Reservation, Yankton, and Vermillion. Sioux City, Iowa, was the next big town, followed by Omaha. Then St. Louis where the river joined the Mississippi. Then south to Memphis and New Orleans.

He'd never even been to South Dakota before, where the exotic place names (*Pierre!*) started. And beyond that it got even more exciting. Kyle couldn't even imagine what Memphis must be like.

And Raheem had shown him YouTube videos of women in New Orleans lifting up their shirts to expose their breasts in the street.

What he didn't want was for the boat and raft to be caught up in the heavy ice floes. Even though Theodore Roosevelt had somehow done it in March of 1886, Kyle couldn't imagine floating downriver surrounded by huge sheets of ice.

September was kind of late already, he knew. The weather could turn any day.

Even if they made good time it would take months, Kyle figured. But every mile they'd be further south and it would get warmer.

That was fine with him.

IT WAS AWKWARD AT FIRST, with Raheem on the oars in the middle of the boat stroking like crazy. They were both wet to above their knees just from shoving the boat and raft out into the water and climbing inside.

The boat veered left and an overhanging branch nearly swept them into the water. The supply raft swung out in a swift current and was bobbing ahead of them on the river.

Neither Raheem nor Kyle had rowed a boat before. Raheem was bigger, though, and much stronger, so it made sense he was on the oars. Unlike Kyle who was two grades behind him although the same age, Raheem was an athlete. He had long arms and legs and ropey muscles. He ran track and played football and basketball at their middle school. Recently, he'd decided to let his hair grow out naturally and it looked like a small black bush on his head, Kyle thought. Raheem kept his back to the bow and pulled hard and the boat went this way and that.

"This ain't working worth shit," Raheem said after he'd thumped the front of the boat into a half-submerged stump. "I can't see anything."

Kyle wasn't sure what to do. He was seated in the back facing Raheem. It was hard to see through his friend or over the bow of the boat to call out hazards. And he couldn't move to the front because they'd stacked it high with their gear. He was glad there were no rapids in the water like he'd seen on television or they'd already be swimming for their lives, he thought.

"You gotta help me with directions," Raheem said to Kyle. He was already breathing hard from rowing so hard.

Kyle asked to try it.

Raheem rolled his eyes but the two changed places. The boat rocked from side to side as they did.

Kyle sat on the wooden bench facing the front. Rather than row, he dipped his right oar into the river until it got stiff to the touch. The bow of the boat swung that direction. When he raised the oar the boat continued to float on a line.

"We don't have to fight the river," Kyle said. "We can let the current pull us along. It's fast enough that all we need to do is steer and keep us away from the trees on the bank and the rocks in the river."

Raheem said he was impressed.

The boat overtook the supply raft and soon the raft was behind them were it was supposed to be.

The sirens got louder as they floated through Grimstad. Kyle caught glimpses of sheriff's department SUVs with their lights flashing up on the bluffs. The column of smoke was now flattening out in the sky and it looked like a giant black T.

He glanced at the few homes along the river as they floated by, hoping no one was looking out at them. He was glad they had waited until Monday, until school resumed, before they embarked on the adventure. There were fewer people out and about during the week.

AFTER HALF AN HOUR, the sirens faded although he could still hear them in the distance behind the boat. The quiet hush of the river took over: slow flowing water, the lap of it against the hull of the boat, a splash when he lowered one oar or the other.

The sun broke out of the clouds and bathed them in yellow light. The river turned from dark gray to green in an instant. Just as fast, the temperature seemed to warm ten degrees.

As they floated around the first big bend they encountered a dozen geese who paddled ahead of them in formation. When the boat got closer a secret signal was sent and they all took off in a noisy cacophony of honks and flapping wings.

"That was cool," Raheem said. "Where's that .22? Maybe we ought to shoot one of 'em and have goose for dinner, bro."

"Do you know how to cook a goose?"

"No," he laughed.

"Me either."

Kyle recalled the only time he'd ever seen a dead goose. It was two years before when his mother was alive and living with T-Lock, her boyfriend at the time. T-Lock's pal Winkie went hunting and brought them a huge dead goose. Kyle had never seen such a huge bird up close before. He'd been fascinated with the depth of the feathers on its breast and the size of its stiff black feet.

When Winkie left, T-Lock marched the carcass out to the dumpster and threw it inside.

T-Lock, Winkie, and his mother. All dead.

To Kyle, it sometimes seemed like he'd made them up in the first place.

KYLE COULDN'T GET over the feelings that grew within him as they floated further away from town. The river sounds came into sharper focus. The early fall colors of the trees seemed more vibrant. He could smell the musky vegetation on the banks and the cold metallic odor of the river itself.

The whole world was opening up in front of him, it seemed.

When he looked over at Raheem he could see that his friend felt the same way. He was beaming.

"This is so fucking cool I can't believe it," Raheem said. He was lounging in the back of the boat with his feet propped up on the bench seat and his fingers trailing in the water.

"Just think," Raheem said. "We could have been in that school right now doin' nothing. But look at us. LOOK AT US!"

Kyle grinned and closed his eyes for a moment, drinking it in.

SIX

TWENTY MINUTES BEFORE and a half mile away from the industrial park, Amanda Lee Hackl was washing breakfast and dinner dishes in the sink of her kitchen when she heard a distant *boom*. Then another, bigger *boom* that shook the glass in the window over the sink and rattled the china in her hutch.

With her hands in the warm water, she leaned forward and peered out the window and squinted. There was nothing much to see: empty lots in a subdivision on a bluff filled with wide empty streets and unfinished houses and lots stacked with building materials that were starting to gray and warp from exposure to the sun and the weather. It was obvious that the subdivision had been created rapidly, started, and then stopped.

That she and Harold were the only actual residents on the block could be chalked up to her husband's unerring gift for bad timing in all things financial. She was still bitter about it. He'd convinced her to pour their life savings into the down payment of the show home they now lived in before the developer finished the subdivision. That way, Harold said, "they'd be on the ground floor of something great!" So they sold their double-wide and moved.

A month later, the bottom of the oil market fell out and the developer and his employees scattered into the wind.

When asked where her home was located, Amanda liked to say that she lived in the "Subdivision of Sadness." Especially when Harold was there to hear her say it.

So hearing anything outside, especially two explosions that rocked the house, was unusual and, she thought, interesting.

Because it gave her something to do.

AMANDA WAS A STOCKY BROWN-HAIRED woman wearing a Santa Claus sweatshirt, jeans, and Crocs. She loved the Christmas season so much that she decorated her house earlier every year and she wore festive clothing in the early fall because it made her happy. Now that she'd been laid off from her job at Walmart she had very little to do after Harold went to his job delivering parts in the Bakken. She'd tried to knit, quilt, sew, and do needlepoint, but she found out she hated them all. She'd listened to nearly every audiobook in the Bakken County Library, many of them twice.

There were no neighbors to gossip with and there were only so many days she could drive downtown and funnel through Main Street with oil field traffic and not lose her mind.

Today she couldn't even do that because Harold's truck wouldn't start in the garage that morning—he'd left his pickup door ajar all night and the battery ran down—so he'd taken her 2009 Kia Spectra to work. So she was stuck, in more ways than one.

She dried her hands on a towel while she walked through the living room and out through the front door.

Amanda noted that the framed high school graduation photographs of her two children—stolid, married Brian and divorced, frowsy Tammy—were tilted at odd angles on the wall as a result of the explosions. She made a note to herself to straighten them later.

She stood on her concrete porch and continued to dry her hands while she looked around. The unfinished houses on either side of hers were framed but not yet covered by sheeting. The rest of the "houses" on the block were no more than concrete foundations set in the ground.

There was no frost on the grass because there was no grass, only bare frozen dirt.

She turned toward the south and was surprised to see a man standing with his back to her on the edge of the chalky bluff that overlooked the town of Grimstad. He was a block and a half away.

There were no pedestrians in the Subdivision of Sadness. Not even door-to-door solicitors ventured up there. The only people Amanda ever encountered were drunk teenagers roaring around throwing empty beer cans on Friday nights and an occasional patrol by the sheriff's department.

Rather than call out to him, Amanda decided to see for herself what he was up to. Plus, the edge of the bluff would give her a very good view of what had happened in town.

She walked across the dirt of her own property and over the "lawns" of the adjacent houses without using the sidewalk. She knew no one was going to object.

As she got closer to him she could see a fist of black smoke punch from the distant industrial park into the pale blue North Dakota sky. She also noticed the tan Ford F-150 CrewCab pickup parked at the curb further up the bluff. It had North Dakota plates and it looked like a farm vehicle. There was a tangle of rusted baling wire in the back of it and a shovel poked out from a slot in the top of the bedwall.

So he hadn't arrived on foot after all.

"Hey there," she said when she was less than ten feet away from him, "did you see what happened?"

He turned, startled.

"Sorry," she said. "I didn't mean to sneak up on ya."

He was an unremarkable man, she thought. Late fifties, early sixties. He was square-built but doughy and he had large hands and a wide pale Slavic face. Dyed jet-black hair and drooping mustache, thick plastic horn-rimmed glasses. Ball cap without a logo. He wore an oversized worn Carhartt parka with a hood, denims stained with grease, and scuffed heavy trucker boots with thick crepe soles. He looked like a lot of the men around town: oil field workers, tool pushers, ex-farmers hustling for a job. He could be Harold, she thought.

He said, "I saw it happen. I was driving down the road and I looked out. There were two explosions down there. I can still see them in my eyes—the flashes, I mean—but they're just now starting to fade away."

As he spoke to her she noticed that he lowered a cell phone he was holding in his right hand into his coat pocket. And that a transmitter of some kind hung around his neck by a lanyard.

"So what *did* happen?" she asked.

"Some kind of explosion."

"Well of course it was an explosion," she said, blowing out a puff of air and rolling her eyes. "I know what an explosion sounds like. They're blowing things up in the oil patch all the time."

"But where did it happen?" she asked. "It sounded close."

"Down there, I guess," he said as he stepped aside so she could better see the plume of black smoke.

"No kidding," she said, approaching the lip of the bluff.

He got close. Shoulder to shoulder almost. She continued to dry her hands by working them within the towel. She noticed he was watching her hands in the towel so she stopped moving them.

"Looks like it was at the industrial park," she said. "I thought that place was pretty much empty these days. Most of the service companies are long gone."

He grunted.

"Hell of a bang," she said. "It rattled the glass in my windows. It reminded me of a couple of years ago when some careless man drove his pickup head-on into that oil train over in the train yard. Were you here then?" she asked.

"No."

"Then you don't know what I'm talking about. That was a hell of a mess and it could have blown up the whole town. Too bad it didn't happen," she said with a bitter laugh.

He said nothing.

Sirens in town cut through the stillness. She saw a flash from the wigwag lights of an ambulance as it sped through Grimstad toward the industrial park.

"Oh no," she said. "It looks like maybe some people got hurt."

He nodded but didn't say anything.

"So you actually saw the explosion?" she asked.

"Yeah. There's a truck down there where the fire is. The truck was backing in and it blew up."

"What was it, an oil tanker?"

"Looked like a normal trailer in back," he said, shrugging.

"I'm glad it didn't happen out there in the oil patch," she said, gesturing toward the flat yellow prairie that was laced with gravel roads connecting working oil rigs as far as she could see. "My husband works out there."

She thought it important just then to bring up the fact that she had a husband. Even if it was Harold.

There were so many sirens going now that they merged into a high whine that hurt her ears. Emergency vehicles from every direction were converging on the industrial park.

"I wonder if they'll tell us what happened on the radio," she said.

"Maybe."

"So you were just driving by and you looked out and saw it happen. Maybe you should call the sheriff and tell him what you saw."

He didn't look at her when he said, "I just seen two flashes of light. That's not exactly unknown information, I wouldn't think."

"But about the truck. You said you saw the truck blow up."

"I think they can probably figure that out," he said.

She nodded. No point arguing with that.

"So, if you don't mind me asking," she said, "what were you doing up here that you saw the explosions happen?"

"I do mind."

When she looked up at him he was glaring at her. His eyes were flat and he had no expression on his face. She felt a chill that started at the base of her scalp and rolled down her backbone.

It wasn't his face, tone, or expression that scared her. It was something else she couldn't explain. Maybe how still he was.

"Well," she said, trying to keep the lilt in her voice, "I guess I better get back to the house so I can listen to the radio."

She stepped back to turn around and he stepped back as well to keep even with her.

"Are you the only people up here?" he asked. "I didn't see any cars. I thought all the houses were under construction."

"Oh, there's a few people around," she lied. She had the urge to run, but she hadn't actually run in years. And even then she wasn't very fast.

"I was maybe thinking of buying a place up here," he said to her. "So I was looking around."

So he was telling her why he was up there after all.

She thought he was lying. She wanted to run, but it would be embarrassing and absolutely not polite. She was from Deer River, Minnesota, where a house was a "hOWse" and you said "yah, yah" while someone spoke and "you betcha" when you agreed with them. If you disagreed, you said nothing at all. She'd grown up polite.

"Are you looking for a place to run your dogs?" she asked, inching away but not trying to look like she was. "I see you've got an electronic training thingy around your neck. My brother is a bird hunter and that's how he trains his dogs. With those electric dog collars, ya know."

The man reached up and grasped the transmitter and looked at it like he was seeing it for the first time. He said, "You saw that, then."

"It's around your danged *neck*," she said, forcing a smile that she hoped wasn't maniacal. She had to raise her voice over the sirens down in town. "Well, good luck," she said, backing away. "I hope you find something up here that suits you. Some of the lots have some real big yards that'd be good for dogs. It's a good neighborhood and all the people here are real friendly. I'm in a group of ladies who go down to the range and shoot our pistols together since we all have them concealed carry permits. They're probably looking out their windows at us right now just wonderin' what we're jabberin' about."

Too much, she thought. Amanda wished that she was capable of not talking so much when she was nervous or scared. But she wasn't wired that way.

She looked from the column of smoke to the man next to her and suddenly asked, "Did you have something to do with that?"

"Why do you ask?"

"Well, that thingy you have around your neck . . . never mind," she said quickly. "Just never mind me. My husband always says I don't have a governor. Things that come into my head come out my mouth."

He said, "Now you're forcing me to make a decision about you."

She pretended she didn't hear what he said and turned toward her house. It was a long distance away and she began to power walk toward it.

WHEN HE RUSHED HER FROM behind and threw a strap over her head Amanda thought: *Yes, dang it, he's going to choke me to death. I knew it.*

It tightened around her throat and she heard the sound of a buckle and she braced herself . . . and he let go.

She staggered a few feet and reached up. There was a thick vinyl collar of some kind cinched tight in between folds of fat on her neck. Amanda was still touching it when she turned around.

He was backing up away from her with the transmitter in his hand.

Why was he backing up?

"What'd you do?" she asked. Her voice was thin because the strap was so tight. "What did you put on me? Don't tell me it's one of those dog collars."

"Okay, I won't tell you."

"Please, mister, this isn't funny at all."

He said, "Now would be the time to pull that pistol you hinted about."

She didn't move.

"Yeah, that's what I figured," he said.

He brandished the transmitter.

"There are three signals on it. The first one does this," he said as he pressed a button with his thumb.

She closed her eyes tight, anticipating the shock. But instead of an electric jolt there was a sharp vibration. It jiggled the flesh of her neck and didn't hurt like she thought it would.

"That's a warning signal," he said. "It vibrates to tell you that the next signal will hurt if you make me push the button."

He paused for a beat. She didn't run. She didn't know what to do.

Amanda ran her fingers along the strap on her neck until she found the buckle. It wouldn't be that hard to undo it, she thought . . .

Electricity coursed through her and the charge weakened her legs and she collapsed to her knees.

He said, "Now don't try to take that off. I see that I need to lock it. I'm still working on the design."

"You hurt me," she said.

"That was just a nick at low power," he said. He seemed pleased with himself. "It was at level forty-five. I can go up to one-forty."

To demonstrate, he twisted a knob on the top of his transmitter. She flinched, but he didn't press the button again.

"So don't try to take off that collar again," he said. "Because if you do, I won't even mess with higher voltage. I'll go straight to button number three."

While he talked she felt around the receiver on her neck to find a second oblong container right next to it. It was smooth and hard on the outside.

"Inside that little box is C-4. Do you know what C-4 is?"

She shook her head.

"It's plastic explosive. It looks just like the modeling clay you used when you were in school. But when there's a detonator stuck into it and I push the third button an electric charge will ignite the detonator and it'll blow up. I don't know if it'll take your head clean off or what. I've only tried it on a goat and believe me the results weren't pretty. The collar is still kind of a work in progress, like I said. If you want to, you can get up and run for your house. That way, I can find out if button number three really works."

The man seemed genuinely curious and it seemed like he expected her to be curious as well.

"Go ahead and run if you want," he urged.

"Not if you're going to kill me."

"What's your name?" he asked.

"Amanda. Amanda Lee Hackl."

"I'm Ron," he said. "Now Amanda, do you think it's the Christmas season?"

"No, why?"

"Your sweater."

"I just wear it to feel happy," she confessed.

"Do you cook?"

"Cook?"

"I'm sure you know what 'cook' means. Do you make meals for your husband Harold?"

She nodded. Tears flooded her eyes. She didn't like being on her knees, being seen by him on her knees.

"Does Harold complain about your cooking?" Ron asked.

Her voice trembled when she said, "Sometimes."

"Often?"

"Not very often."

"Are you one of those fancy cooks or do you make good old-fashioned American food?"

"You mean like meat loaf?" she asked.

He nodded.

"Yeah, I make a good meat loaf," she said.

"No arugula or crap like that?"

"No."

"Can you make a peach pie?"

"Maybe not from scratch, but I can do it."

Ron seemed to be studying her. Making up his mind about something. She wanted to get up, but she didn't dare run.

Oh, how she hoped there would be a random drive-by from the sheriff's department. But with all of those sirens down below, it was unlikely any law enforcement would be in the area.

"Okay, we can give it a shot," he said. "Amanda, I want you to get up and go get in that tan truck. Get in the passenger-side door and curl up on the floor. I don't want you looking out the window and I don't want anyone seeing you in there when we drive away."

She closed her eyes tight and cried. Then she felt the vibration on her neck and she recoiled from it.

"Amanda," he cautioned, "you know what comes next. Now get up and walk to the truck. We're going to drive for a couple of hours and you'll get to meet another woman who is along for the ride. Maybe you two will hit it off, or maybe not.

"And quit blubbering, will you?"

SEVEN

FOR THE LIZARD KING that dusk the planet had stopped rotating.

It was no longer rolling toward him on a ribbon of asphalt where he sat motionless above it all in the high cab of his Peterbilt as he had for decades.

His mind and body had not adjusted to being stopped and it was jarring. When he closed his eyes he could still feel the motion of the road inside him. It was as if he were slightly drunk or drugged or he was a longtime sailor who was stepping on land for the first time in years.

The ground beneath his feet felt still and dead as he emerged from the double-wide trailer west of Sanish, North Dakota. From a place that smelled of greasy dirt and spilled alcohol. Weed smoke clung to the curtains, the fabric of the furniture, and the gray-tinged unmade bedsheets in the back bedroom.

He turned and locked the door behind him with the same set of keys he'd used for the tan Ford. He pulled on the door handle to make sure it was secure. It was.

Constructing the second explosive collar had gone much smoother than the first. Now he knew how to pack the C-4 into the receiver, and how to place a metal stud through a hole in the strap to secure it on so it couldn't be unbuckled without a tool.

He walked around the perimeter of the double-wide making sure all the windows were sealed tight and the back door was locked as well. He was disgusted with the place itself and couldn't see how a man could actually live there and still look at himself in the mirror in the morning.

He'd lived in his truck for years with no permanent address and he'd kept it in immaculate shape inside—both the cab and the sleeper. It wasn't that hard to keep things neat and clean. An organized living space was the sign of an organized mind.

And vice-versa.

HE STEPPED BACK AND BEHELD the trailer home that was really no better than an isolated shack on five acres of grass-land. The location itself was good—no close neighbors, two miles off the state highway, en route to nowhere. The big river flowed quietly through a maze of tangled brush and trees at the edge of the property.

But the structure itself and the condition in which it had been kept made his stomach churn.

A dozen tires had been thrown on the roof to keep the sheet metal from blowing away in the wind. The yard, what little there was of it, winked with broken glass. Two motorcycles, neither fixed up to run, occupied the lean-to carport on the side.

Inside were three filthy bedrooms, a bathroom, a kitchen, and a living area. One of the bedrooms served as a cramped office of sorts. Another was so packed with boxes, auto parts, and trash bags filled with clothing that he couldn't even step inside. He thought: *A hoarder.* Just like his mother had been.

In the front room was a fifty-four-inch HDTV. The set was gaudy and too large for the space and it told anyone stepping inside as much about the former owner as the cheap Indian prints and rugs that covered the walls.

The Lizard King learned nothing from searching inside the trailer about the man who had owned it—Floyd T. Eckstrom—that he didn't already know.

Floyd T. Eckstrom was a wannabe. A wannabe long-haul truck driver, a wannabe monster. Wannabe.

But he'd been too goddamned stupid and obvious.

The cardboard box in the bedroom closet was stuffed with newspaper clippings including a *USA Today* story about the formation within the FBI of a "Highway Serial Killer Task Force" charged with investigating over a thousand cases of missing truck-stop prostitutes across the nation. There were printouts of alleged sightings and a ream of stories about a forty-eight-year-old long-haul driver who'd been arrested in Georgia after being pulled over for malfunctioning running lights. The trooper noticed a severed human foot sticking out of a plastic Walmart bag in the trucker's cab and immediately arrested him. The trucker later confessed to thirty-nine victims. There were also highway trooper reports of body parts found along the nation's highway system, a filled-out application for employment at a long-haul trucking firm that had apparently never been sent, and an entire self-published "true crime thriller" written by a man named "Tub" Tubman who was the sheriff of Lewis and Clark County in southern Montana. The thriller described how Tubman's efforts—and his efforts alone—had broken up a sadomasochistic "gang" that included the man known as the Lizard King. The fact that the Lizard King had escaped custody in the end was laid at the feet of Tubman's subordinates.

The search engine on the desktop computer inside on the kitchen table was bookmarked with hardcore snuff pornography sites. And there was a large encrypted file of over four gigabytes that wouldn't open without a password. He assumed the file was filled with video downloaded from the Internet. There was no point in even trying to open it because it was so obvious what was in there. He'd seen it all before but none of it compared to the cache of home movies he had with him.

Wannabe, the Lizard King thought.

Eckstrom had kept a loaded 12-gauge shotgun in the closet of his bedroom, a .30-06 hunting rifle on the wall, and a Colt 1911 .45 in his bedstand. That was it for weapons, and the Lizard King had removed them from the house and stashed them inside a shed and locked it.

He fished inside his jacket for the transmitter and pressed the button to vibrate.

There was a closed-ended cry from inside from the fat housewife followed by a muffled curse from the lot lizard from Eau Claire. He'd observed closely when they both saw each other for the first time, when he'd ushered Amanda into the trailer. Would they be happy to be with another person in the same situation?

The lot lizard had looked up with disgust on her face and said, "Who in the *hell* is she?"

"She can cook," he said.

"Fuck," the lot lizard said.

He leaned close to the closed window and said, "Stay in there and don't try anything stupid. Look through those groceries I brought back and make some dinner. I got steaks in there."

SATISFIED THAT THE TRAILER was secure and no one would try to get out, he walked away from the double-wide toward the bank of the river. Gravel and small pieces of glass crunched under his thick-soled trucker boots. His legs felt strange and weak, and once he had to stop and take his bearings. He wondered how long it would take for the world to stop rotating. And whether he really wanted it to.

There was too much tangled brush near the water to get to the river's edge so he chose a massive branch of driftwood and sat down on it and stretched his legs out.

The sun was ballooning as it slipped toward the flat western horizon and it made the light orange. He could hear the river flow. There was a shriek of a nighthawk. These were things he'd missed for years but not that much.

He turned and looked at the double-wide over his shoulder. It was quiet although someone had turned on a light in the kitchen. Good.

MOST OF ALL, HE THOUGHT, he was tired.

So tired.

He was tired of having no fixed address at fifty-nine years of age and tired of being downtrodden. He was tired of idiots in four-wheelers on the highways and tired of smug and judgmental "citizens" who despised men like him while feasting on the food he'd delivered to their grocery store so they could eat while watching reality television programs about rich amoral celebrities.

He was tired of the government imposing more and more rules and regulations on him for simply trying to make a living. More and more permits, licenses, random drug tests, the Federal Motor Carrier Safety Administration coming up with "scores" for every driver and constantly threatening to decrease driving hours allowed. The state "authorities" weren't any better, always looking to shut a truck down for some chickenshit rule, especially in Minnesota, Ohio, California, Oregon, and Washington.

He was sick of being on high alert every minute of his day while he was calculating mileage, pickups, deliveries, and protocols that changed from state to state. They were trying to make it impossible for an independent trucker to survive.

He was even tired of lot lizards. They were more tatted up and drugged out than ever. They never learned that making themselves available to people like him by going from truck to truck was stupid and dangerous.

And they were so quick to scream.

It was time, he thought, for his next stage of life. He didn't need to force it to make it happen. Like the countless lot lizards over the years, that next stage was coming to *him*.

HE'D BEEN ON to the bogus LTL posts on the log boards for months. The wording just wasn't right and he knew it instinctively. Farmers who posted were cheap but these offers—all coincidentally from the Bakken in North Dakota—were written as if money were a second thought.

He knew that it had to be that overweight investigator from Montana who had—*coincidentally*—taken a job in North Dakota. She knew too much about him and she'd seen him in person twice. She was a threat.

State troopers, assholes in chicken coops, even the feckless FBI task force had lost interest and lost their edge. Time did that. But this woman—she was relentless.

HE'D LEARNED ABOUT C-4 on the Internet after he'd purchased two cases of it from a nervous Mexican trucker in Brownsville, Texas. The Mexican didn't explain why he was unloading the cases surreptitiously to interested drivers at the truck stop and the Lizard King hadn't asked. But he knew it might come in handy, as it had.

The stuff was as safe as a brick of clay until it was ignited by a detonator. It could be jostled and banged around in his trailer and nothing bad would happen.

As he drove back and forth across the country with the two cases of C-4, an idea came to him prompted by a cryptic message on an Internet trucker forum that read LOOKING FOR LK APPRENTICESHIP. It had a 701 area code. North Dakota.

The Lizard King didn't respond at once but he thought the message was too bold for his relentless investigator and too clever by half for the feds.

There was no way that there would be two simultaneous efforts to lure him to North Dakota by law enforcement, was there? That didn't make sense. But as he thought about it as he drove, an idea slowly developed.

First, he had to vet the wannabe and make sure there was no connection with the other effort to lure him in. So he placed a call from a pay phone in West Virginia to the 701 number and was introduced to Floyd T. Eckstrom.

Eckstrom, a local auto mechanic, was so starstruck by the call from the Lizard King he could barely speak. He offered to ride along for free, to assist with whatever he could, to learn the ropes from a master.

The Lizard King hung up on him and waited a week to see if the call would be traced back to him somehow. Then, after seeing the latest LTL post requesting a rig in Grimstad for ten pallets of remanufactured oil field parts, he called again and asked Eckstrom if he could drive a truck.

"Not just drive it, but back it up safely to a loading dock."

When Eckstrom eagerly said he could do that, the Lizard King asked him to meet him in four days at a Flying V truck stop on the outskirts of Rawlins, Wyoming.

"Keep your cell phone on when you get there," he instructed.

FOUR DAYS LATER, the Lizard King sat in the cab of his truck at the Flying V and watched the scene around him with his truck running. He was parked fifth from the end of the first long row of rigs facing the facility. He watched as dozens of tractor-trailer operators came off I-80 for fuel and food, and dozens left the truck stop to rejoin the mechanized river of commerce of the interstate. Many of those coming in had reached the end of their federally mandated driving shift and they'd carefully pull their rig into an empty space on the lot to get some sleep.

The truck stop was designed like most of them: big commercial trucks on one side, private passenger cars on the other. On the big rig side there was a driver's-only lounge with Wi-Fi, showers, and a business center. A restaurant was in the middle of the facility but partitioned off between drivers and civilians. On the civilian side was a large gift shop, fried food and snacks for the road, and gasoline pumps instead of diesel.

Eckstrom wouldn't know what kind of truck the Lizard King drove or what he even looked like. Very few people did. And he had no way of contacting his potential mentor when he arrived.

The first thing the Lizard King determined was that there appeared to be no special surveillance by law enforcement at the Flying V that afternoon. If it was a trap the cops had been much more careful and sophisticated than usual. There were standard video cameras mounted within and outside the facility, but no out-of-place panel vans, no "civilians" standing around on the corners of the building pretending to be busy with something, and no significant conversations between civilians who might actually be undercover cops.

But that wasn't enough. He had to be sure.

He decided that the tall, gawky man wearing a canvas farmer coat and black plastic glasses who had circumnavigated the trucker-side parking lot four times, looking more and more vexed, must be Floyd T. Eckstrom.

He punched in the number for Eckstrom in a prepaid cell phone he'd picked up in Utah that morning. He watched as the man in the farmer coat suddenly stopped near the side of the building and dug into his pocket for his phone.

"This's Floyd." He sounded, and looked, nervous.

"Hello, Floyd. It's me."

"I've been looking for you. When will you get here?"

"Oh, I'm here. I'm watching you right now."

Eckstrom slowly looked up from where he stood to the line of thirty-five truck grilles out in the parking lot. Scores of other trucks were lined up behind them, and more behind them.

The Lizard King knew he couldn't be identified through the smoked glass of his windshield.

"Which rig are you in?"

"Nope. How do I know you're not a cop?"

"Shit—do I look like a cop?"

"No, but that doesn't mean anything."

"Tell me where you are. I'll prove to you I'm not a cop."

"How are you going to do that?"

"I'll show you my CDL, maybe. I'll show you my ID. I'm who I say I am."

"Those documents are easily made. Especially for an undercover cop."

"Man . . ." He was fidgeting now, shifting his weight from foot to foot. What he wasn't doing, the Lizard King observed, was trying to catch the eye of anyone on the public side or within the building who might be doing surveillance. He had all the appearances of being alone. But that wasn't enough, either.

"You need to prove you're not a cop or I hang up and I'll never be in contact with you again."

"How in the hell do I prove that?" Eckstrom asked, holding his free hand out as if pleading.

"Do you have a knife on you?"

"A what?"

"A knife."

"Well, yeah, I got a Buck knife in my pocket."

"Take it out. I want to see it."

Eckstrom hesitated a moment, then drew a large folding knife out of his jeans.

"Open it."

"Open it?"

"Open it."

A sigh. "Just a second . . ."

It took two hands. Eckstrom clamped his phone between his neck and shoulder while he pulled out the blade. It locked into place.

"Okay," he said.

The Lizard King sat back and scanned the facility until he saw what he was looking for.

"There's a red Subaru wagon that just pulled into the gas pumps. It has California plates. Walk to the end of the building and you'll see it."

Eckstrom did. He stopped at the corner and peered around it to the rows of gasoline pumps and dozens of cars that had briefly exited the interstate.

"Yeah, I see it."

"The husband just filled up the car and went inside. I want you to walk over to the car and open the passenger door. There's a woman inside and you need to cut her throat."

"You're kidding, right?"

"Do you think I'm kidding?"

"Right here in broad daylight? With all these other cars around?"

"Do it fast and run. That way, I'll know you aren't a cop."

Eckstrom hesitated. He looked nervously around and for a moment it appeared he would retreat to the vehicle he'd arrived in. Then he took a deep breath and strode with purpose toward the red Subaru.

The Lizard King felt the hairs on the back of his arms rise. His eyes widened as Eckstrom got within three feet of the car.

He was going to do it.

For a brief moment, the Lizard King thought of calling it off. Not to show mercy but because there was no doubt in his mind Eckstrom would do anything he asked.

But what if Eckstrom really was law enforcement and was just going through the motions until the last possible second?

Either way, Eckstrom had apparently dropped the live phone into his pocket and there was no way the Lizard King could call him in if he tried.

The Lizard King watched as Eckstrom reached out his his free hand and grasped the Subaru door handle and threw it open. Quickly, he lunged inside. A spray of blood flecked the interior of the windshield glass.

Then Eckstrom backed out and slammed the door shut and walked stiffly away. No one else at the pumps had looked up while it happened. And after it did, no one shouted, honked, or tried to chase him down.

When Eckstrom bolted around the corner of the building and was out of sight from the gas pumps, he pulled the phone from his jacket and held it to his face.

"*Did you see that?*" he said. His voice was exuberant.

"I tried to stop you."

"Never mind that—did you see it? Do you believe me now that I'm serious?"

"I do," the Lizard King said. "Right now you need to get out of here."

"I thought we had a deal," Eckstrom hollered into the phone. I thought you were going to teach me."

"Here's your first lesson: Drive away calmly and no more than two miles over the speed limit. Don't put your head on a swivel. Don't give the cops a reason to pull you over. Text me your address—I'll be in touch."

He put his truck into gear and pulled away from the line of

trucks toward the exit. In his rearview mirrors he could see Eckstrom shouting into a dead phone and running toward his vehicle with a bloody knife in his hand.

On the public side, the driver of the Subaru pushed his way out through the double doors with soft drinks and snacks in his hand to deliver to his wife.

HE'D HAD NO IDEA the fuel tanks would ignite that quickly or that the burner cell phone he'd embedded in the C-4 under the seat of the driver would work so well. It was a bigger and messier scene than he could have hoped to create. He'd not been sure whether to use five pounds of the stuff or ten pounds, so he'd gone with ten.

Good call, he thought. *Death of a wannabe. Death of a relentless bitch of a cop.*

Eckstrom wasn't completely without a legacy, though. The man known as the Lizard King was now sitting on his property near Sanish with Eckstrom's ID, trailer, weapons, and Ford pickup.

Plus, the Lizard King thought, he had six hundred thousand dollars of hard-earned cash and a couple of women wearing explosive electric dog collars to serve him.

HIS STOMACH GROWLED when he smelled meat broiling. It had been over a day since he'd eaten. He couldn't recall the last time he'd sat at a kitchen table in an actual home—not a truck stop—and eaten a good meal. Probably, he thought with a frown, it had been in his mother's home before she burned up in the fire. And it probably hadn't been very good. Not memorable, anyway.

As he stood his knees and back crackled from stiffness and age.

When he heard a shout he froze and looked around. There

were no close neighbors with lights on and no sounds of vehicles on the dirt entrance road. He doubted anyone inside the trailer had the temerity to call out even though he reached for the transmitter on the lanyard around his neck.

Then he heard it again. It came from the river behind him. Sound carried on the water.

He noticed a light blue object passing in a slow current just beyond the thick brush. It was a small raft packed with parcels.

A moment after the raft was caught fast in the undergrowth he heard a male voice shout, "There it is. I see it. Can you get us over there?"

"Yeah, I think so."

"You might have to row forward to get out of this current."

"I'm doin' that."

The Lizard King neared the river and reached into his jacket pocket to grip his .380. There was a boat on the water beyond the brush and it was getting closer.

At first he thought it was a man and a boy, the boy on the oars. The boy talked in a garbled, high-pitched way. He could make out the gist of what he was saying if not the individual words.

Then he realized it was two boys, a black one and a white one. The black one was sprawled over baggage in the front of the boat. He was reaching out to try and grab a loose rope that was attached to the raft.

"Got it," the black one said with triumph. "Now pull over to the bank and we'll tie it back on the boat."

"I'm tying the knot this time, Raheem."

"Fucking right you are," the bigger boy said, laughing. "I guess I can't tie knots worth shit."

The boy on the oars was scrawny, undersized, and there was something obviously off about the way he moved and talked. He was damaged in a unique way and the Lizard King felt something stir inside him.

When he looked at the damaged boy he saw himself at that age. When he was young he was on his own in the world and he had a speech impediment as well that was cruelly mocked by those around him.

There had been no one to look up to, no one to take his interests to heart.

He kept his hand in his jacket pocket when he stepped through a thick willow and said, "You boys look like you could use some help. I'll give you a hand."

No one had ever offered *him* a hand up. Or nurtured him within a family.

"I'll help you boys," he said.

PART TWO

BISMARCK,
NORTH DAKOTA
ONE MONTH LATER

EIGHT

CASSIE DEWELL AND SHERIFF Jon Kirkbride sat on opposite sides of a coffin-shaped conference table in a too-hot room in the state capitol building in Bismarck. Outside, the sky was the light gray color of weathered barnwood. She could see the yellow crowns of autumn trees in the distance.

Down the hall was the office of the state attorney general as well as the Bureau of Criminal Investigation. The door was closed but Cassie could hear snippets of urgent conversation out in the hallway and she could see shadows of passersby through the frosted glass.

She looked down at the lukewarm Styrofoam cup of coffee between her hands and saw that the surface of the liquid was trembling.

She let go of the cup and placed her hands on her lap beneath the table so Kirkbride couldn't see what condition she was in.

But he knew. Which was why, she surmised, that he talked about everything except for why they were there.

"Lotta people drive right by this building and don't realize it's the state capitol building," he said, referring to the twenty-one-story tower in the heart of Bismarck. "The house majority leader of Minnesota said it looked like a State Farm insurance building. You can guess how that went over around here."

Cassie tried to smile. The fact was, it *didn't* look like any capitol building she'd ever seen. Certainly not like the neoclassical building she'd seen in Helena with its copper-clad dome, or in Cheyenne or Denver with their glistening golden domes.

"It's art deco style, I guess," Kirkbride continued. "Not that I know anything about architecture. All I know is it's the tallest building in the state and the historian types like to call it the 'Skyscraper on the Prairie,' for what that's worth. The other thing I know is I've spent most of my career doing everything I could to *not* come to Bismarck, especially during the legislative session. All these politicos and lobbyists make me damned nervous. I've learned that whenever politicians get together in one place bad things happen." Then: "First time here?" he asked.

"Yes."

"Sorry I couldn't drive up with you," he said.

She nodded. She was sorry, too. She'd driven the three and a half hours in her personal Ford Escape. She knew the sheriff had traveled to Bismarck the previous day to testify at a committee hearing for the legislature. He was there to talk about rampant drug use in the western part of the state where oil was pumping.

"How are you holding up?" he asked.

"Do you mean with the suspension?"

"Ian."

Hearing his name jolted her. "He didn't deserve what happened to him. If I would have not had him driving that forklift . . ."

"*Stop*," Kirkbride said. "It could have been any of us. It could have been *us*—you or me. You can't think like that."

But she did. And late at night when she was not sleeping she fought back thoughts that Ian's blind love for her should have been reciprocated to a higher degree. The guilt that thought produced gutted her.

Cassie changed the subject and said, "Do you know if there's been any progress finding Kyle Westergaard or Raheem Johnson? The two boys who left town in the boat?"

"I'm aware of them," Kirkbride said. "I know you're close to Kyle. I haven't heard anything and I haven't been in the office to follow the case.

"Honestly, Cassie," the sheriff said with a sigh, "I'm not sure what's been going on in the office while I was out—if anything. That explosion blew up the department in more ways than one."

She nodded.

"I don't know what's keeping them," he said changing the subject and nodding toward the door. "Do you want me to go find out what's going on?"

"Maybe give them a couple more minutes," she said.

"Okay."

"Jon," she said, "thank you for being here. I know you didn't have to."

He waved it off and sat back in his chair without comment. She wasn't used to seeing him wear a tie with his uniform shirt, a concession he'd apparently made for the legislators. He noticed her staring at his tie and in response he reached up and loosened it with a tug.

"How are you really holding up?" he asked.

"Don't worry about me," she said.

"I *am* worried about you. I'm afraid they might be looking for a scapegoat. Especially Tibbs."

She nodded.

"I think this might be a setup," he said. "Tibbs and the head of BCI were college roommates. It ain't right."

Before she could reply Kirkbride swiveled his head toward the door at the sound of approaching footsteps.

"Here they come," he said.

AT THE FUNERAL SERVICE for Deputy Ian Davis, Ian's parents had approached Cassie to assure her they didn't blame her for what happened in the industrial park. It was the first time she'd met them. Ian had been planning for them both to fly to his childhood home in Wisconsin at the end of September so he could introduce his fiancée.

"Really," Ian's mother had said after taking both of Cassie's hands in her own, "it's just such a tragedy. Such a useless tragedy. But we know he died doing what he loved."

She could see Ian's eyes and facial expressions in his mother. His father, though, was inscrutable.

Tragedy.

Cassie hated the word. And until that moment she hadn't grasped the notion that there were people in the community and state who were whispering that she was responsible for the deaths of deputies Ian Davis, Fred Walker, and J. T. Eastwood. Not to mention what double amputee Tigg Erger had to endure, or the third-degree burns Tom Melvin had sustained trying to drag Walker's body out of the fire. Shaun McKnight had survived without a scratch but was so traumatized he'd quit the sheriff's department a week later.

Kirkbride had suffered a concussion when a piece of metal from the exploding truck hit him in the forehead, leaving an angry red scar. The injury was severe enough to keep him hospitalized for a week, with two weeks at home under observation. He'd only recently returned to his office in the Law Enforcement Center.

During the services for Walker and Eastwood the word "tragedy" had not been used. Instead, the eulogies were about sacrifice and duty. The speakers had focused their anger and rage at the man who had self-immolated and taken fifteen percent of the Bakken County Sheriff's Department with him.

The explosion had resulted in the largest loss of life of law enforcement personnel in state history. Tibbs made the recommendation that the incident be turned over for review to the BCI and it made sense at the time to Sheriff Kirkbride, who was still in the hospital. Kirkbride said he was too close to his dead and injured deputies to do the job right. Plus, he wanted an outside investigation to clear the air since he wasn't in good enough condition to oversee it. He told Cassie his experiences with the agency had been straightforward and professional when BCI was brought in to investigate officer-involved shootings.

Cassie was too devastated at the time to have an opinion. She could barely remember surrendering her badge and gun although she recalled feeling grateful to be rid of both of them.

The suspension had been hell on her. Although she tried to put on a good face with Ben and her mother, she agonized constantly about what had taken place at the industrial park and how it had happened. She second-guessed herself and had too many sleepless nights. Her hard-charging world had come to an abrupt stop and all she could do was wallow in it and relive that day over and over. She didn't read the *Grimstad Tribune*, listen to the radio, or watch regional news. It was as if her life couldn't resume until the suspension was lifted.

Ben told her that Kyle and Raheem had "escaped" Grimstad and were somewhere miles away on the Missouri River. Kyle, once again, was considered a legend by the boys in school who wished they were on the river.

IT WAS LATER—AFTER three weeks—that it dawned on her that Avery Tibbs was manipulating the narrative. She couldn't prove that the whispering campaign against her had originated in the office of the County Attorney but she thought the odds were high that it had.

That there were people in Grimstad who considered her solely responsible for what had happened took her by surprise and gutted her. She felt it wherever she went—to school to drop off Ben, or at the grocery store. Eyes lingered on her just a little too long. No one had made an accusation to her face, though.

Instead, like Ian's father at the funeral, they said absolutely nothing. It was the worst thing people accustomed to treating each other "North Dakota nice" could do.

She wondered if the BCI report would change their minds. She'd been so eager to read it she'd come to Bismarck at her own expense and in her own car the day it was scheduled to be released.

Bakken County Attorney Avery Tibbs entered the conference room holding it in his hand.

"WHAT A SURPRISE that it's you," Kirkbride said, not bothering to disguise his sarcasm.

Tibbs sat down at the head of the table nearest the door with the report in front of him. Although he tried to appear solemn, Cassie thought she could see tiny muscles dancing on his temples.

"Anyone else coming?" Kirkbride asked.

"No, just me. I volunteered to deliver the news."

"Good of you."

"I'm here for the press conference," Tibbs said defensively. "It's scheduled for one this afternoon."

"Press conference?" Kirkbride said.

"The head of the BCI wants to present the findings in the most transparent way possible," Tibbs said. "He believes in transparency."

"And you just happen to be here to help him," Kirkbride said.

"It's my county, too, Sheriff," Tibbs sniffed. "In fact, I'd like you to be there as well. So it looks like we're presenting a united front, so to speak."

"It depends on what the report says."

Cassie noted that Tibbs had yet to meet her eyes since he'd entered the room. That, and the fact that he'd not asked her to be at the press conference as well told her what she needed to know.

She suddenly felt cold and numb.

"We can't bring back those fine officers," Tibbs said, as if addressing a jury, "but we can make sure nothing like this happens again. We can make sure procedures are in place so that one rogue operator can no longer run a lone-wolf operation that results in the unnecessary deaths of law enforcement personnel and suspects alike."

He continued to look at Kirkbride when he said, "What I need you to do publicly is agree that mistakes were made that will never happen again. From now on there will be no major initiatives taken within your department that have not been signed off on by my office. You need to assure the public that you and your department have entered the twenty-first century and that it's no longer the Wild West in Bakken County run by good ole boy Jon Kirkbride in complete control. If you do that you can ride off into the sunset with your reputation intact."

Kirkbride narrowed his eyes but said nothing. His full mustache hid the set of his mouth. Cassie looked from Kirkbride to Tibbs. They were glaring at each other.

Although she'd been prevented from going into the office during her suspension, she'd heard from Kirkbride's administrative assistant Judy Banister that Tibbs had practically installed an assistant county attorney named Deanna Palmer into the sheriff's department to serve as his eyes and ears until Kirkbride came back. In fact, she'd been given Cassie's vacant desk on a temporary basis.

"I'm not telling you what to do, Sheriff," Tibbs said. "God knows you've got a mind of your own and a stubborn streak as wide as the Missouri. But you know as well as I do that if my office brings charges against your chief investigator, one that you hired and apparently stand behind"—he briefly glanced at Cassie for the first time—"you'll be as tainted as she is. I don't think either one of us wants that. What do you say?"

Kirkbride took a deep breath and expelled it slowly. Then he said, "I say you can stick it up your ass, Tibbs, you third-rate political hack."

Tibbs raised his eyebrows and pursed his mouth. "I was kind of afraid you'd take it that way."

"She didn't cause the death of my officers any more than you or I did," Kirkbride said. "The person who killed and injured them was Ronald Pergram, that psycho son of a bitch."

"Granted," Tibbs said, "but who lured that psycho son of a bitch into the heart of our community? Who literally entrapped him in a sloppy plot and forced his hand?"

"It wasn't like that and you know it," Kirkbride said.

Tibbs tapped the pages with the tips of his fingers. "That isn't what this report says."

Cassie started to speak but Kirkbride held his palm out to her. To Tibbs he said, "I'll go you one better. I'll go to your press conference and when you're done spouting off I'll tell them how I feel about that report and how wrong it is. I'll tell them you've got your fingerprints all over it. Then I'll probably resign on the spot and say it's because you're such a horse's ass. How's that? Does that work for you?"

"Please," Tibbs said, stalling for time. Cassie could see his mind working.

"*No*," she said with force.

Both men looked over.

To Tibbs she said, "You have my badge and gun. Keep them because I quit. You'll get your scapegoat. If you want to press charges you can track me down somewhere. I'm sure the voters will want a congressman who spent his time prosecuting a single mom war widow who resides in another state."

She stood up and leaned toward him across the table. "I'm not saying this because I'm a victim. I don't play that game. I'm just telling you what it'll look like and I know that's what you care about—how you look."

To Kirkbride: "You will not resign. Grimstad needs you to finish out your term. You will not go down because of me. You gave me a chance and I'll always appreciate it. But you *will not resign because of me*."

Kirkbride looked stunned.

She said to Tibbs, "What pisses me off the most about this is all of your energy has been devoted to saving your butt so you can come out looking good. You started with the explosion and worked backwards for the purpose of finding fault instead of thinking it through."

"I voiced my concerns about your operation at the time," Tibbs said to Cassie.

"But you didn't stop it, did you?" she asked. "And you were ready to take the credit if we took the Lizard King into custody."

"I don't remember it that way."

"I do."

Tibbs cocked his head to the side, obviously confused.

"I lost my fiancé and three other good men who were my friends. I've looked around for you at the funerals and I didn't see you anywhere. And I hate it that you've made this about me and how you can one-up the sheriff and about how you come out. I *hate* that.

"But what I hate even more is that there are too many things that don't make sense about what happened that aren't even on your radar screen. Pergram *was* a psycho son of a bitch but I spent years thinking about him. He didn't stay on the road for all those years because he was lucky. He's convinced he's the smartest man in the room, that he can outthink everyone in law enforcement. He's a reptile who only cares about himself. He might go down in a hail of gunfire, but he's not a man who would commit suicide by cop."

"What are you saying?" Tibbs asked.

"Figure it out," Cassie spat. "And while you're at it, consider how good you'll look if we find he's still out there."

Tibbs turned to Kirkbride. "This is nuts. She's nuts. Pergram is dead." Then: "*We were there.*"

Cassie said, "Someone died behind the wheel. But what's the FBI analyis say?"

"The explosion was caused by military grade C-4," Tibbs said. "That didn't happen by accident. He waited until he was backed into the dock and law enforcement was all around him before he hit the button. He wanted to take as many of you out as he could."

"What's their DNA test results?" she asked.

"There isn't a positive analysis," Tibbs said. "Even though the body was badly burned the FBI was able to obtain samples. The problem is—and you know this—there's no DNA from Pergram on file. So there's nothing to match it up with. But it was his truck, his ID, everything."

"*Everything*," Cassie repeated, mocking Tibbs. "Except I'm the only person still alive who knows him and knows the way he thinks. He wouldn't end it that way."

Tibbs had a pained grin. He shook his head as if asking himself, *How long do I have to listen to this?*

"What about the lot lizard?" Cassie asked. "Did you find her body in the kill room in his trailer?"

"There was no body," Tibbs said. He sounded bored. "But no doubt he dumped it between Wisconsin and here. Not having a body right now means nothing. As you of all people should know, he's been disposing of bodies for years and none of them have been found."

Tibbs was correct, Cassie knew. It was the single most infuriating aspect of the years'-long pursuit of the Lizard King: no bodies found.

Tibbs asked, "If it wasn't Ronald Pergram then who was it, Chief Investigator?"

"Not Ronald Pergram," she said, gathering up her coat to leave the room. "And call me Cassie."

NINE

CASSIE DIDN'T STOP WIPING ANGRY tears out of her eyes until she got past Dickinson and was nine miles from the border of Theodore Roosevelt National Park. But she was still fuming.

She'd listened to the Bismarck news on the AM radio and had heard snippets of Tibbs' statement before the press. She'd turned it off after he assured the reporter, "Don't worry, we'll get Grimstad and Bakken County law enforcement cleaned up once and for all."

There was no mention of Sheriff Kirkbride at the event.

SINCE SHE WAS now a civilian and couldn't show her badge to a trooper and expect leniency, she had to remind herself to reduce her speed on I-94. Dickinson was considered the start of cowboy country in North Dakota, where farms gave way to ranches, and grazing cattle and horses began to override wheat fields.

The sky was lighter than it had been in Bismarck, but it was still close and oppressive.

Every few miles, she thumped the steering wheel or dashboard with the heel of her hand and yelled, "Shit!"

LESLIE BEHAUNEK IN NORTH CAROLINA answered on the second ring.

"Cassie," she said as a greeting.

"I'm out of the department," Cassie said. "I resigned before they could fire me."

"Oh, Christ. I'm so sorry." But she sounded more angry than sorry, Cassie thought.

They'd discussed her situation every few days while Cassie waited out her suspension. Behaunek felt as responsible for what had happened at the industrial park as Cassie, although neither could have anticipated that it would happen the way it did. Both were obsessed with catching the Lizard King and they wanted him rotting away in prison for the rest of his life—or dead.

"Those bastards," Leslie said. "Can you appeal?"

"I'm sure I can but I don't want to," Cassie said, telling Leslie how Sheriff Jon Kirkbride had followed her out of the state capitol building to her car. He'd begged her not to resign, to fight Tibbs, to sue the county he worked for to get her job back.

"He kept saying, 'It just ain't right,'" Cassie said.

"What did you tell him?" Leslie asked.

"I said I was through, then I gave him a hug. I'll miss that guy," Cassie said. She fought back another wave of tears. She was proud that she'd waited to cry until Kirkbride was no longer in the rearview mirror. She hadn't wanted him to see her break down.

In their many late-night conversations, Leslie and Cassie had become comfortable enough with each other to share feelings, discuss relationships, and dish on their colleagues. They were kindred spirits—unmarried women in the rural, male-dominated field of law enforcement. It wasn't the first time one of them had cried while on the phone with the other. Especially after Ian Davis was killed.

Cassie recounted the proceedings in the conference room and Leslie cursed throughout.

"I wish I could have been there as your lawyer," Leslie said. "I'd eat Tibbs for lunch."

"You would. But the deal was done when he walked in the door."

"It's overwhelming, isn't it?" Leslie said. "Every agency has its own political intrigue and you spend way too much time just trying to figure it out and survive. You don't know where the threats are coming from until they get you. And in this case, it sounds like the real target was your sheriff and you were collateral damage."

Cassie agreed. Her previous job in Lewis and Clark County, Montana, had more than its share of backstabbing and innuendo.

"But at least I grew up in Helena," Cassie said. "I knew the players and I had a pretty good understanding of the sheriff and the political types going in. Here I'm still learning. Or I should say, I *was* learning. And what I was learning was that I could trust the sheriff and just about nobody else. It hurts."

"Of course it does, Miss Cassie," Leslie said. She knew Cassie had been amused when she was in North Carolina by the Southern affectation of *Miss Cassie*. "And worst of all, that son of a bitch is probably still out there. I lost him the first time, and now you lost him."

"Again," Cassie reminded her. "I lost him *again*."

"And we know more women are going to die," Leslie said.

There was a lull in their conversation. They'd talked enough that long pauses were okay.

After a few moments, Cassie told Leslie about the DNA that had been recovered from the burned body of the driver and the absence of a body in the trailer and Leslie cursed again.

"If they'd allowed us to do a DNA swab on him when we had

him here there would be a match," Leslie said. Pergram, who was using the identity of Dale Spradley at the time, had refused to agree to a swab.

She continued, "Or there *wouldn't* be a match which would mean he's still out there for sure."

"I know."

They speculated on other methods of determining whether Pergram was the driver but could come up with no good ideas.

Finally, Leslie asked, "What are you going to do now?"

"That's the question, isn't it? I'm not looking forward to telling my mother or Ben."

"Maybe Ben would kind of like his mother around more," Leslie offered.

Cassie laughed. "He would have a few years ago but now he's twelve. Having his mother hovering around him is the last thing he wants, believe me."

"Are you going to stay in North Dakota?"

"I've still got a lot of thinking to do." Then: "Probably not. I love my sheriff but he's struggling along until he can retire. Tibbs has placed a spy in the office and he's slowly but surely easing Jon out. I'll probably go back to Montana, but I really haven't thought about it until this second."

"Doing what?" Leslie asked.

"I don't know," Cassie sighed. "I don't have a clue who would hire a fat, disgraced ex-cop with a hippie mom and a twelve-year-old boy. And did I mention I'm fat?"

Leslie started to give a pep talk to Cassie, telling her not to get down on herself, when Cassie said, "Really, Leslie, not now. I appreciate it and all, but I have to think this through."

"Maybe I can put in a good word for you here?" Leslie said. "Maybe you can get a new start."

"North Carolina? I'm getting too old for a new start, I think. I'm a Rocky Mountain girl at heart."

"What's your choice?" Leslie asked.

After a beat, Cassie said, "I don't think I have one."

AFTER ARRIVING IN GRIMSTAD at dusk, Cassie slowed down her car and joined a long caravan of oil field vehicles from the south where they were funneled through town. She'd been a part of the traffic parade thousands of times since she'd arrived, but this time it seemed more annoying than usual. Once she reached the downtown she took a left and drove around aimlessly, waiting for the shift change at the sheriff's department. The last thing she wanted to do was arrive as the afternoon shift and evening shift of deputies converged around their lockers. No doubt, she thought, they would have heard what happened in Bismarck. News like that travelled lightning speed through the law enforcement community and she didn't want the drama.

She knew there was a contingent of deputies who blamed her—at least somewhat—for the explosion and the deaths of their fellow officers. Tibbs had more than a few of them in his camp with vague offers of promotions and better assignments when and if he had more power within the department. Even if most of the deputies thought she'd acted entirely above board or disliked Tibbs—which she thought most of them did—a high-profile press conference from the state capitol targeting her actions would likely shake their confidence in her decisions.

As she had felt with Sheriff Kirkbride, Cassie didn't want her presence in the department to serve as a wedge. In her experience, cops did two things really well: drink coffee and gossip with each other. If she tried staying in the department and fighting Tibbs as Kirkbride had suggested, the pro-Kirkbride and pro-Tibbs factions would harden. She knew she couldn't do her job in that kind of poisoned workplace environment, and she didn't want the last months of Kirkbride's tenure to be filled with acrimony.

Her intention now was to enter the building to clean out her desk after the afternoon shift had gone home and the evening shift was on patrol. She hoped she timed it right.

KIRKBRIDE HAD NOT CHANGED the key code on the double front doors of the Law Enforcement Center and Cassie quickly entered the lobby and headed toward the elevators with her head down. She sensed a presence near the left bank of windows but she didn't look over.

As she reached out her finger to punch the button for the second floor a female voice behind her called, "Cassie? Is that you?"

She turned. A frail woman in her mid-seventies sat primly in the middle of one of the low benches. She had white hair done in a swept-up style that was the thing a quarter century before, and she wore gold-rimmed glasses, a scarf, and a calf-length coat. Although Cassie couldn't see her dress because she was so bundled up, there were two thin bare ankles above sensible brown shoes.

It had been months since Cassie had seen Lottie Westergaard. Lottie had been injured two years before at her own home but had since recovered.

"Hi, Lottie."

"I'm glad you're here," Lottie said. "I asked for you but instead they made me talk to a woman who wasn't very helpful."

Since there were only two women on staff in the department and one of them was Judy Banister, Cassie said, "You must have spoken to Assistant County Attorney Deanna Palmer."

"Yes," Lottie said with distaste, "I think that was her name."

Cassie paused. It was obvious Lottie had no idea she was talking to an ex-cop. Cassie didn't know how much to tell her, if anything.

Before she could respond, Lottie said, "I'm here about Kyle. He's been gone a month and nobody here will help me find him."

Cassie had a decision to make. Go to her office on the second floor while no one was around, or take a minute with Lottie and risk running into some of her colleagues. She took a deep breath, then walked away from the elevator and sat down next to Mrs. Westergaard.

"Lottie, I know that Kyle and Raheem Johnson are missing—"

"Raheem," Lottie interrupted. "He's a nice young black boy. His father and I camped out in this lobby for the first week and we got to know each other. We got along even though the reason we were here was not good."

Cassie looked away to keep from smiling. Lottie was from another time before the oil boom when there were no African Americans in Bakken County.

"They've been gone a *month*," she said again. "Mr. Johnson is pretty sure they took his boat and went downriver. Kyle kind of talked about that ever since I took him to Medora and he saw those old photos of Theodore Roosevelt on the river. But I never thought he'd actually do it, you know. They could be in South Dakota or someplace even worse by now and nobody is doing a thing about it. It'll be winter soon."

Cassie nodded for her to go on, but instead Lottie reached into her purse and handed over a folded sheet of lined school paper.

"Kyle left me this."

Cassie read Kyle's letter and felt a lump form in her throat. She could hear his voice as she read. Then she handed it back.

Lottie said, "You know what Kyle is like. He's a good boy and I love him but he lives in his own head. We always got along well, even when his mother was alive. I think I was the only stable person in his life. We always communicated even though he's hard to understand at times. I can't imagine him not calling me at some point, or you know, texting."

When she said that she withdrew a cheap flip-phone from her purse and opened it.

"Kyle made me get one of these things. You can see that he

texted me just about every day when he left school. Then nothing for a month.

"What if they had an accident? What if their boat overturned and they drowned in the river? I just need to know."

"I understand your concern," Cassie said, reaching out and patting Lottie's small hands in her lap. "I wasn't assigned to the case.

"The fact is, Lottie," Cassie said while squeezing the old woman's hands, "I've been on suspension since that explosion in September. I haven't been in the office until today so I don't know much."

It was Lottie's pleading eyes that got her, Cassie thought. The old woman had been through so much: the death of her husband, the overdose of her daughter, the trauma that led to Kyle staying with her. She was just a kind and resourceful North Dakota native who wanted to live and let live and bake *lefse*. Suspensions and politics within the sheriff's department weren't of concern to her. Kyle was.

Cassie asked, "What did the investigating officer tell you when you reported Kyle missing?"

"He told me to come back later."

"Really?"

Lottie nodded her head. "He was trying to be nice but I could tell he had a lot on his mind that day."

Then it sunk in.

"Lottie, what day did Kyle go missing?"

"September fifteenth," she said. "A month to the day."

Cassie said, "That's the day the truck blew up at the industrial park. I'm sure you heard of it. We lost three good deputies and had two others very seriously injured. The sheriff got a concussion and he was off duty for three weeks. I'm sure this place was absolute chaos at the time."

"It was. Nobody really wanted to talk to me." A thin tear rolled out of her left eye as she said it.

"So you came back the next day?" Cassie prompted.

"Yes. I talked to a another nice officer. Mr. Johnson was also here that day. The officer wrote down what we told him about Kyle, Raheem, and the boat. He said he'd alert all the police down-river from here to look for a boat with two boys in it. He assured me they should be pretty easy to find. Then I talked to the sheriff himself."

"You did?"

"I know where he lives," Lottie said with a slight grin.

"What did the he say?"

She looked away. "I've known Jon since he rodeoed a hundred years ago," she said. "He's a good boy. But on that day when I knocked on his door and talked to him about Kyle he just looked at me like he wasn't hearing what I was saying. He was . . . distant."

"He'd just lost his men," Cassie said.

"I understand. But that doesn't bring Kyle back."

Cassie didn't know what to say. Kyle was unusual and too eas-ily dismissed and misunderstood, she knew. Beneath the halting speech and inscrutable facial expressions was a very determined young man. That's why Ben looked up to him. Kyle wasn't the kind of boy who would simply abandon his only remaining family member for a month without a call or text. His concern for Lottie was reinforced in the letter he'd written to her.

"You stay right here," Cassie said. "I'm going upstairs and I'll try and get you some help."

"Oh, I'm not going anywhere," Lottie said with a nod of deter-mination. "I've decided to make a nuisance of myself until they find him."

TEN

JUDY BANISTER, SHERIFF KIRKBRIDE'S administrative assistant, looked up with surprise from her desk when Cassie stepped out of the elevator doors. She appeared frozen in place.

Cassie thought, *She knows what happened in Bismarck.*

"I'm just here for my things," Cassie said. "I'll grab them and get out."

"Sheriff Kirkbride is on his way back," Judy said. "I'm sure he'd like to talk with you."

"Not tonight."

Judy nodded. She wore her usual dark suit and there were a few strands of silver in her severe black haircut Cassie hadn't noticed before. Judy was hard to get close to, Cassie thought. The two of them had tiptoed around each other when Cassie first joined the department but they'd later formed a kind of professional relationship based on mutual respect.

Judy looked left and right down the empty hallway and lowered her voice. "I'm very sorry about what happened today. I think you didn't deserve it and . . . I'm just sorry it happened that way."

Cassie paused for a moment. "Thank you, Judy."

"I know the sheriff feels the same way. So do a lot of other people."

"That means a lot," Cassie said. "It really does."

Judy implored Cassie to come to her desk and Cassie got closer.

"Let me know if there's anything I can do to help," Judy whispered. "Really. I'll give you my number at home."

Judy scribbled the number on a pad and tore off the top sheet and handed it to Cassie.

"Thank you," Cassie whispered back while folding the sheet and slipping it into her jacket pocket. She wasn't sure why Judy had done that.

"Why are we whispering?" Cassie asked.

"Because there's someone in your office," Judy said, gesturing with the tilt of her head down the hallway.

"I thought she was supposed to be here only until the sheriff came back from his injury."

"We all thought that," Judy whispered.

ASSISTANT COUNTY ATTORNEY DEANNA Palmer said "Come in" when Cassie knocked on the slightly open door. Cassie knocked with enough force to fully open it so she could step inside.

When Palmer saw it was Cassie the forced welcoming smile on her face faded.

"It's me. I'm just here long enough to gather up my personal stuff," Cassie said.

Palmer wore a camel-colored business suit over a white blouse. She had short red hair and a smattering of freckles over the top of her cheeks and the bridge of her nose. Cassie had never worked with her, but her reputation was that she was as fiercely loyal to Tibbs as Cassie was to Kirkbride.

"Everything is boxed up along the wall," Palmer said.

Cassie noticed that the credenza behind the desk no longer had her photos of Ben and Jim and that her diplomas from the University of Montana and the Montana State Law Enforcement Academy were no longer there. Instead, there were framed shots of Palmer on a ski trip, on a rafting trip, with Tibbs shaking hands with the president in Washington, and her two small children. No husband, though. Palmer was divorced.

Palmer had added a banker's lamp to the desk that illuminated her in a soft yellow glow. Cassie's computer—*maybe it was Palmer's computer now*—was on but turned at an angle so she couldn't see the screen. The rest of the room was dark.

"Can I ask how you got in here?" Palmer asked while Cassie's eyes adjusted to the gloom. She could see two small open-top boxes on the carpeting near the wall. She recognized her photos and diplomas stacked neatly inside as well as spare makeup and medication she'd stored in her desk.

"I used the keypad outside and in the elevator."

"We'll need to get that changed."

Cassie said, "Not for me you won't. I won't be coming back."

"So I heard," Palmer said. "Do you want me to get you some help with your belongings?"

Not, Cassie noted, *Can I help you?*

"I'm fine," she said, putting the smaller box inside the larger one and lifting it up. Together, they weighed practically nothing.

"If I find anything else I'll leave it at the front desk and give you a call," Palmer said. "But I think that's everything."

"Seems like it," Cassie said.

Palmer nodded and turned back to her computer screen. When Cassie didn't immediately step out of the doorway, she looked over with her eyebrows arched.

"Is there something else?"

"Lottie Westergaard is down in the lobby. She's hoping

someone up here will take a personal interest in a missing person's case. Her grandson Kyle has been missing a month and she isn't feeling any love from the sheriff's department about the progress of the investigation."

Palmer took a deep breath and waited a moment before answering as if she were putting aside what she *really* wanted to say.

"As you can imagine, we've had a lot on our plate this past month."

"Oh, I can imagine it. But maybe if you took a few minutes and reviewed the file and just talked to her—"

"That's not what I do here." Crisp. Abrupt.

"I guess I'm not sure what it is you do," Cassie said. "If nothing else, you could ask one of the deputies to speak with her. I think if she was assured that someone up here was taking Kyle seriously that might really provide some comfort to her."

"Shouldn't you be talking to the sheriff?" Palmer asked.

"He's not here, but I will."

"Then I think we're done."

"There's another boy missing with Kyle named Raheem Johnson."

Palmer practically threw herself back in her chair in exasperation. She said, "It's not that I'm uncaring or unsympathetic so don't you dare put that on me. You have no idea how many things are going on around here right now. We're grossly understaffed and the sheriff hasn't been back long enough to get a handle on all of the problems that occurred during his long sick leave."

"He had a concussion," Cassie said.

"And we know why, don't we?" Palmer snapped. Then: "We get calls every day about missing people because folks around here are *transient*. Some guy wants to collect the money he's owed from another guy but he can't find him. A landlord is looking for the tenant that skipped rent. So many of these 'missing' people didn't really put down roots here. They just go without telling anyone else at the time and leaving mortgages, leases, and car payments. They came to work for big money in the oil field and when they find the jobs have dried up they just pack up in the middle of the night. Every day, folks drop off the keys to their houses at the bank on their way out of town and a lot of them don't even bother to do that."

"They're both *fourteen*," Cassie said.

Palmer threw up her hands. "There was a man in here a few weeks ago saying his wife had gone missing. According to him, he came home for dinner and she just wasn't there. So add her to the list of unsolved cases, I guess.

"Talk to the sheriff you love so much," Palmer said with finality. "Tell him to get his act together before the whole county spins out of control. But don't bring your problems to me."

"Go tell that to Lottie Westergaard down in the lobby," Cassie said.

Deanna Palmer huffed and turned back to her computer.

Cassie resisted the urge to hurl the boxes at the woman's head. At that moment she was grateful they'd taken her gun away.

SHE CONSIDERED BYPASSING THE LOBBY on her way down to avoid Lottie but the thought overwhelmed her with guilt.

Lottie stood up expectantly when the elevator doors opened, and Cassie said, "Let's talk tomorrow morning and review the facts on Kyle. Will you be home?"

"I'll either be home or right here in this lobby."

"I'll come by after breakfast, but keep in mind I'm no longer with the department. So it isn't like an official interview."

Lottie clasped her hands together and said, "Bless your heart."

"Lottie, I'm not sure you understand what I'm saying here. I'm no longer a cop anymore. I'm a civilian just like you. The best

I can do is listen, take notes, and maybe offer a recommendation to the sheriff."

"At least you're doing *something*," Lottie said with a mist of tears in her eyes.

ELEVEN

CASSIE PADDED INTO HER HOME office at three in the morning and closed the door because she couldn't sleep. Her "office" consisted of a chair, a battered card table, and a space heater in the only spare bedroom. While her laptop booted up she rubbed her eyes and wished she could go back in time and relive the previous day but with a different outcome.

Dinner had been awkward. Cassie had brought home pizza—Ben's favorite food—and they'd all eaten at the breakfast bar with the television providing background noise in the living room. When the evening news on KXN came on and led with Tibbs' press conference in Bismarck, her mother Isabel rushed away from the counter. With her robes flowing behind her, she searched for the remote control in the living room, found it, and turned the television off.

"What was *that* about?" Ben asked when his grandmother returned.

Rather than answering, Isabel implored Cassie with her eyes to explain.

Cassie had sighed. "I was going to tell him in my own way."

"Tell me what?" Ben asked, looking from his mother to his grandmother.

"I quit the sheriff's department today," Cassie said to him.

After a moment, Ben asked, "You're not going to be a cop any-more?"

"Not for a while, I don't think."

Isabel said, "I knew it would come to this. It's a corrupt system and you have been wasting your time being a part of it."

"Please mom," Cassie begged, "Not now . . ."

Ben was crushed. "But I like it that you're a cop."

She knew that was true because he'd told her the older kids at school who bullied or teased others left him alone. He attributed it to their fear that he would report them to his mother.

"Does this mean we're moving again?"

"I don't know," Cassie said. "I'm trying to figure everything out."

"Did you get fired?"

"Technically, no."

"What does that mean?"

Isabel said, "It means your mom was thrown to the wolves by a male-dominated institution. That's what those people do."

"*Please*, Isabel."

Isabel sat back in a huff and looked away. Ben's eyes bored into Cassie and she could see that he wasn't far away from tears.

"We'll figure things out," she said to him.

He threw the uneaten slice of pizza on his plate and said, "First my dad dies, then we move from Montana. Then Ian dies and Kyle leaves. *And now this.*"

She didn't know he could be so dramatic. Despite how upset he was, it almost made her smile.

When Ben stormed into his room and slammed his door shut, Cassie turned to Isabel and said, "Thanks for getting that started. I would have rather handled it on my own."

"I was trying to help by shutting off the news."

"You didn't. Instead you called attention to it. Do you think Ben pays attention to the local news?"

In what Cassie would deem a righteous snit, Isabel said, "He would have found out on his own at school tomorrow. Everybody at my pottery class was talking about it before you even got home."

"... *and Kyle leaves.*"

The words hung in the air as Cassie tapped on the keys of her computer.

The *Grimstad Tribune*'s Web site was a poor one—the publisher obviously wanted people to subscribe to the print version, not read it online—but she did find a small item about the search for Kyle and Raheem next to their school photos. She ignored the extensive coverage of the industrial park explosion and the photos of the dead and injured deputies, as well as her own photo.

Kyle looked small and feral, and Raheem wore a big confident smile. Kyle was described as five-foot-four and 110 pounds, Raheem five-ten and 175.

If anyone fitting those descriptions saw them, the article said, they should immediately contact the Bakken County Sheriff's Department.

The few comments under the piece were unhelpful as anonymous comments often were, but she read them anyway. She knew of multiple instances in both Montana and North Dakota where newspaper commenters—often inadvertently—provided intel and even leads to investigators working particular cases. In a couple of instances commenters fingered suspects who turned out to be guilty but until that moment had not been suspects. Often, though, locals used their false identities to post disparaging things about law enforcement, or they used the article to further ride their personal hobby horses. Back in Helena, she recalled cops laughing at one particular citizen who cited global warming as the root cause of every arrest or traffic accident.

The first post commended the boys for "being smart enough to get the hell out of Grimstad while they still could." The second lamented the fact that if Raheem didn't come back, the quarterback of the Vikings wouldn't have anybody good to throw to. The third blamed racism for why Raheem must have left. The rest of the comments argued with the commenter who played the race card.

Two days later, on September 18, another missing persons item appeared. According to the story, forty-seven-year-old Amanda Lee Hackl was reported missing by her husband, Harold.

Harold was extensively quoted.

> *"She just wouldn't do something like this,"* Hackl told the Tribune.
>
> *"Amanda is a homebody. She wouldn't just wander off so somebody must have come in the house and taken her. There were dishes in the sink and hamburger thawing on the counter when I got home from work."*
>
> Hackl said Amanda didn't have use of a car that day and her clothes and suitcase weren't missing.
>
> *"Some sicko got her,"* he said.
>
> *Amanda Lee Hackl is described as being 5-foot-3 and 190 pounds. She has dark hair, brown eyes, and wears bifocal glasses. According to her husband she was likely dressed in a Christmas sweatshirt.*
>
> *"Come home, honey,"* Harold Hackl said in a direct plea to Amanda. *"If I done something wrong I'm sorry and I'll fix it. And if whoever might have taken her hears this you can bring her back now and I won't press no charges."*

The comments beneath the item were just as useless as the Kyle and Raheem comments, and most of them went with the theory that she had run off with a delivery truck driver, specifically the Schwan's frozen foods man. Schwan's' yellow freezer trucks were ubiquitous throughout the Midwest.

The first comment read: "I knowed Amanda little bit before she moved up on the hill. She used to have the Schwan's man deliver ice cream every week because she thought he was hot. She told me that herself!"

"If you ever met Harold Hackl," another comment read, "you'd run off with the Schwan's man, too."

DESPITE WHAT DEANNA PALMER had told her, Cassie couldn't find other stories about additional missing people in the area in the past month. At least none who made the paper.

Kyle and Raheem vanished on September 15, the day of the explosion. From what Cassie could discern from the story about Amanda Lee Hackl, she disappeared the same day although it took three days for the item to appear in the *Tribune*.

Three missing in the same day? On the day of the explosion?

She wondered if Sheriff Kirkbride or any of the other deputies found that as unusual as she did.

CASSIE WAS GRATEFUL the sheriff's department had been so overwhelmed the last month that no one had thought to change the passwords on the law enforcement databases they had access to.

Cassie accessed the FBI's NIBRS (National Incident Based Reporting System), NCIC (National Crime Information Center), ViCAP (Violent Criminal Apprehension Program), and MOCIC (Mid-States Organized Crime Information Center) which regionalized crime reports to Illinois, Iowa, Kansas, Minnesota, Missouri, Nebraska, North Dakota, South Dakota, and Wisconsin. Similar regional databases covered other sections of the country.

She was looking for possible crimes committed by boys of Kyle and Raheem's description and perhaps the discovery of bodies matching them.

It took until breakfast and the searches resulted in nothing that helped her. Another man in Sanish reported missing by a neighbor a week after September 15; teenage runaways from two different Indian reservations late that month—but nothing really connected.

Cassie didn't specifically search for any hits on Amanda Lee Hackl, but she kept her eye out and found no helpful information.

Maybe, she thought with a slight smile, she should key in *Schwan's man* in the search criteria.

But she didn't.

CASSIE STOOD OVER BEN'S BED after her shower, with a damp towel on her head. "What's this Isabel says about you being sick and not wanting to go to school?"

"My stomach really hurts," Ben said with a protracted groan. "I think I have a fever."

She leaned over and placed the back of her hand on her son's forehead. "You feel cool to me."

He groaned again. It was as theatrical a groan as his statement had been at dinner the night before. He writhed around under the covers and flipped the top sheet up so it covered his face so she couldn't see it.

"Ben, I know you're upset but I don't think you're sick. At least get up and get dressed and get something to eat."

Another groan but this one had less flair, she thought.

"Staying away from school won't help anything."

"Grandma Isabel could call them," Ben offered.

"She's already gone to her yoga class, and I'm not calling the school if you're not really sick. Man up, Ben, or look me in the eye and convince me you really are too ill to go to school."

After a beat, Ben pulled the sheet down but didn't recant. She held his gaze for a moment before he broke it and looked away.

"Avoiding a situation doesn't solve the problem," she said, sitting down on the bed next to her son. "You know who told me that?"

He shook his head.

"Your dad," she lied. Jim had not actually ever told her that.

"Your dad met problems head-on, which is something I try to do in my life and you should try to do in yours. You'll hear some things at school you probably don't want to hear about me, but *they're not true*. You can get through this but not by staying in bed."

He blinked and she thought he understood.

"Put some clothes on," she said while stroking his cheek. "I'll take you to school and you'll march in there like a man with your chin up. And if someone gives you a hard time—and I mean beyond just a few words you can shrug off—you call me and I'll get things straightened out.

"Just because I'm no longer a cop doesn't mean I won't protect you," she said. She considered explaining to him how a she-bear would protect her cubs, but she didn't.

He looked away, embarrassed. She'd said too much and gone too far, she realized. No boy his age wanted his mother to fight his battles for him.

It was times like this, she thought, she wished Jim was still there. Or Ian.

"Okay," she said, patting him on the shoulder while she rose, "Thirty minutes. Showered, dressed and breakfast, Little Man."

AS HE GOT out of the car, Ben said, "I'll walk home tonight—okay? You don't need to pick me up."

"Are you sure?" she asked.

"Yeah."

She watched him shoulder his backpack and walk away from

her car toward the front doors of the school. He didn't look back and she was glad he didn't or he could have seen the tears in her eyes and the concern on her face for him.

None of the other kids gave him undue attention that she could tell. That would come later.

TWELVE

OVER HOMEMADE NORWEGIAN SNACKS of rolled-up *lefse* spread with butter, sugar, and cinnamon, and baked apples with *gjetost* cheese, Cassie listened to Lottie Westergaard talk about Kyle. Her spiral pad was open on the table in front of her and she dutifully took notes.

Lottie's small house was located on the edge of the thick band of cottonwoods that choked the river. The other homes in the bottomland swale were scattered in the trees and could only be seen from her house in the winter when the leaves dropped. Builders had been prevented from constructing additional houses in the area because it was in a floodplain, but older homes like Lottie's had been grandfathered in.

Cassie had been there dozens of times before to drop Kyle off after he'd spent time with Ben. The first time she'd seen the home, though, was when it was occupied by two MS-13 gangbangers from Southern California, their local drug distributor, and Kyle's mother. Lottie herself had been taped up so she couldn't move or call for help. It had been a bone-chilling night and when it was over, three men and Kyle's mother had been killed.

"**I JUST DON'T THINK** he's dead," Lottie said. Then: "More coffee?"

Cassie declined. The coffee was hot and weak, just the way older North Dakotans seemed to like it. They drank it throughout the day and into the evening.

Lottie filled Cassie's cup anyway and said, "Don't think ill of me when I talk about my grandson being dead. I grew up on a farm and I've been around death all my life. It's how things go."

"I don't think ill of you."

Lottie said, "Good. Now if he was dead and Raheem was dead— like if they drowned on the river or something bad like that—I think their bodies would have been found. Bodies don't sink, do they? Don't they kind of bloat up and float to the top? I remember seeing a drowned heifer do that in the river when I was a little girl on the farm. It bobbed along like a beach ball or something."

Cassie nodded. It was a tough subject to discuss but that didn't seem to effect Lottie. She was a tough old bird who could serve slices of baked apple and *lefse* at the same time she was talking about the bloated body of her grandson.

"That's true," Cassie said. "When bodies decompose in the water they create gas that buoys them to the surface sooner or later."

"Unless of course they're weighted down with chains or something," Lottie said. "But that just sounds a little too crazy, doesn't it?"

"Well . . . we have no reason to believe that someone murdered them, do we?" Cassie asked.

"Nah, I guess not." She shook her head. "Maybe I watch too many of those TV shows."

Lottie pushed herself up from the table to get the pot of coffee. It didn't seem to matter that Cassie had said she didn't want more.

On the way to the kitchen counter, the old woman slid a loose rug aside that was in front of the stove to reveal a star-shaped burn in the linoleum.

"That's where one of those tear gas things went off that night," Lottie said. "It burnt my floor. The sheriff said he'd replace the flooring afterwards but I thought that was a wasteful use of taxpayer money. I just asked him to buy me a rug at Walmart to cover it up."

"That was nice of you," Cassie said. The thought of Sheriff Kirkbride browsing through kitchen rugs for the right one at Walmart made her smile to herself.

"Of course, it took months to get the smell of that gas out of the house," Lottie said. "It clung to the curtains and the sofa fabric. It was worse than old tobacco smoke, you know?"

"I can imagine," Cassie said. Like most cops, she guessed, she hadn't really given a lot of thought to the long-lasting effects of a police raid to the homeowner afterwards. The scars, the smells, the ghosts that lingered.

"When it was warm enough I tried to air it for days on end," Lottie said as she came back and refilled Cassie's cup. "Finally I think it's gotten to the point where I can't smell that smoke anymore. Can you?"

"No."

"Well, good. When I smell that smoke it always takes me back to when it happened."

CASSIE CONTINUED TO WRITE DOWN the pertinent details of the missing person's case as Lottie laid them out, including a list of all the items Kyle had taken with him that had been collected over the years in his "River Box." She did it to keep herself busy, primarily because she had no doubt the information was already in a file at the Law Enforcement Center. She did it to suggest to Lottie that something was being done.

"Is there anything else?" Cassie asked after an hour and too many bites of *lefse* and baked apple.

Lottie answered, "Yes. If you find Kyle, you don't have to make him come back."

"Excuse me?" Cassie had no idea that Lottie expected her to start an immediate investigation herself.

But Lottie misunderstood the question. "There's no need to force him back to Grimstad to attend high school. He's learning very little of value as far as I'm concerned. I've looked at his homework assignments. I can't even figure out what they're teaching him that can be of any real benefit to a boy like Kyle."

Before Cassie could break in and steer the conversation back, Lottie continued.

"Kyle is a very poor student but as we know he's very smart in his way. He'll learn a lot more about the world by being out in it. That's the way things used to be in this country. Not every person went to college and a lot of people I know never even finished high school. Instead, they went to work and moved from place to place. That's how you get wisdom. It isn't from school papers about diversity and gay rights and that sort of thing they teach these days.

"Kyle will learn and get smart in his own way," she said. "If you find him I want you to tell him I said that. He's always welcome back here and he should give me a call because I worry about him, but he doesn't *have* to come back if he's healthy and he's doing okay. I just want to be assured he's alive and on his journey, whatever that is. So will you let him be if he's in a good place?"

Cassie didn't know what to say to that.

"It's more important to me to know he's alive and well than it is to drag him back here to waste his time at that school and have to live with a little old lady," Lottie said. "I just want to be sure. And I'm sure that nice Mr. Johnson wants to know that Raheem is okay."

Cassie sat back. "Lottie, I think there's been a misunderstanding here. I'm no longer law enforcement. I really can't investigate this. I'm just here to get all the information and relay it to the sheriff now that he's back."

"There's no misunderstanding," Lottie said with a mischievous grin. "You were the only person who helped Kyle when he really needed it and you're the only person I trust to find him or learn what happened to him.

"Here," she said, digging into her purse on her lap and withdrawing a thick envelope. "This is eight thousand, three hundred and twenty-eight dollars. It should get you started."

"Lottie, I'm not a private detective."

"Whatever you are, this will help with expenses. Gas, motel, food, that kind of thing."

"I can't take it," Cassie said.

"Of course you can," Lottie said. "What am I going to do with it—die with it in my bank account? I'd rather spend it on finding Kyle."

"I won't take your life savings," Cassie said.

"Oh," Lottie said, waving away Cassie's concern, "I got a lot more money than this stashed away. This is just one of my accounts from the First International Bank and Trust in town. I've got a lot of other accounts and a whole bunch of stock I've picked up over the years. I'm not worried about running out of money before I go meet Jesus. So if you need more, just say so."

Cassie stuttered, "I'm not . . . I can't do this kind of thing. This will take some time and travel and I have a son of my own."

Lottie nodded eagerly as if Cassie had played right into her trap. "What would *you* do if Ben went missing and the police didn't seem to care?"

Cassie closed her eyes and admitted it. "Everything I could."

"Well, I'm not asking you to do that for Kyle," Lottie said. "But this is all *I* can do."

Then, after a long pause: "So, you'll help me?"

WITH EVERY INTENTION to return later in the day and hand the thick envelope back to Lottie, Cassie drove out of the river bottom toward the state highway that ran from Grimstad to Watson City.

Maybe rather than facing her again—the old woman was deviously persuasive and she had the ability to melt away Cassie's willpower—she could put the money in Lottie's mailbox with a note saying she couldn't accept it.

Instead, she could meet with Sheriff Kirkbride and brief him on the case. She could light a fire within the department to investigate the disappearance of Kyle and Raheem. That, she decided, was the best she could do.

The only thing she *could* do.

Cassie fished her cell phone out of her purse.

"SHERIFF KIRKBRIDE'S OFFICE."

"Judy? This is Cassie. Is the sheriff in?"

"He's in but he's in a meeting with County Attorney Avery Tibbs and the entire county commission. They asked not to be disturbed."

Cassie knew that given the participants it was likely a contentious meeting. She guessed Tibbs was negotiating Kirkbride's exit with the commissioners there to rubber-stamp it.

The coup was underway.

"Can you have him call me when he gets out? It's important."

AS SHE DROVE THROUGH TOWN she said, "Damn you, Lottie."

At the same time, though, she couldn't deny that she was personally invested in what she'd been asked to do. Kyle was special to her, and for the past month she'd been without purpose, just waiting for the final BCI report so she could get back to work. Decelerating from the roller coaster, new-crisis-every-day world of law enforcement had been miserable.

Lottie had given her a reason and a purpose for moving on.

It enraged her that the investigation into the missing boys had been given such short shrift. She suspected that if one of the boys had been Avery Tibbs' son—and not a developmentally disabled teenager and his African American friend—it would have been a different matter altogether. In fact, she was sure of it.

And there was something nagging at her from the computer database research. The complete lack of any information—sightings, crimes, credible leads—about Kyle and Raheem over the past month made her recall something her mentor Cody Hoyt had once told her about standard investigative procedure.

This was right after he told her *the* most important tenet in law enforcement was to never pass up an opportunity to eat or use a clean bathroom.

"A lot of times our biggest problem is we get focused too tight on a suspect or on our own stomping grounds. Douchebags"—the term he used for any and all criminals—"don't give a shit about our jurisdiction. We forget there's a great big world out there."

And she thought: *Which way does the river flow?*

BACK AT THE COMPUTER in her home office, Cassie expanded the database search beyond North Dakota and MOCIC to include the states downriver: South Dakota, Nebraska, Iowa, Kansas, and Missouri. Because the Missouri was the longest river in North America—2,341 miles—she guessed that even if the boys had traveled on it for a solid month they would yet to have reached the Mississippi.

They could be as far as Omaha, she thought.

FOR THE NEXT THREE HOURS she ran keyword searches. The results were disheartening. So many missing boys, so many missing girls. It reminded her of when she first started research-ing the number of missing truck-stop prostitutes on the original Lizard King case. She was astonished that the numbers climbed from the hundreds into the thousands.

What she couldn't find, though, were any records that matched the descriptions of Kyle and Raheem. She searched for drowning victims and unidentified bodies found in or near the river and al-though there were scores of them, they didn't match up. Ninety-five percent of the unidentified bodies were of men who were too old or boys who were too young. The other five percent were girls or women. Only two unidentified bodies were suspected vic-tims of homicide and they were categorized as likely homeless men. Probably living under bridges when the water rose and washed them away.

The majority of victims had been found in the summer months when it was much more likely people would be wading, swim-ming, fishing, or boating in the river. There were no victims at all, in fact, for the past two weeks of October.

How could it be that they'd simply vanished, she asked herself. Was it possible Kyle and Raheem had negotiated dams, reser-voirs, cities, and entire states without being reported? Did they travel at night and take on the risk of foundering in the dark?

Or maybe they'd decided to ditch their boat somewhere along the way and take off on their own.

That didn't work either. Kyle wasn't devious. In fact, in his way, he was the most straightforward and single-minded teenager

Cassie had ever met. He wouldn't have gathered items and gear for years for a river journey and then not followed through. She doubted Raheem had the influence to convince Kyle to use the boat as a ruse so they could slip away and go elsewhere. When Kyle's mind was set *no one* could change it.

She was flummoxed.

BEFORE GIVING UP ENTIRELY to start dinner for Ben after he got home from school, she recalled how Cody Hoyt sometimes spouted off wild scenarios that seemed to have nothing at all to do with the case they were investigating. He did it, he said, because it was just as important to rule things *out*. By ruling out even implausible theories it helped them focus on what *was* plausible.

Which meant her search would have to expand beyond the Missouri River states to include the entire nation. That's where NIBRS, NCIC, and ViCAP should come in. But she'd already looked at those the night before. Maybe she'd used the wrong criteria, she thought.

The most implausible theory she could come up with was that the boys got in their boat and went *upriver*.

She'd assumed from the start that they would be at the mercy of the river flow and could travel no faster downriver than that. But what if they somehow obtained an outboard motor with enough horsepower to push them against the flow? The river near Grimstad was wide and slow. Steamboats had at one time sailed upriver.

Even though it made no sense to her, she accessed RIMN—the Rocky Mountain Information Network that included Arizona, Colorado, Idaho, Montana, Nevada, New Mexico, Utah, and Wyoming. It was the database she'd used the most when she worked for Lewis and Clark County in Montana.

Upriver was Montana, her home state, where the headwaters of the Missouri River originated.

She scrolled through incident reports from Montana and gasped when she found an item from three weeks before from the tiny (population 332) town of Ekalaka in Carter County, the most southeastern county in the state.

The Carter County Sheriff's Department is seeking information on the September 22 discovery of a headless body discovered south of town. The victim was a young African American or dark-skinned Native American and/or Hispanic male in his late teens or early twenties. The victim was found 180 feet from County Road 154 wearing boxer briefs (lg.) and no other clothing. Victim is estimated to have been five-eight to five-ten and 160 to 175 pounds. There are no identifying marks on the body except for a two-inch (apparent) surgical scar on the inner left ankle. Cause of death, according to Sheriff (and Coroner) Bebe Verplank, was not determined due to possible post-mortem decapitation. There were no other wounds on the body. Montana DCI is involved in foren-sic pathology procedure.

Cassie reread the post and sat back, her heart whumping in her chest.

One victim, not two. Ekalaka was a town so small and isolated that it listed only three law enforcement personnel: a deputy, an undersheriff, and a sheriff named Bebe Verplank who also served as the coroner. Confusion over whether the body was African American, Native American, or Hispanic.

The timing—three weeks—kind of worked. Did Raheem have a surgical scar on his ankle?

But Ekalaka was the absolute *wrong* direction: west. And it was found over two hundred miles due *south* of Wolf Point and the Missouri River in Montana.

It made no sense. None. But it was the only thing she'd found in hours of searching that might be a lead.

As she spun out scenarios in her head her cell phone burred and skittered across the top of the card table. She snatched it up.

Sheriff Kirkbride was returning her call.

She couldn't wait to talk to him. She wanted to know if Kirkbride knew of Bebe Verplank in Ekalaka, or if Raheem had a scar on the inside of his ankle.

FROM THE SECOND HE SAID, "Cassie, it's Jon," she knew something was wrong on the other end. It came through in his tone.

"Thanks for calling me back."

"Sure," he said. Then: "Well, it's over. Avery Tibbs won and I lost. I'm in here cleaning out my desk."

"*What?*"

"I came to an agreement with the county commission. I really didn't fight very hard. They're letting me retire as of today with my full pension. Tibbs is putting Deanna Palmer in charge until the next election. She'll do fine . . ."

Cassie didn't know what to say.

"I'm not even all that pissed off at Tibbs," he said. "He wanted me out more than I wanted to stay. That's how the game is played at this level. It's pure power politics and I'd be lying if I said I wasn't pretty damn good at it myself back when I was rising through the ranks. That's just how it goes.

"I guess I'll finally get the chance to spend some quality time with my horses," Kirkbride said. "I can't say I mind that one bit."

Cassie asked, "How much of this had to do with the explosion?"

Kirkbride hesitated for a moment. "That was the thing Tibbs could latch onto," he said with a sigh. "We've never lost any officers before, so someone had to take the fall. I don't mind that it's me."

Cassie said, "I'm just so sorry you have to leave because of me—because of what I did. You trusted me and I let you down."

"*Stop it*. Just stop it," Kirkbride said with a flash of anger. "I was your supervisor and I was all in. Nobody could have prepared for what happened because we were up against a guy using his own sick set of rules. I'm sure we both have had plenty of sleepless nights where we ask ourselves what we would have done differently. But there was no way anyone could have guessed he'd blow himself up and take as many of us with him as he could."

"Did you tell the commissioners that?" she asked.

"Not really. I've pretty much lost my enthusiasm for another political fight after all these years. I did fight for you, though."

Cassie sat back in her chair. "You did what?"

"I told them they ought to come to you on bended knee and beg you to stay. That they really don't want to lose the best investigator in the department."

"I'll bet Tibbs loved that," Cassie said.

"He wasn't too happy about it," Kirkbride said. "But I'm afraid if I was you I wouldn't wait for them to show up at your door."

"Thank you," she said. She was going to say more but she could feel her emotions taking over. For the second time in two days she didn't want the sheriff to know she was going to cry.

"But that's not what you called about," Kirkbride said.

"No it isn't but never mind," she said. Something was burning in the back of her throat.

"Don't be a stranger," Kirbride said with his usual good cheer. "Come by the place and have a cup of coffee if you don't have anything else to do. And if you want a good laugh you can watch a fat old guy try to ride around on his horse."

She discontinued the call and lowered the phone to her lap.

Then she closed her eyes and took a ragged breath. She thought she knew how Lottie Westergaard must feel: that something unusual had happened and the aftermath was unfair and unjust.

Cassie pushed back from the card table and opened the blinds of the window and looked out on the quiet street. A knot of grade-school kids were on the sidewalk coming home from school. Ben should be on his way home as well.

As for Kyle Westergaard and Raheem Johnson . . .

THIRTEEN

Location Unknown

KYLE HAD NO IDEA where he was but he knew it was different from any place he'd ever been before.

The air was thinner. He'd thought at first when he got there it was the hood over his head that made it hard to breathe, but when it finally came off he realized he couldn't seem to get a full breath—more like half a breath. It gave him a headache and made his lungs hurt and when he stood up too quickly he became dizzy.

The trees were different, too. He could see them through the cloudy window cut into the log wall as well as the window above the old-fashioned sink. Tall and skinny—really skinny trees. Christmas trees, sort of. Not like the kind of full trees he was used to, the ones that looked like upside-down pears. And he could smell a waft of pine on the rare occasions when the front door opened.

It got cold faster when the sun went down and it warmed up more quickly in the morning.

And there were very few normal sounds outside. No traffic, no voices, no train whistles. A few times he heard a jet airplane high in the sky and the sound of it passing seemed to wash down through the air, crescendo, and vanish again.

The cabin they were being held prisoner in was old, dark, and small with a close ceiling. It was built of logs that had been there so long they'd turned as hard as stone and gray in color. It was essentially two rooms. The main room had a woodstove and propane stove for cooking, a table, cupboards, nails and pegs inserted into the logs to hold coats and clothes, and a double bed pushed up against one wall and a single bed pushed up against the other. There was only one door and two windows. Adjacent to the main room was a smaller bedroom Ron occupied. There was no door between the main room and his bedroom but it had been established early on that no one was to enter his room for any reason or they'd be severely punished.

When Ron was gone, like he was now, the only sound inside the small structure was when the wind rattled something above the rafters or on the roof. It sounded like a playing card clipped to a bike frame so the spokes would make it go *rat-rat-rat-rat-rat*. And the pop of flames in the potbellied stove.

That, and the two women talking.

"HE'S BEEN GONE a really long time," the older woman named Amanda said to Tiffany. Her voice dropped to a whisper.

"Maybe he's not coming back. What do we do if he doesn't come back this time? What if he gets in an accident or something?"

Her voice and accent were familiar to Kyle, kind of like a cross between Grandma Lottie and his mother. Amanda had a round face and tight curls and she had large hands. She was a heavy woman with big thighs encased in jeans. She wore an oversized sweatshirt with a jolly Santa face sewed on the front of it. There was a smear of black soot on Santa's beard from her feeding lengths of wood into the old stove.

"Oh, he's coming back," Tiffany said. "He *always* fuckin' comes back."

"But what if they arrest him, you know? Do you think he'd tell the cops about us?"

"What do *you* think?"

She was younger, Tiffany was. Really thin, too, almost bony. She had narrow shoulders, improbably large breasts, long stringy blond hair, big brown deep-set eyes, and a hard-edged husky voice. She was always complaining that she was cold no matter how much wood Amanda stuffed into the stove. She'd staked out her spot on the iron-framed bed in the corner nearest to the heat. Linty blankets covered her bare legs. Tiffany had lost one of her long dangly earrings somewhere along the way but the right one was still attached to the lobe. She was still wearing her short black skirt.

"What if he doesn't come back, though?" Amanda asked her.

"Then we can get the hell out of here, I guess," Tiffany said.

"What about the bolt and the lock in the door?"

"What about it?"

"How do we break it?"

"Shit if I know."

Amanda chinned toward the window on the wall above them. "If we got that open could you squeeze out?"

"I know *you* couldn't."

Amanda ignored her and said, "Maybe if you could get outside you could use an ax or something to break the door down and let us out."

"So it's up to me, huh?" Tiffany said. She shot a look at Kyle to take his measure. He knew his shoulders were too wide for consideration. She sighed when she realized it, too.

She turned to Amanda. "So it's my job to get out of that window, find an ax, and chop you out of this cabin? All the while Ron is someplace out there. What if he comes back when I'm halfway out the window? What if he comes back when I'm trying to chop the door down?"

Then Tiffany's mouth twisted up into a cruel grin. She had two rows of small, dark-yellow teeth. "Maybe you can go lose some weight and climb out through that window yourself. If he doesn't blow your head clean off I'll follow you. How's that?"

"Don't be so mean," Amanda said, hurt. "Why are you always so *mean?*"

Tiffany crossed her arms over her chest and looked away, obviously annoyed.

"Really," Amanda said. "We're in this together. We should work together, shouldn't we?"

Tiffany refused to answer.

"Well?" Amanda asked.

"You're trying to get me killed," Tiffany said finally. "This is bad enough without you trying to get me killed, Grandma."

Amanda shook her head and looked down at her lap. Kyle could barely hear her say, "I'm not trying to get anybody killed."

They talked as if Kyle wasn't even in the room. He sat on his very small bed in the far corner of the room. Amanda had addressed him a couple of times since they'd all been together but he'd refused to look at her or answer her questions. He'd done the same once when Tiffany scowled at him and asked, "*What the fuck is wrong with you, anyway? Do you even know what's going on?*"

Kyle had nodded that he did.

IT HAD BEEN THAT WAY since that night near the river when the man he now knew as Ron showed the pistol and ordered both Kyle and Raheem to pull their boat out of the water into the thick brush. Then the raft.

In the dark, Ron had marched them toward the old house trailer and made them sit on lawn chairs propped up around a cold campfire.

On the way there, Raheem asked Ron questions.

"Why are you doing this?"

"Why do we have to go with you? Just let us get back on the river.

"Is there a reward for us or something? Who would spend that kind of money, anyway?

"Are we trespassing or something? What's wrong?"

But Ron—Kyle didn't know his name at the time—never answered.

Instead, Ron kept his gun on Kyle as he wrapped Raheem's wrists together with silver duct tape, then his ankles. Then his mouth with a particular flourish. Ron put the gun in his coat pocket as he did the same to Kyle. Kyle didn't resist.

Ron wasn't violent with them, or particularly rough. He said as few words as possible to get the task done.

Kyle didn't know what Ron meant when the man said to himself, "Looks like I need a couple more dog collars," and sent them one by one into the trailer house where Amanda and Tiffany were.

The two women had simply stared at them for a long time. They weren't taped up but Kyle noticed in the gloom of the trailer that each had a small green blinking light emanating from a black collar on their necks.

"Oh this is fucking great," the skinny one said to the other. "He's collecting even more people."

"Maybe they can help us?" the older woman said.

"The big one, maybe. That little one—I doubt it."

Kyle had ignored them. He managed to stand up with his legs and wrists bound and he watched through the louvred windows that night as Ron fed their clothing and gear from the boat into the fire pit and burned it.

Ron broke up their boat with an ax he'd found in the shed and threw the staves on the fire. Raheem soon joined him at the window.

"What in the hell is he going to do with us, man?" Raheem asked Kyle.

"I don't know."

Hours later, Ron fired up an ancient front-end loader that had been parked on the side of the shed and scooped up the entire smoldering fire pit and dumped the debris and earth into the Missouri River with a loud hissing sound. There had been a lot of sparks as each load hit the water, and Kyle could smell the acrid steam even that far away.

THE NEXT DAY RON PUT hoods over their heads and taped them on securely. Kyle listened as Ron led Tiffany and Raheem outside and told them calmly to lay down on the back floor of the pickup truck.

Kyle felt Ron's presence as he entered the trailer and his grip under Kyle's arm.

"You're next," Ron said. "You get the seat but you have to lay down on it. Don't sit up no matter what."

Kyle had no idea why he got the seat and Raheem and Tiffany got the floor. He felt guilty about it as he wriggled into the back of the cab.

"You're next to me," Ron said to Amanda, who apparently didn't have a hood over her head. "Sit there like you're my wife. Don't look at anyone and don't make eye contact. Don't take off that scarf over your collar. You know what'll happen if you do."

And they drove away from the trailer house. Eventually, Kyle could hear the singing of the tires as well as passing vehicles. Ron didn't say a word to anyone.

Kyle wished at the time he knew his directions better. He

couldn't tell where they were headed in the truck, only that it was taking hours upon hours. For a while he tried to count the minutes and then the hours by saying in his head "one-thousand-one, one-thousand-two" so he could figure out how far away from the trailer they would end up. But he messed up his count and couldn't recall where he'd left off.

He could hear Raheem breathe at times, and sometimes his friend moaned in frustration. Tiffany was extremely still when she wasn't quietly crying.

A LONG TIME later Kyle could feel the truck slow down and take a long turn on pavement. It stopped a couple more times and he could hear the ambient sounds of cars around them. He guessed Ron had stopped at a stop sign or under streetlights. Then Ron swung off the street into what Kyle guessed was a gas station or parking lot.

"You're coming with me," Ron said to Amanda.

The springs in the front seat groaned as Ron turned in his seat to address Raheem, Tiffany, and him in back.

"Nobody fucking move," Ron had said.

Kyle had felt the truck rock a little as Ron and Amanda got out and shut their doors. Then the back door opened and he knew it was Ron.

"Hold your hands out."

There was rustling and Tiffany cried out, "Not so tight!"

Kyle was confused about what was happening until his own bound hands were jerked away from the seat. He felt the bite of wire being wound around his wrists.

Ron ran the wire over Raheem and Tiffany and tied it off somewhere under the seat, probably to the frame.

"Just in case anyone was thinking about getting out," he said and shut the door tight.

KYLE HAD THOUGHT about what he should do. Should he writhe around on the cushion until he was in a sitting position where someone might see a hooded boy in the back of a truck and call the police? Or would the person who saw him turn out to be Ron?

Both Raheem and Tiffany were moving around and grunting on the floor. They seemed to realize Ron was gone and they were trying to get up.

He hadn't heard the sounds that would have resulted in the truck being fueled—the gas cap being opened, the gasoline pumping into the tank—so Kyle assumed they were parked elsewhere.

But where?

Before he could make up his mind to try and sit up he heard the familiar bass of Ron's voice not far from the truck. Tiffany and Raheem heard it, too, and both became still.

The truck doors opened and Kyle could sense both Amanda and Ron climbing in.

"That man might wonder why you're buying two shock collars at once," Amanda said.

"People around here train their dogs to hunt birds. He only saw cash," Ron said back. "Now shut up, please. You talk too much. I don't need your help or advice."

Later, when Kyle thought about it, that had been the only real chance in the past month he'd had to draw attention to his situation and possibly escape. He *might* have been able to tug hard enough on the wire that it became unfastened, or he could have started shouting with the hope that someone outside would hear him. But he hadn't acted.

Since then, he, like Amanda and Tiffany, had gotten used to a new and terrible way of life. He heard Amanda say it had been four weeks, but it seemed much longer. So much longer that when he recalled pushing out on the river with Raheem on that glorious day it now seemed like a dream.

Raheem would have hated this new life, Kyle thought, but at least it was life.

IN THE LATE AFTERNOON, Kyle heard labored breathing outside and he turned his head toward the door. Both Amanda and Tiffany clammed up.

The lock clicked and a bolt was thrown and the door opened.

Ron stood in the threshold covered with blood. It was on his face and hands as well as his clothing. He peered inside because it was dark and let his eyes adjust. A rifle was slung over his shoulder, the muzzle behind his back pointed up in the air.

"There you all are," he said, slightly out of breath. "I was gone longer than I planned to be."

"We're just fine," Amanda said. She always felt she had to say something, Kyle thought. Unlike him.

"Good, 'cause I hope you know how to butcher a deer," Ron said to Amanda. "I field dressed it already so you don't need to worry about that."

Kyle let his eyes drop from Ron in the doorway. A two-point gray buck deer was slumped behind Ron. The buck's eyes were open but dried out and its tongue lolled out of the side of its mouth like the deer was smoking a swelled-up pink cigar. Ron had dragged it from far enough away that he was obviously worn out from the exertion.

"I've cooked venison," Amanda said cautiously. "But I've never actually skinned out a deer or cut one up."

Ron nodded in that way that meant he could care less what she said. He reached behind him and produced a small bone saw designed for big game. He reversed it and pointed the handle toward her to grasp.

"Here," he said. "I'll show you how."

As an aside, Ron winked at Kyle and said, "It's the first time this saw's been used on a game animal."

Then he grinned as if sharing a joke.

PART
THREE

EKALAKA

FOURTEEN

CASSIE KEPT A CLOSE EYE on the gas gauge of her Escape as she got within five miles of Ekalaka, Montana, on State Highway 7. She regretted not stopping back in Baker for fuel fifteen minutes earlier. A gaggle of men standing around in coveralls surrounding the only open pump had convinced her to keep going.

The digital display on the dashboard had gone from 12 MILES REMAINING to LOW FUEL.

If she ran out of gas—which was very possible—she didn't know how long it might be before someone came by to help her. Since she'd passed through Wibaux fifty miles north of where she was, she'd not encountered a single car on the road.

The terrain was as flat as it had been in North Dakota but even more desolate. There were ponderosa pine–covered buttes every few miles, and weather-beaten signs for distant ranches, but no place to stop for fuel.

Thanks to Jon Kirkbride she had the cell phone number for Carter County Sheriff (and Coroner) Bebe Verplank entered into her phone. Kirkbride and Verplank were both officers of the Western States Sheriffs Association and knew each other well. Cassie knew she could call Verplank if she ran out of gas and was stranded—but what an inauspicious way to meet, she thought.

People in small towns loved to talk about knuckleheads like her—city types who didn't have the sense not to run out of gas in the most remote and least populated corner of the entire state. Her North Dakota license plates would work against her as well. Montanans, as she knew, loved to make fun of North Dakotans. That Montana was her home until two years before would only muck up the narrative.

She'd checked a map before she'd departed that morning. Ekalaka—pronounced *Eek-ah-lack-uh*—seemed to be the dead center of Nowhere. It was twenty-six miles from the North Dakota border, twenty-four miles from the South Dakota border, sixty miles from Wyoming, and one hundred miles from the nearest town in Montana of any size: Miles City.

Everybody growing up in Montana had heard of Ekalaka because the name kind of rolled off the tongue. Few actually knew where it was. Fewer still had ever been there.

She'd concluded there was no logical explanation for Kyle and Raheem to push off on the Missouri River in Grimstad and wind up hundreds of miles away and upstream in Ekalaka.

Yet, here she was.

And she had an appointment with Sheriff Verplank at 5 P.M.

SHE PULLED OFF THE HIGHWAY at the first gas station she saw a half-mile north of town. It was a tiny A-frame building she assumed was open because there was a light on inside. A hand-painted sign on the side of the building read WE ASSASSINATE DRIVE-AWAYS.

When she climbed out of her car and stretched she blew out a long breath. It had been nerve-wracking driving on fumes.

The pumps were old-fashioned and instead of a digital display that showed the cost and the volume of fuel dispensed, there were spinning dials and no way to use a credit card.

She cursed and grabbed her purse from the front seat and walked across the gravel to the office. She could see a man's face peering at her through a cloudy window.

Inside it was dark and musty. The small space was crowded with shelving with very few items for sale outside of .22 shells, beaded jewelry from what was no doubt a local artisan, and used paperback books. Dust-covered mule deer heads looked down at her from the walls.

"I need to fill up," she said to the man seated behind the cash register. The top of his head barely cleared the top of the counter.

"Well, go ahead."

He had a large bald head and owl-like eyes. She wondered why he didn't stand up until she got closer and realized he was in a wheelchair.

"Here's my credit card," she said, offering it to him. That's when she saw the large caliber revolver in his lap.

"Just pay for it when you're done," the man said. "But this isn't full-serve. You have to pump it yourself."

"That's fine."

"And we don't take credit cards. Cash only."

"I see," she said. "I can't remember the last time I paid cash for gasoline. Probably high school."

The man shrugged. "You can always go on into town, I guess."

"No, it's fine," she said, thinking of the envelope of cash Dottie had given her and refused to take back. She had only twenty dollars herself. "Is the women's bathroom open?"

He handed her a key.

When she brought it back he asked, "What brings you to town? Here to see the dinosaur museum? This is dino country, you know. Bones everywhere."

"Is that so?"

"That's so."

"Do you always keep that gun on your lap?"

He paused as if the question confused him. Finally, he said, "Yep, I do."

"I'll be back," she said.

"Yep."

SHE ALMOST DROVE OUT the other side of Ekalaka before she realized there was no more Ekalaka, only one short main commercial street and unpaved roads to scattered homes. She did a U-turn and parked on the shoulder of the highway. The tiny community was in an oasis of trees in the high desert landscape. The whole of the town spanned her windshield.

Cassie punched in the number Kirkbride had given her.

"Yullo?" A man's deep voice.

"Is this the Carter County Sheriff's Department?" she asked.

He chuckled and said, "This is Sheriff Verplank. You're calling my cell phone."

"Oh, I'm sorry. This is Cassie Dewell from North Dakota. I made an appointment with your receptionist this morning."

"That was my wife, but yeah. You want to meet at the Old Stand Saloon?"

"Sure," she said. "Where is it?"

He laughed again and said, "You can't miss it. Are you in town?" Then the sheriff said, "Oh yeah, I see you."

She looked up. A stocky man in a beige uniform had stepped out the side door of the only three-story building in town. It was a square wooden structure with a cupola on top.

He waved. "You're looking at the Carter County Justice Center. We're on Pine Street. The Old Stand is on Main Street," he said, indicating the area on the other side of the building. "Everything," he added, "is on Main Street."

"I'll see you there," she said.

"If it's open," he said cautiously.

OVER THE PAST FEW DAYS Cassie had gone to the office supply store to replicate the things she had on her desk at the Law Enforcement Center—stapler, paper clips, highlight pens, and other items. She fell back on her police training and assembled a case file. It included printouts from the databases, copies of her interview notes thus far, photos of Kyle and Raheem, and the missing persons reports filed by Lottie and Raheem's father. Both reports were public records although she'd received them more quickly than usual because Judy Banister made sure she did.

She constructed a timeline of what had happened so far: the disappearance, the initial contact with law enforcement, the follow-up—and lack thereof—up to when Lottie cornered her in the lobby of the Law Enforcement Center. The list of contacts for the case was short.

She assembled the file meticulously with the thought in mind that when her investigation was complete—one way or other—she could turn the entire thing over to law enforcement.

Cassie was grateful for the distraction the work provided, and whenever she hit another dead end she thought about Lottie. And the work kept her at arm's length from her mother, who would pop in and out of the house at any time depending on her activities.

The day before she'd purchased a used .40 Glock 27 at the Work Wearhouse in Grimstad that was just like the piece she'd turned in after her suspension. Cassie was used to carrying that particular weapon—nine rounds in the magazine and one in the chamber—and it was perfectly legitimate to do so. She still had her Concealed Carry permit from Montana, and North Dakota offered reciprocity.

While waiting for her background check to clear to take possession of the weapon, she pushed a cart around the store and added items from the shelves: three-cell Maglite flashlight, a handheld radio with a police scanner frequency, binoculars, a Swiss Army knife, and plastic bindings for fencing that could conceivably be used as flexible handcuffs.

Because she'd heard Lottie's version of events Cassie thought it important to talk to the other complainant as well.

She tracked down Raheem's father in Minneapolis via a law enforcement database she still had access to on her home computer.

He answered his cell phone on the second ring.

"MR. JOHNSON? MR. CLYDE JOHNSON?"

"That's me. Who are you?"

"My name is Cassie Dewell. I'm calling from Grimstad to follow up on the case of your missing son Raheem."

She could hear him take a sharp breath.

"He's dead, isn't he?"

"No, no—that's not why I'm calling. I'm investigating the disappearance of Raheem and Kyle Westergaard. I'm trying to find out what happened to them."

"You with the police?" His tone was aggressive.

"No. It's a private investigation on behalf of Lottie Westergaard. I'm not a member of law enforcement."

"Well, you couldn't do much worse than those fools, that's for sure. I went into the sheriff's department four times before I left town and nobody could give me any answers at all. I understand why they didn't do much that first day," he said. "That was the morning that truck blew up in town and killed them cops. You know about that?"

"Yes, I do."

"Some woman cop was responsible is what I heard."

"There *is* a dispute about that," she said. "But go on."

"Anyway, there's no damned excuse for why they didn't do anything the second, third, and fourth time I went in there to see 'em. They weren't doing *nothing* to find him I could see."

"I'm sorry to hear that, Mr. Johnson. I really am. But I've got the missing person's report you filed and I'm trying to find out everything I can. I hope you'll spare me a few minutes."

"I got time," he said. "I'm at my brother's place in the Twin Cities trying to find a job. There isn't any work in North Dakota no more."

"Believe me, I know."

"Yeah, the bottom fell out. I didn't want to leave with Raheem still gone. I feel bad about that. But I sat around for three weeks waiting to hear from either Raheem or the cops and the rent came due. I had to clear out."

"So Raheem has made no attempt to contact you since he went missing on September fifteenth?"

"I don't know if he made an attempt or not but he didn't contact me if that's what you mean."

"That's what I mean."

"Okay then. I *did* leave a message on the house phone where I was at if he tried. I think he'd try my cell phone anyway, though. Man, every morning I wake up and look at it to see if he called or texted me."

"And nothing so far," she said.

"Nothing so far. I've heard as much from Raheem as I have from the damn cops."

"I know you and Mrs. Johnson are divorced but did you check with her to see if Raheem had been in touch?"

"I did," he said wearily. "She said she hadn't heard from him. All she did was ream me out and say what a shitty dad I must be if Raheem felt he had to run away. This from the woman who left with a salesman and moved to Texas when Raheem was four."

She nodded even though she knew he couldn't see it. "Can I ask you a few questions?"

"Yeah, sure."

"We assume that Raheem and Kyle left Grimstad in a drift boat on the morning of September fifteenth. But that's just what it is—an assumption. Do you recall Raheem ever saying he wanted to visit a special place?"

There was a long pause. "Are you asking me if I think Raheem and Kyle faked leaving in the boat and went somewhere else?"

"Yes, I guess so."

"Hmmm, that's a weird one. I guess I never really thought about it that way."

"I've got no reason to suggest it, Mr. Johnson. I'm just trying to rule everything out."

"Yeah."

"So shall we move on?"

"Yeah, next question."

"I'm looking at your report and I don't see that you list any identifying marks on Raheem. Is it possible you left something out?"

"*New Orleans*," he said suddenly.

"Excuse me?"

"Raheem used to say he'd like to go to New Orleans so he could see women take their shirts off, you know? I always laughed about that. Even his favorite team is the Saints. So maybe New Orleans."

She wrote that down. New Orleans, she knew, could be the end of their journey if they were somehow still on the river.

"About those marks. Anything?"

"Why?" he asked suspiciously. "Did someone find a body?"

"I can't confirm that," she said.

"Let's see," he said. "Well, when he was nine he fell out of a damned tree! Climbed to the top and fell down through the branches like a dumbass. I thought he might have broken his neck but he's like a cat—he doesn't get hurt. He jumped right back up on his feet. I think all he needed was stitches on his leg. That's it."

"Where on his leg?"

"His ankle."

"Which ankle?"

"Right. It was his right ankle."

She glanced over at the RIMN printout. The body supposedly had a scar on the inside *left* ankle.

"No, I'm wrong," he said. "I was thinking that when I looked at him head-on the scar was on the right. But it was *my* right. The scar was actually on his left ankle."

"Where on the ankle?" she asked, trying to keep her tone even and professional.

"On the inside. Why you asking me about his ankle?"

"Like I said—I'm trying to gather as much information as possible as well as rule things out."

"Uh-huh," he said. "You've already asked me more questions than the damned cops ever did. Maybe you ought to be a cop."

She let that go.

WHEN SHE'D CALLED EX-SHERIFF Jon Kirkbride at home and told him what she was doing, he'd laughed and said, "What are you, a private detective?"

"Kind of," she admitted.

"You know what I think of private detectives," he said.

"I remember," she said. "You said, 'TSA agents are folks who were too dumb to pass the test for a job at the post office, and private investigators were folks too dumb to qualify for the TSA.'"

He laughed.

"Well, I'm not an official private investigator. I don't have a license. I'm just trying to help out Lottie Westergaard and Clyde Johnson."

"What can I help you with, Cassie?"

"Do you know the sheriff in Ekalaka, Montana? His name is—"

"Bebe Verplank," Kirkbride said. "Yeah, I know Bebe. Good guy. But why are you interested in him? Have you ever been to *Ekalaka*?"

THE OLD STAND BAR and Grill had a covered porch outside supported by four-by-fours. Inside was a bar with two big-hatted cowboys separated by a single stool. It was an ancient place. A cavernous room to the right was scattered with steel and formica tables, most not occupied. The ceiling sagged in the room and looked like it might give out any moment.

Sheriff Verplank waved her over from a table. As she approached he stood and removed his tan cowboy hat with his left hand and extended his right.

"Bebe Verplank."

"I'm Cassie Dewell," she said. "Thanks for agreeing to meet with me."

"Jon said you'd be coming. He said you're one of the good ones."

"That's nice to hear."

He nodded, waited for her to sit down, and did the same.

Verplank was in his mid-sixties, with light gray eyes and a white bristly mustache that hung over his top lip like the head of a toothbrush. He had faint smile lines on both sides of his mouth.

"Jon told me what happened up in North Dakota," he said to Cassie. "Let me say that I'm very sorry for your loss."

She nodded. "Ian was a good man. I miss him."

"Jon said the same. He also said you two both got railroaded."

"You can put it that way."

"And that you're now trying to help an old woman out by doing a private investigation of some kind?"

She nodded. "I'm not a licensed private investigator. I'm a civilian with a law enforcement background. When it comes to arresting someone I'll call the cops, hand over what I've found, and let them take over. I just want to make sure we're clear on that."

"Crystal clear," he said. "You get to do investigative work without all the bureaucracy and politics of a sheriff's department. I envy you there."

She smiled.

"We're in luck," he said, gesturing around the room of The Old Stand. "No one ever knows when this place is going to be open or closed. The owner just kind of does what he wants to. I don't know why he even posts hours on the door because he doesn't pay any attention to them."

"It's interesting," Cassie said.

He looked up and grinned while he took her in. He had a friendly, half-amused-at-everything demeanor, but behind it were the cool eyes of a lawman.

"It was either here or the Church of Hank Williams," he said.

"The Church of Hank Williams?"

"That's what they call it," he said. "It's really an old garage down the street where locals bring their own beer and sit around and listen to old country music and shoot the shit when The Old Stand is closed. I've wound up there a few times myself.

"Wife's gone to Miles City," he said. "I hope you don't mind if I order some dinner here while we talk. I missed lunch today because I was chasing a cow that jumped the fence and got on the highway. So I'm damned hungry."

"Did you catch the cow?" she asked.

"Sadly, yes," he said with a roll of his eyes. "But it was a rodeo for a couple of hours. As you can guess, my life as a sheriff is filled with nonstop action."

That made her smile.

"It's not like the big city," he said. "We don't spend much time trying to stop a gang war—or chasing the Lizard King."

"So you know about those things," she said.

"I did my homework on you and Jon filled in the gaps. Damned impressive work you did."

"Thank you," she said. She knew she was blushing.

"Jon said you were the best chief investigator he ever had."

She wanted to get to the point but not offend him. And Cassie couldn't deny that the compliments made her feel good. She also knew that innocent small talk from a sheriff wasn't always innocent. It was a technique to disarm while verifying the subject at the same time.

"I'm sorry to call you on your personal cell phone to request a meeting," she said.

"Everybody here calls me on my cell phone," he said. "I used to joke that nobody in Carter County knew how to dial the numbers nine-one-one."

She smiled.

"So, first time in Ekalaka?"

"Yes."

"You won't get lost, that's for sure."

"I appreciate that."

"Do you know the story of this place?" he asked.

"The town or this bar?"

"Both," he said with a grin. "A man named Claude Carter—hence the county name—was pulling logs and whiskey across the state in the 1880s to build a bar down by Miles City. He got his wagon stuck in the creek out there and he said, 'Hell, anyplace in Montana is a good place for a saloon,' and he built this place right here where it still stands.

"You think I made that up, don't you?"

Before she could answer, a waitress in a dark red smock approached the table with a pad and pen. "Do you know what you want?"

"What do you think?" Verplank said.

"Baseball steak medium-rare, burnt fries, salad with Thousand Island."

He nodded and said to Cassie, "Try the baseball steak. They cut all their own meat here in the back."

"Baseball steak?"

"Exactly like it sounds," he said. "The size and shape of a baseball. A damned nice piece of meat."

Cassie looked up at the waitress and said, "I'll have what he's having. Only blue cheese instead of Thousand Island."

"We don't have blue cheese," the waitress said.

"Then Thousand Island."

"Good choice," she said and departed the table with a knowing wink to the sheriff.

When she left, he said, "Everybody knows Mrs. Verplank is gone and here I am sitting at dinner with a nice looking lady. It'll be the news at the Church of Hank Williams within the hour."

"So," she said, "about that body you found . . ."

FIFTEEN

"IT'S NOT LIKE WE NEVER see any dead bodies around here," Sheriff Verplank said to Cassie as he cut into his steak. Juice from the meat pooled across his plate.

"We see our share," he said, taking a bite. He chewed slowly and closed his eyes because he obviously enjoyed it so much.

After he swallowed, he said, "Car accidents, mainly, and once in a while a suicide. But ninety-five percent of the bodies I've been called out on died by natural causes. We *thought* we had a double homicide a while back but it turned out it wasn't. The story is a weird one even for here.

"A local rancher called to say there was a car with South Dakota plates parked off to the side of a service road on his place. The rancher looked inside and didn't see anybody so he called me.

"We checked it out and found a dead female in the trunk. That looked highly suspicious," he said. "Then we found her husband dead a quarter mile away. He'd been shot in the chest with a deer rifle that was laying there next to him in the mud."

He jabbed his fork at her.

"Hey, you had better eat up before yours gets cold."

Cassie cut into the baseball steak. It was delicious.

"Turned out it was a drug thing," he said. "The woman OD'd and the husband apparently stuffed her in the trunk because he was high on meth and didn't know what else to do with her. Then he offed himself in a hayfield."

Cassie must have looked skeptical because Verplank said, "I know what you're thinking. But we had agents from the South Dakota and Montana divisions of criminal investigation here and they both came to the same conclusion.

"Before that," Verplank said, "The last outright murder was in 1992. Guy shot right out there on Main Street. But that's about it. We don't have many violent deaths but what we do have I'd call end-of-the-trail deaths."

"Meaning what?" she asked. She knew she shouldn't be enjoying the steak as much as she was given the subject matter being discussed. But she did.

"If you look at Ekalaka on the map it's about as isolated as you can get," he said. "We didn't even have a paved highway to here from Baker until recently. This place is absolutely not on the way to anywhere—you don't *pass through*. If you find yourself in Ekalaka you are coming here for a reason, as you no doubt learned today."

She nodded.

"So we're literally the end of the road. An enterprising bad guy or a meth head like the South Dakotan might figure it's a good place to hide out or dump a body. Two years ago a rancher found a couple of mutilated bodies in his irrigation ditch. The FBI showed up and concluded they were gangbangers from either Fargo or Minneapolis. Somebody killed them and drove their bodies here thinking no one would ever find them and connect them to anywhere. That's what I mean."

"Gotcha. So do you think this boy's body was dumped here?"

Verplank concentrated on eating the last few ounces of his meat, then swabbed French fries through the juice on his plate and popped them into his mouth.

"Between you and me," he said. "I do not."

When she arched her eyebrows he said, "I'm waiting to find out what the DCI concludes from their autopsy and investigation. They've got the body at the state lab in Missoula and they haven't sent me any results yet. So I'm keeping my theory to myself for now and only sharing it with you. I don't want to assume a homicide like I did with those South Dakota tweakers and turn out to be wrong again.

"I've got an election coming up," he said as explanation.

"Okay, it's just between us," Cassie said. "And we'll start from the premise that what you think is simply a theory at this point."

The sheriff leaned back so the waitress could clear his plate. Cassie did the same.

When she was gone, Verplank said, "It was easily the creepiest thing I've seen since I've been the sheriff here. I still think about it."

Cassie reached inside her purse for her notebook. "Can you describe what you found?"

"Not here," he said after he looked over both shoulders to see if any locals were eavesdropping. "Let's go to my office."

"I'll get the check," she said.

"Not in a million years. My county, my treat."

AT THE CARTER COUNTY Justice Center, Cassie followed the sheriff through the back door into his small office. An inside window looked out over three small cubicles and a lone deputy seated at a desk. The deputy looked up and saw them and waved hello.

Verplank signaled back to the deputy and gestured to Cassie to take the hardback chair positioned in front of his desk. He sat down heavily and opened a file drawer behind him and placed a folder on the desk.

Before he opened it he said, "Some of these photos are pretty graphic. Are you okay looking at them?"

"I'm okay," she said. But she wasn't sure. She'd met Raheem several times when he was with Kyle. He was brash but polite to her and she always thought he was overplaying the role of a fish out of water; a cool street kid stuck in rural North Dakota even though he had been in Grimstad most of his life.

It was one thing to look at deceased bodies of strangers. It was quite another to possibly see the dead body of someone she knew and liked.

The sheriff opened the file and slid a full-color eight-by-ten to her.

She glanced at it and gulped.

The shot was taken from about ten feet away so she could see the entire body. He was naked except for partially pulled-down boxers. The body was chest-down and sprawled crosswise across three rows of a freshly plowed field. The victim's skin was the same color as the clumpy dirt it lay in. The soles of his feet were pinkish.

There were several deep red abrasions near the shoulder blades and another on the small of his back. The victim's limbs were long and well muscled.

There was no head.

"That's what the scene looked like when I arrived," the sheriff said. "The photo was taken by me on my cell phone as I walked from the state highway out into the field. Obviously there was nothing obvious there to identify the victim. No wallet, no clothes, no tattoos. No teeth to check dental records."

She tapped on the photo. "Any idea why his underwear is pulled down?"

"First thing I thought, too," he said. "But I think we can discount sexual abuse. Those shorts got pulled down from falling forward into the dirt. The fabric was caught by the ground itself. It's hard to see that from the angle you're looking at."

She breathed a sigh of relief.

"Who reported it?" she asked. Her voice was husky and unsure.

"The school bus driver. She said she was on the way into town from picking up rural kids and she saw a bunch of crows perched on something in the field about fifty yards from the road. The ranch is owned by the Wilson family. The driver's name is Jean Spires and she knew that crows sitting there all together meant something was dead. She called in to say there was a dead Indian or a migrant in the hay meadow."

"An Indian?"

Verplank expelled a long puff of air from his nose. "We don't see many other dark-skinned citizens around here. The reservation is west of here. She assumed."

"Those wounds on his back?"

"The crows. Meaning birds and not Crow Indians."

She nodded.

He slid a few more photos to her of the field itself. The soil was dry and chalky and made up of small clods of dirt. In one photo bare footprints could be seen clearly. In the other were boot prints just as obvious.

"Those are mine," the sheriff said. "The only footprints in that field besides those of the victim."

It took her a moment to understand the point he was making.

Then: "So the victim ran across the field from the road without anyone chasing him?"

"That's what it looks like. He wasn't dumped there. I measured the distance between his footprints and you'll notice the balls of his feet made deeper impressions than the heels. He *ran* there."

"How is that even possible?" she asked. She deliberately didn't say, *without a head?*

"I've got some thoughts on that," he said. "But I want to see if you come to the same conclusion on your own. The DCI boys didn't seem to think much of my theory. They were operating under the impression that the victim was killed somewhere else and dumped out there somehow. They thought whoever did it dragged the body out there while the ground was frozen and didn't leave tracks."

She nodded for him to go on.

"How the victim could leave tracks but the killer didn't makes no sense to me even if it had gotten below freezing the night before—which it did. But those Missoula boys think they know it all sometimes.

"This one's rough," he said, showing her a close-up photo of the victim's neck and shoulders. After a split-second glance she deliberately focused on the upper right corner of the photo so she couldn't see it again. But she couldn't un-see it.

"The decapitation is unusual," Verplank said. "The head isn't cut off with a knife or hacked off with an ax. It was blown off. See the singeing of the skin? See how the edge of the flesh is discolored?

"At first I thought, given the distance from the road, that somebody took a shot at this poor guy with a high-powered weapon. But in all my years I've never seen a head get blown clean off by a bullet no matter how big the gun was.

"So what do you think?" he asked.

He paused while she thought.

"It doesn't seem to make sense that he was dragged there but no footprints were found," she said.

"Exactly," he said. Then: "I was in the Army during Operation Desert Shield when we had Saddam's forces on the run. I saw more bodies along the Road of Death than I ever care to see again. I saw men who'd been burned, decapitated, and mutilated. We found four Iraqi soldiers—deserters, we figured—who'd been buried up to their waists in the sand and killed by close range cannon fire from Saddam's tanks. I remember one guy in particular who was shot point-blank in the face from a cannon. His head was blown clean off his body. Just like this," he said, tapping the photo in front of Cassie.

"So you're thinking he was killed by a cannon?" she asked, trying to keep the skepticism out of her voice.

"No, of course not. But maybe an RPG, a rocket-propelled grenade fired from the road. Maybe the explosive charge detonated on impact. It would be a tough shot—fifty yards—but not impossible for someone who was trained."

Cassie sat back in the chair. The sheriff was merciful and retrieved the photo and put it back into his folder while she did.

"There would be additional injury to the shoulders and upper body," she said. "A grenade wouldn't work that cleanly."

"I concede that and I don't have an explanation for it."

"What other evidence was gathered in the field?"

He shrugged. "Pretty much nothing."

"They didn't sift the dirt around the victim to see what else might be present?"

"No."

"So maybe there is evidence still out there?" she said.

He brightened. "Like maybe fragments from an RPG?" he said, nodding his head to indicate she was on the right track—or at least *his* right track.

"Something like that."

Verplank got up and strode toward the interior window and rapped on it to get his deputy's attention. When the deputy looked up the sheriff motioned for him to come in.

"I'll have my deputy get a sifting screen from the hardware store and we can go out to that field before it gets dark," he said to Cassie.

"Good. I'd like to see it. But while we wait for him can I see all the photos? Do you have any of the victim's torso, the lower legs in particular?"

The sheriff looked at her with a squint. He obviously knew she was looking for something in particular she hadn't revealed.

"There's a missing boy back in Grimstad, an African American. He had a distinctive scar."

"Ah," he said, handing over the entire file.

As she riffled through it the deputy stuck his head in.

The sheriff said, "Go down to True Value and buy some furnace filters we can use as sifting screens. You know, for dirt."

The deputy and sheriff got in a short discussion about what that meant until Verplank was able to convey what he wanted.

"Meet us out at the Wilson place where we found the victim," he said.

Then to Cassie, "Are you finding what you're looking for?"

She shook her head and closed the folder. "No. The incident report said he had a surgical scar on his lower left ankle. I was hoping for a clear shot of his ankles or lower legs that are close enough to see a scar. We could show it to the father of the missing boy."

The only close photos she'd seen of the victim's legs were at the wrong angle. The legs had been turned in and the ankles were in shadow.

"Sorry," the sheriff said. "If I'd had any idea . . ."

"Could you check with DCI?" she asked. "Can you ask them to send us a good photo of the scar?"

"First thing tomorrow," he said ruefully. "They're state employees. They go home at five."

"Also, please ask them to send the DNA results to . . ." Her voice trailed off.

"To where?" the sheriff asked.

To where? She couldn't have them sent to the Bakken County

Sheriff's Department where she no longer worked, where they'd likely be mishandled or relegated to the bottom of a pile.

Maybe Minneapolis, where Raheem's father was located? But that would mean asking Clyde Johnson to produce materials that might contain his son's DNA. It would be traumatic. And she wasn't yet prepared to make that request of him. Not until she had more to go on.

"I'm not sure yet," she confessed. "I'm at a real loss here doing this as a private citizen. Let me think on it. But please ask them to be *prepared* to send the DNA results . . . somewhere."

SIXTEEN

THE SUN BALLOONED OVER the flat western horizon. As deep shadows formed in the furrows from the setting sun and the deputy palmed loose dirt onto the screen and sifted it, Cassie studied the location. From Verplank's detailed description, she could imagine where a vehicle had been on the road and in her mind she could see the victim running across the field to where they where now.

There were no ranch houses or structures in sight. It was unlikely anyone could have seen what happened that day unless they were driving along the highway at just the right time. The sheriff confirmed that no one had reported seeing anything unusual on the highway that day.

Cassie and the sheriff designated a twenty-foot grid around where the body had been found. On his hands and knees, the deputy sifted through the churned-up dirt with the screen.

The temperature cooled down quickly and within a half-hour they were working in the dark. Verplank turned on his flashlight and the deputy strapped on a headlamp. Cassie's job was to hold out an open large evidence bag so the deputy could pour in whatever was caught in the screen.

She observed carefully what he came up with. It wasn't unique for the most part: rocks too large to fall through the screen, bits of plastic that might have been out there for years, spent .22 casings, a Copenhagen chewing tobacco lid. But they did find some tiny slivers of black plastic—it looked like vinyl—and a couple of small metal pieces.

She plucked one of the metal parts out of the bag and asked the sheriff to illuminate it in the palm of her hand with his flashlight. It had a green color and small wires, like spider legs, extended out from it.

"What do you think this is?" she asked.

"Don't know for sure but it kind of looks like a part of a circuit board. Like maybe it was from a cell phone, radio, or walkie talkie."

"That's interesting, don't you think?" she asked.

He nodded. "I'll send this into DCI for analysis."

"So maybe it wasn't a rocket or grenade," she speculated. "Maybe there was a bomb of some kind attached to his neck. That would explain the close-contact burns. Whoever did this to him didn't shoot him from a distance. He sent the victim running and triggered the explosives by remote control."

"I never even considered that," the sheriff said. "But what kind of person could do such a thing?"

It was a question she was asking herself. She couldn't help but think of the last situation she'd been in that involved explosives.

But where that thought took her was a whole other place.

"ONE MORE THING," she said to the sheriff as they drove back toward Ekalaka in the dark. "Are there any closed-circuit cameras in town that might have seen the victim or whoever drove him here?"

"There are a few cameras around," he said. "Nothing like in

the cities, though. We've got them inside the bank, at the convenience stores, all the ATMs of course. But it isn't like London or New York. The likelihood of finding whoever did this on video is remote at best. Plus, the DCI team checked the few cameras we had and they didn't find anything worthwhile."

She thought about that and said, "I was just speculating."

"Speculating is okay. That's what we do. Your speculation of screening that field might lead to something even though it might shoot my RPG theory to hell," he said with a grin. "So where can I drop you off?"

"My car," she said.

"I can recommend a motel if you're staying the night. You've got all of two choices."

She laughed. "I hadn't even planned that far ahead. I guess I thought I'd be driving back tonight."

"That's a long drive," he said.

She thought about the journey back to Grimstad and something struck her.

"That gas station before you get to Grimstad—I stopped before I met you today."

"Yes?" he said, not understanding where she was going.

"It's the only place to get gas between Baker and here. When I turned in I was literally running on fumes."

"Okay."

"What if the killer was in the same situation? If he was on the same route? Wouldn't it be more likely he'd stop outside of town at a place like that than risk being seen in Ekalaka?"

The sheriff nodded and said, "Assuming he came that way, I guess. And not from the south."

"Even then he wouldn't want to risk being seen in the middle of town, right?"

"I'll play along," he said. "What are you getting at?"

"Let's drive out there and talk to the man in the wheelchair.

That place has old-fashioned pumps so you have to go inside personally to pay. Maybe the owner remembers someone coming in that day."

"Worth a shot." Verplank sighed and said, "Kirkbride was right. You *are* a bulldog."

"He said that?"

"It was a compliment."

THE A-FRAME GAS STATION was dark in front when Sheriff Verplank pulled off the highway onto the gravel lot.

"Closed," Cassie said with a sigh.

"He lives in back of the place," Verplank said. "I'll roust him."

"Should we do that?" she asked. "It can probably wait until tomorrow."

"My cousin owns this place," he said grimly. "His name is Bodeen Verplank. He's a creepy little pervert if you want to know the truth. About fifteen years ago I responded to a Peeping Tom call in town and when I got there the son of a bitch took a shot at me and took off running so I returned fire and hit him in the spine. Turned out it was my cousin. He's been in a wheelchair ever since. I wish my aim would have been better because to this day I don't like him."

"Still . . ."

The sheriff reached down and turned on his flashing lights. The front of the gas station erupted in revolving blue and orange beams. Then he triggered his siren and made two loud blasts of sound.

WHOOP! WHOOP!

"That ought to get his attention," the sheriff said, baring his teeth.

Cassie sat tight.

Finally, lights came on in the front of the station and she caught a glimpse of Bodeen's head as he propelled himself in his chair from his living quarters in the back to the front of the store.

"Here he comes," the sheriff said as he opened his door. Cassie did the same. She stayed a step behind him as he clamped on his wide-brimmed hat and approached the front of the station.

The door cracked a few inches. The sheriff shot his arm out and wedged it into the opening to prevent it from closing again.

"Bodeen, you little reprobate, let us in."

The door swung fully open and the owner filled the threshold. Bodeen glared up at the sheriff with undisguised hatred until his eyes slid off and found Cassie.

"Who is she and why are you here?" Bodeen asked.

"That's Cassie Dewell and we're working on a case. Now roll yourself back so we can come in."

Bodeen thrust out his jaw. "I don't have to do that if I don't want to. And you know it."

Cassie knew he was right. "Sheriff . . ."

"Damn you, Bodeen," Bebe Verplank said as he lifted up his right boot and placed it on the front of the wheelchair seat between Bodeen's legs and pushed it back hard. The chair rolled back into the store.

"Come on in," he said to Cassie over his shoulder.

AFTER THEY CLOSED THE DOOR behind them, the sheriff crossed his arms across his chest and tilted his head to the side as he and his cousin began an epic stare-down. Cassie stood helplessly near the counter. It was obvious there were years of history on display.

At about half a minute, Bodeen broke. "What now?" he asked, resigned.

"I thought you'd tell me."

Bodeen looked away.

Cassie had no idea what was going on. She edged behind the counter so she could be further away from them if a fight broke out.

"I been good," Bodeen said. "I kept my nose clean."

"First time ever, then."

"Really, man. You've got no right to come here and harass me."

"Did you get those pumps adjusted like I told you to? Are they honest pumps?"

"They're honest, Bebe. I don't overcharge anyone anymore."

"Are you still buying weed from the Sorensons? I can smell it in here."

So could Cassie.

"Medical marijuana is legal and you know it, Bebe."

"And you've got a card to prove it you can show me?"

"I'm gonna get one," Bodeen said. "I promise."

The sheriff looked over his shoulder at Cassie and winked. He was enjoying himself.

She wasn't and he could tell that.

"Okay, enough foolishness," he said to Bodeen. "We need to know if you remember any particular customers you might have had about a month ago. Late in the night on September fifteenth or early the next morning September sixteenth. I assume you were working on those days."

Cassie saw panic on Bodeen's face. He said, "Man, how do you expect me to remember that far back? What is this, anyhow?"

She wondered that herself. She knew what *she'd* been doing those days only because they were among the most traumatic days of her life.

"Think, cousin," the sheriff said. "For once, think."

"Tuesday the fifteenth through the twenty-second," the sheriff said. "Who bought gas from you?"

"How can I possibly remember?"

"Don't you keep records?"

"We're an all-cash business, Bebe. I don't take no credit cards so there ain't any receipts."

Embarrassed for Bodeen, she looked down. It was obvious Bodeen had no memory of those dates or of any customers on those dates.

And there it was: a small computer monitor tucked away up under the counter where it couldn't be seen by a customer on the other side.

"Maybe it's on his security camera," Cassie interjected from behind the counter. "There's a monitor back here."

Verplank put his hands on his hips and leaned toward his cousin. "You have a camera?"

"No!" Bodeen shouted. He raised both hands toward his cousin as if to ward him off if he attacked. Then: "The camera don't even work."

"Which is it, Bodeen?" the sheriff asked. "You don't have one or it doesn't work?"

"*Both*," Bodeen cried. He dropped his hands to the rims of his chair and tried furiously to get around the sheriff to where Cassie was behind the counter. The sheriff stepped to the side and blocked Bodeen's path.

"What have you got back there, cousin?"

"Nothing. *Now go away and leave me alone.*"

Cassie found the power button on the monitor and turned it on. It took a moment to warm up. While it did she looked up to see Bodeen's face twisted up with rage.

"Get that bitch out of my store!" he screamed. "She's got no right to be here."

Again he was correct, she thought. But she was in Sheriff Verplank's county and she deferred to his judgment.

Then the monitor lightened to blue and the forms it showed came into focus.

It was a view from above looking down. She could see a sink, a stall, a toilet inside the stall, and the top of a sanitary napkin dispenser.

"You bastard," she said to Bodeen. Then to the sheriff, "He's got a camera in the ceiling of the women's bathroom."

"I told you he was a pervert," Sheriff Verplank said.

BODEEN SAT SLUMPED OVER with his head in his hands as Cassie tapped the keyboard of the monitor to zoom in and out. It was aimed squarely at the toilet seat.

"You're sick," she said.

He mewled.

Then she noticed a series of icons on the bottom of the screen and she clicked one with the mouse. It was a video folder.

When it opened she could see at least twenty-five video files. She chose the most recent file and clicked on it and watched herself enter the bathroom, put aside the key, take off her coat, and enter the stall.

Cassie watched no more.

"You sick bastard," she said again. "I'm on this, Sheriff."

Sheriff Verplank bent over Bodeen and asked, "Where's the hard drive?"

"Please, leave me alone. I never touched any of them."

"Where is the hard drive?"

"Under the desk," Bodeen said through wails.

Cassie turned and saw it down there. Two blinking green lights in the dark.

"Now, Bodeen," the sheriff said, "I'm going to take that with me. Then I'm going to go into the women's bathroom and tear that camera out of the ceiling. You aren't ever going to use it again.

"Then I'm going to come back here tomorrow and arrest you. That gives you a little time to call your lawyer and get your affairs in order. You're going to Deer Lodge for a few years."

She could barely hear Bodeen as he spoke and cried at the same time, but she got the gist of it. The sheriff, Bodeen was saying, had no reason or right to come into his gas station and search, much less remove anything.

For the third time, Bodeen was legally on track.

But Sheriff Verplank said to Bodeen, "I've got every right in the world, cousin. It's called probable cause. Cassie here told me she had a very strange feeling when she went into the women's bathroom today. She said she felt she was being spied on. Turns out, she was right."

Cassie mouthed "*What?*" to the sheriff, and he winked at her to play along.

Bodeen bent further over in his chair and wept.

To Cassie, the sheriff said, "How about you unhook all that equipment and I'll go pull that camera from the bathroom. We'll take it all with us."

She nodded in agreement and the sheriff grabbed the key to the women's and went out the door.

WHILE SHE BENT UNDER the desk she could hear Bodeen's wheels rolling slowly across the floor toward her. She paused and reached inside her purse and gripped the handle of the Glock inside.

"What do you want?" she asked him. She used her flat cop voice.

"I don't want to go back to prison. I hate Deer Lodge."

"You'll have to talk to the sheriff about that."

"He don't have any right to take all my equipment without no warrant. Those cameras are expensive."

She unplugged the server and it wound down into silence. It was warm to the touch and she picked it up and placed it on the desk. Then something struck her and she slowly turned around and leaned over the counter at Bodeen.

"Cameras?" she asked. "You said cameras. Is there more than one?"

He looked up blankly. Then, "Yeah. There's two."

"Where is the other one? In the men's?"

"Shit no," he said, offended. "I ain't queer."

Then he nodded toward the front of the station and raised his eyes to indicate where it was.

"It's out front under the eave where it's hard to see from the pumps. It's there so I can get the license plates in case somebody fills up and don't pay me. Drive-aways are a real problem. Of course, our great sheriff could care less about real crime like that—crime against small business owners trying to make a living. Not when he can spend his time abusing his cousin—"

"*Stop*," she commanded.

He shut up and looked like he was about to cry again.

"Do you have video records of all of your customers on this server?"

He nodded.

"How far back does it go?"

He shrugged, "Maybe a couple months. I don't look unless I have a drive-away. I haven't had any for—"

"*Stop*."

SEVENTEEN

WHILE SHERIFF VERPLANK took a call from his wife in his office, Cassie set up the computer and monitor from the A-frame on an empty desk in the squad room. She appreciated him giving her such free rein when she knew he could have easily asserted his authority over the chain of custody of the evidence and sent her away.

She used the time it took for the computer to boot up to call one of the two motels in town and make a reservation. The woman on the other end laughed and said, "Reservation? You'll have the run of the whole place. I'll give you our best cabin . . ."

The motel owner described the virtues of the motel unit while Cassie focused on the monitor.

"You've got your own kitchenette, a queen-sized bed, free Wi-Fi . . . all for seventy-five dollars per night."

"It's a deal," Cassie said. She was distracted and she terminated the call.

IT TOOK A WHILE to get the hang of the video folder system Bodeen had set up. There seemed to be no rhyme or reason why certain folders were where they were and the labeling didn't help. The folders contained at least three years of digital video from when the system was installed. Bodeen didn't appear to use the computer for much of anything else except accessing the Internet.

Before opening any of the folders, she downloaded them all onto a 128-gigabyte thumb drive she'd brought in her purse. That way, they'd have a clean backup of all of the files on Bodeen's entire hard drive in case she accidentally deleted anything. The data on the thumb drive would, she hoped, insulate Sheriff Verplank from being accused of planting or manipulating evidence.

She quickly determined that the "Cam#1" folders were clips taken from the outside camera, while the "Cam#2" folders were made up of raw unedited videos taken in the women's bathroom. Except when they weren't.

She thought she found the folder for Cam#1 for September but it turned out to be what she thought of with disgust as a "Best of" anthology of woman after woman using the bathroom over the past few years. Bodeen must have spent hours amassing the collection and putting them into a sequence that pleased him.

Like the close-up of the victim in the hayfield, she couldn't unsee it afterward.

SHE PROCEEDED BY IGNORING all the Cam#2 folders entirely and she focused on the Cam#1 files. She was heartened to see that the surveillance video provided a time stamp in the lower left corner and she was able to zero in on the right dates even though the video quality was very poor.

When she found a series of Cam#1 files starting with September 9 she slowed down her search and became more methodical.

When Cam#1 went live it was programmed to take a wide-angle shot when a customer pulled into the pumps. She guessed it was triggered manually by Bodeen inside when he heard a vehicle arrive. Bodeen then had the capability to zoom the camera in on the vehicle and focus on the plates in back or on the fuel dials on the pump itself. After that, she noticed, he usually turned the camera off.

Some days he had as few as four customers, others as many as twenty.

Most of the cars captured on video were ranch and utility vehicles that she guessed were local. Montana offered a slew of different license plate designs—from Montana Livestock Board to Montana Quilters to Montana Hunter to Support the NRA—but every fifth or sixth vehicle was from out of state. South Dakota, Wyoming, North Dakota.

When she reached September 16 she took a deep breath. The first customer was a Montana rancher or cowboy in a new-model GMC pickup. The second was a group of local students, likely high school, pooling their cash and putting four dollars and cents worth of unleaded into their older SUV. The kids did a round of "paper-scissors-rock" to determine the loser who had to go inside the station and hand over the change to Bodeen.

The third customer drove a battered beige crew-cab Ford pickup with North Dakota plates. The bed of the truck was piled high with duffel bags, full black trash bags, and tools.

She could see the silhouettes of two people inside the cab—a man and a woman. The angle of Cam#1 made it impossible to see further inside the vehicle.

A man got out of the driver's side and quickly turned away but not before there was a split-second view of his face lit up by early morning sun. The driver wore a bulky tan coat and baggy jeans and a ball cap pulled down low.

He inserted the fuel dispenser into the gas tank and stepped back while it filled. He stretched, removed his cap for a moment, and smoothed his hair before pulling it back on.

When he was done filling the tank he said something to the woman inside the truck and he vanished from the frame.

To pay Bodeen, she thought.

She wished she could see the woman better but the angle of the camera prevented it. At least she *thought* it was a woman.

But something about the man triggered recognition in Cassie. The stiff way he moved, his posture, his squared head.

"*No*," she said loud enough for Sheriff Verplank to hear her through the glass and look up. "No."

IT TOOK A FEW MINUTES to figure out how to run the video back and freeze it. Her fingers trembled on the keys while she did. Her heart whumped in her chest.

Five times, then six, she watched the driver exit the vehicle and turn away. The flash of sunlight fuzzed out a clear view of his face but each time she viewed the clip she thought she could see more: wavy black hair, bushy eyebrows, prominent cheekbones set in a face that had gone to fat. Huge hands, stocky build.

And something on a lanyard hanging from his neck when he got out that wasn't there when he went into the office. Obviously, he'd zipped up his coat while filling up so it couldn't be seen.

Before sliding back behind the wheel, the man turned slightly and addressed the back of the cab. Did he have a dog back there?

Cassie sat back and rubbed her eyes. She could barely breathe.

When Sheriff Verplank tapped her on the shoulder she jumped.

"What is it?" he asked, obviously surprised at her reaction.

"I think my mind is playing tricks on me," she said.

"Meaning what?"

"This guy who got fuel on September sixteenth looks a hell of a lot like the Lizard King."

She turned in her chair. Verplank had a confused look on his face. He indicated his skepticism by closing one eye like he was trying not to chuckle.

"He's dead," he said. "You of all people should know that."

She said, "I have my doubts about that."

"Why do you think it's him?"

"I'm one of the few who have ever seen him up close," she said.

She turned back around and ran the clip. This time, she managed to freeze it before the driver turned away.

Frozen, she thought, it looked less like him than she imagined. But when he was moving, that stiff but sure gait . . .

"Now I'm not so sure," she confessed.

"Who else is in the truck?"

"It looks like a woman in the passenger seat. I can't see anyone else."

"I don't recognize him," the sheriff said. "He must not be from around here."

"North Dakota plates," she said, letting the clip run until the field of view narrowed in on the front plates.

"JLS-011," she called out.

"I'll run 'em," Verplank said after writing it down.

"THE PLATES BELONG to a guy named Floyd T. Eckstrom of Sanish, North Dakota," Verplank told Cassie.

She looked up from where she'd copied the video clip of the man in the blue Ford from the hard drive onto her thumb drive.

"Something about that name is familiar," she said.

"He was reported missing three weeks ago," Verplank said. He'd printed out a report in his office and as he skimmed it he read from it. "Eckstrom was reported missing September twentieth after a couple of local hunters went onto his property to ask permission to construct a duck blind. Apparently he owns a little tract right on the Missouri River inside the reservation there.

"But instead of talking to Eckstrom they found his trailer burned to the ground. Eckstrom wasn't around and his truck was gone. The local officials there think it might have been an insurance deal. Apparently the guy had back payments due on an 18-wheeler from a dealership in Bismarck and maybe he burned his own place to collect on it."

Cassie nodded her head. "That was it. That's where I heard the name. He was one of the missing persons in the area around the time Raheem and Kyle were reported. So he's a long-haul trucker?"

The sheriff continued to read. "Yep, looks like it. His employer is an outfit out of Dickenson. His rig is there now because he left it there for some service work. They reported that he didn't show up to pick it up and he hasn't called in since the twentieth. Apparently they're on the hook for his truck as well."

"Do they list a description of him?" she asked.

"Let's see . . . yeah. Thirty-two years old, six-foot, brown eyes. We've got the photo from his CDL."

She rose and stood shoulder to shoulder with Verplank. In the photo for his Commercial Driver's License Eckstrom looked bug-eyed into the camera. He had dark hair, black-framed glasses, a small mouth, and an intense, unnerving stare.

"Tell me," she said to the sheriff while pointing at the frozen image on the monitor, "does this guy look to you like that guy?"

He studied the photo and then the screen. "Nope."

"So who was driving his pickup and why?" she asked. "And what was he doing in Ekalaka?"

The question hung there.

Finally, the sheriff said, "I think you might have a better idea than I do."

She rubbed her eyes and then her temples. She said, "I need to sit down with a glass of wine and my files and this new information and puzzle it out. I need to talk to a couple of people and get their take."

"And I need to get home and feed the dogs," he said.

Cassie looked up and the sheriff smiled at her. "Don't forget to get some sleep. And don't hesitate to call me if you need anything. You have my cell phone number after all."

She said, "I'll come by here in the morning."

As she shut down Bodeen's computer and gathered her belongings she knew she'd be up all night.

Because the scenario that was forming in her mind was too disturbing to push aside.

THE STATE LIQUOR STORE was closed for the night but Cassie bought a bottle of cheap red wine at a gas station/convenience store and checked into her cabin at the Home Ranch Motel. The owner, a jolly round woman in a housecoat and slippers with her television blaring in the background, outlined where the thermostat was located and scribbled down the password for the Wi-Fi. Cassie listened with a pleasant expression on her face and pretended she was listening but her mind was back at the sheriff's department.

HER CABIN WAS LARGE, spare, clean, and paneled with knotty pine. It smelled like disinfectant. The walls were decorated with Frederic Remington and C. M. Russell cowboy prints as if to remind her she was back in Montana.

With a full glass of wine in a flimsy plastic cup, she sat down at the small desk and tried to get her head right before she called home. Cassie wanted to think "Ben" and not "Lizard King."

Unfortunately, Isabel answered the landline.

"What do you mean you may not be home tomorrow?" she asked after Cassie explained that her plans had likely changed. "I have things to do, you know."

"I know. But I might need to extend the trip. Progressive Grimstad can wait a day or two, can't it?"

"I also have my Zumba."

"That's during the day when Kyle is at school."

"I hope this doesn't become a habit."

Cassie bit her tongue. Isabel shared the house, didn't cook or clean, and paid nothing toward the mortgage. But she loved Ben and was a wonderful caretaker. Plus, she was family. Finding someone to be in the house with a twelve-year-old in Grimstad wasn't easy.

Cassie said, "I appreciate you being home when Ben is there, I really do. I couldn't do this without you."

She took a big gulp of wine after that. It warmed her throat and built a fire in her belly and took the edge off the guilt she felt for being such a manipulator.

Isabel sighed her familiar sigh. It was the sigh of a martyr.

Cassie ignored it. "Is Ben there?"

"He's doing his homework but I'll go get him."

Cassie heard the receiver on the other end clunk on the kitchen counter.

"Mom—did you find Kyle and Raheem?"

Cassie was startled by the question. "Who told you I was looking for them?"

"Grandma Isabel."

Cassie briefly closed her eyes. "No, I haven't found them yet. I'm looking hard, though."

The last thing she wanted to do was mention the headless body in the hayfield to Ben or anyone else until she was absolutely sure of the identification.

"So where are you?" Ben asked.

"Montana."

Ben said, "It's weird. I can hardly remember Montana. I can

remember our house and all of that but I can't remember *Montana*. Do you know what I mean?"

"I think so."

They discussed his homework and his day. When she asked if anyone gave him any trouble at school because she lost her job, he said none of the kids mentioned it but his gym teacher gave him a weird look.

"Does that bother you?" she asked.

"Naw. Nobody likes Mr. Schustler anyway. He's kind of lame."

Ben talked more to her on the telephone than he did in person anymore. She found that interesting.

When he handed the phone back to her mother, Isabel said, "I didn't hear. Did you find them?"

"No," Cassie said. "And please don't tell Ben everything I'm doing. I don't want to give him false hope that we'll find those boys."

The sigh, again.

SHE OPENED THE ROAD ATLAS showing the North Central United States and it was large enough to cover the entire desk. With a black pen she circled Eau Claire, Wiconsin; Grimstad, Sanish, and Dickenson, North Dakota; and Ekalaka, Montana.

They had video of the Lizard King from the truck stop in Eau Claire on the night of September 14. On the fifteenth, his truck was sighted east of Dickenson en route to Grimstad, which meant he'd driven west on I-94 from Wisconsin. From Dickenson north to Grimstad, the logical route was U.S. 85 through Watson City.

Cassie drew a line connecting those locations and sat back. Sanish was northeast of Watson City and not on the way to Grimstad. To go there and still get to Grimstad, the Lizard King would have had to backtrack in the wrong direction. Unless . . .

Unless he took two-lane North Dakota State Highway 22 which

went north through Manning, Killdeer, and within eight miles of Sanish.

They'd *assumed* he took U.S. 85 that day, she recalled. But they didn't *know* it.

A stop in Sanish might account for the one-and-a-half-hour delay they'd experienced before he got to the industrial park.

She said, "Damn," and finished the cup of wine and poured another. On a fresh sheet of her legal pad she began to construct a timeline.

CASSIE WAS INTERRUPTED FROM HER work when her phone lit up and skittered across the desk. She grabbed it and was surprised to see the caller was Jon Kirkbride.

"Hello, Sheriff."

"I'm not the sheriff anymore. How'd things go in Ekalaka?" he asked.

"Actually, I'm still here."

"You are?" She could hear the smile in his voice. "I spent a month in Ekalaka one night," he said.

"Thank you for putting in a good word with the locals."

"You bet. Glad I could help."

She filled him in on the discovery of the body outside of town and what they'd found at Bodeen's gas station. He listened quietly.

When she was done he said, "*Damn*. This is getting interesting."

"It is."

She was grateful he'd called to check up on her but she guessed that wasn't the only reason.

He sighed and said, "When I left the department I swore to my wife and myself I'd leave it all behind me—all the politics and bullshit. I didn't want to be one of those bitter old guys who spends his retirement criticizing the new regime and telling everybody who will listen how *I* would have done things. I know too many former sheriffs like that and feel sorry for them."

"Right," she said. In the back of her mind she sincerely hoped that despite Kirkbride's preamble he wasn't going to do exactly that. It would be too distracting.

He said, "But as you know, I still have a lot of friends on the inside. I worked with some of those people for years and I hired just about all of them. They call me and I can't just not answer the phone. I heard something today that I thought I ought to pass along to you so you won't be blindsided if it happens."

Cassie perked up. "If what happens?"

"Well, apparently your old FBI contact has been meeting with Tibbs."

"Special Agent Rhodine?" she asked.

"Him."

"What about?"

"You, I suspect," Kirkbride said. "I do know they requested your personnel file from the department."

Cassie suspected his source to be Judy Banister. She was the only employee with access to personnel files.

He said, "Think about it, Cassie. Both of those guys are ambitious as hell. They went all in on getting the Lizard King at the industrial park because they both wanted to take credit for it. Then things turned out the way they did and you became the scapegoat. They've got to figure out a way to come out on top again."

Cassie shook her head. "Wasn't forcing both of us out of the department enough?"

"Apparently not."

"So what are they up to? Why are they meeting?"

Kirkbride said, "That I don't know—yet. But whatever it is they're hatching is being done on the sly. They've met at restaurants and other nonofficial locations but not in the office.

"I do know Tibbs seems especially interested in your activities of late. He's been asking around about where you are and what you're doing."

"So why doesn't he just call me directly?"

"That's not how he operates."

"But why does he even care what I'm doing?"

"Again, Cassie: Think about it. Tibbs has taken over my department and has the resources of the entire sheriff's office and prosecutor's office under his control. Rhodine is the tip of the spear of a federal agency with hundreds of agents and an 8.3 billion dollar budget. How would it look if a private individual operating on her own located a couple of missing runaways *and* tracked down Ronald Pergram? Answer: It wouldn't look good for them."

"My God," Cassie whispered.

"So keep alert," Kirkbride said. "And don't be surprised if they somehow try to take you down."

TWO HOURS LATER Cassie paced the floor of her cabin. It was so quiet inside that her footfalls echoed off the walls. Outside, except for two saloons, Ekalaka was asleep.

She checked her watch and saw it was only nine-thirty although it felt much later. Plus, she'd gained an hour entering the Mountain Time Zone.

Nevertheless, Cassie sat down at her laptop and inserted the thumb drive she'd loaded at the sheriff's department. After copying the clip of the Ford at Bodeen's to her hard drive she attached it to an e-mail with the subject header PLS LOOK AT THIS.

She sent it to an address in the Eastern Time Zone—two hours later.

It would be a long night, she thought. She wished she could somehow zip back to Grimstad, see Ben and sleep in her own bed, and reappear in the morning. By then the e-mail should have been opened where she sent it and she'd hear from Sheriff Verplank about what the Montana crime lab techs had found.

She grinned when her cell phone came to life in her hand and she saw the familiar 252 area code prefix. North Carolina.

"Hey," Leslie Behaunek said. "My phone chimed. Did you send me something important?"

"I did."

"Cassie, you sound keyed up."

"I am."

"And maybe you've had a glass or two of wine."

"Not a glass but a plastic cup. And yes, I've had several. And probably more to come."

Leslie laughed. Her voice was husky from being tired or perhaps a little drunk herself. She, like Cassie, liked to drink wine at night.

"Where are you?" Leslie asked.

"A place called Ekalaka, Montana. I'll guarantee you've never heard of it."

"And you'd be right. What brings you there?"

Cassie hesitated a moment, then asked, "I don't want to tell you quite yet. I want you to have a totally open mind when you open the video clip I sent you and watch it."

"Right now?"

"I'll wait."

"Okay," Leslie said. "I've got to get my housecoat on and get my computer in the other room. I was just turning in when I saw you sent me something."

"I'm sorry it's so late there."

"It's fine, it's fine . . ."

Cassie paced and kept the phone pressed to her ear, stopping only long enough by the desk to pour more wine into her cup.

After five minutes Leslie said, "Oh my God—it can't be."

This time, she sounded fully awake.

"What do you see?" Cassie asked.

"I see someone who looks a lot like Ron Pergram putting gas into a truck."

Cassie closed her eyes. She felt both elated and terrified in equal measures

Leslie asked, "Where did you get this?"

"Here, in Ekalaka."

"When was it taken?"

"September sixteenth of this year."

There was a pause. Leslie said, "But he blew himself up on the fifteenth. Can there be a mistake on the time stamp?"

"I don't think so."

"My God, my God. What can this mean?"

Cassie said, "I have a theory but it's pretty off the wall. But first I want to catch you up."

"I couldn't go back to sleep now if I wanted to," Leslie said, letting her drawl creep in. "But first I need a glass of wine."

AFTER SHE'D COVERED the investigation thus far, Cassie said, "I'm waiting until morning to find out if the body has the identifying scar on the ankle. If so, I'll ask the sheriff to proceed with a DNA request from Mr. Johnson so we can get a positive ID."

"And if so, what?" Leslie asked. "Even if it turns out to be Raheem Johnson I don't see how you can connect him to the Lizard King. Or if that even *is* the Lizard King."

"I understand," Cassie said with a sigh. "I know you have to look at everything from a prosecutorial point of view. Right now, all I've got is a video clip and an unidentified body. You're asking me to connect them and I can't. All I can do is speculate."

"Mmmm-hmmm."

"There are advantages to working as a civilian," Cassie said.

"I don't have to follow any protocol and I don't have to deal with politics and red tape. And I don't have to build a case like I would if I were planning to turn it all over to the DA for prosecution. So I can go farther out on a limb.

"But the downsides are obvious," she said. "I'm at a real disadvantage at times like this when I need to access evidence techs and light a fire under different law enforcement personnel. I got lucky that Kirkbride knows Sheriff Verplank and was so nice about everything . . ."

"It's amazing that you live in a place where everybody knows each other hundreds of miles away. That must be smothering at times."

"Anyway," Cassie said in her let's-get-back-on-track voice, "listen to my theory and then shoot all the holes in it you want to."

"Okay."

"Start with the date September fifteen. On that day a lot happened in this area. Too many things occurred to dismiss them all as random."

"Go on," Leslie said after taking an audible sip.

"On September fifteenth a lot of things happened within a few hundred miles of each other. First, the Lizard King drove across the entire state of North Dakota from Wisconsin so he could blow himself up in Grimstad. That event was so terrible for everyone that it overshadowed other events—or crimes—that went on that same exact day."

"Keep going."

"Kyle Westergaard and Raheem Johnson started floating the Missouri River and vanished. Amanda Lee Hackl was later reported missing by her husband. In Sanish, seventy-three miles away, Floyd T. Eckstrom burns down his own home and disappears as well. From what I was told, Eckstrom's house is right on the river.

"Leslie, I see how you could say that all those incidents are unrelated but keep in mind we're talking about western North Dakota and eastern Montana. There aren't many people around here at all—it's probably the least populated area in the lower forty-eight—and most of them look out for each other. There aren't any trees like you have, so you can see for miles. People can't hide as easily, is what I'm trying to say, and they can't just all disappear on the same day."

"But they did," Leslie said.

"They did. And on September sixteenth, a man who appears to be Ronald Pergram fills up with gas in Ekalaka driving Eckstrom's truck—"

"*Hold it*," Leslie interrupted. "Did you just say that was Eckstrom's truck?"

"Yes, but that isn't Floyd Eckstrom on the camera. And if you watch that clip as many times as I have you'll see the form of a woman in the passenger seat. She's unidentifiable because of the camera angle but she's there. And when Pergram gets back into his truck to pull away he says something into the back of his cab like there was a person back there. Watch it again and tell me I'm wrong. I'll wait."

While Leslie Behaunek ran the clip again on her screen, Cassie saw that the battery on her phone was running critically low. She fished the power cord out of her briefcase and plugged it into an outlet under the desk. Unfortunately, the cord tethered her to one place so she could no longer pace.

"Okay," Leslie said. "I see what you're talking about. But are you trying to say that the Lizard King scooped all these people up and piled them in Floyd Eckstrom's truck and drove off—*after he killed himself*?"

"No, I'm saying the driver of Pergram's truck has never been positively identified as Pergram. We all assumed it was him, of course. But what if it was Eckstrom?"

"Whoa," Leslie said. "You're giving me a headache. You're saying that Pergram somehow coerced Eckstrom to drive his truck to Grimstad and commit suicide?"

"I don't know what happened," Cassie said. "I'm wracking my brain on that one. The only thing that makes any sense is that Eckstrom didn't know there were explosives wired into the truck. Only the Lizard King knew that."

"So Pergram set him up," Leslie said. "He sent him to his death."

"Which sounds a lot like something our man would do, doesn't it?"

"It does."

"Not to mention that this wouldn't be the first time he burned down a house to hide his tracks."

"But where do the others come in? This Amanda, or Kyle and Raheem? How do they fit?"

"Again, I don't know," Cassie said. "But Sanish is downriver from Grimstad. I worked it out and it's about an eight-hour float. Think about that."

Leslie did and Cassie waited.

"Pergram was there at the Eckstrom house," Leslie said. "He somehow encountered Kyle and Raheem that night."

"It works in my timeline," Cassie said.

"Why wouldn't Pergram just let them float on by? He's never targeted teenage boys before that we know about."

"I agree it doesn't fit his profile. But it could be something else. Maybe they got a good look at him and he couldn't risk letting them go. Maybe they caught him in the act of something. Or maybe he wanted hostages just in case law enforcement moved in. It's one of the parts of my theory that doesn't have a good explanation . . . yet."

Leslie asked, "But what about Amanda Hackl? From what you told me she doesn't fit his profile either. Didn't you say she vanished from Grimstad?"

"That's what her husband reported."

"Do you know when?"

"What hour?—no. Sometime between when he went to work in the morning and when he came back that night. She disappeared in the daylight hours."

Cassie could envision Leslie nodding, putting things together. "Which means she could have gone missing long before Pergram encountered the boys. So how does she fit in?"

Cassie said, "Maybe it was just as simple as she saw something or somebody she wasn't supposed to see. Her home address is right on the bluff overlooking town. No doubt she saw the explosion down at the industrial park."

Leslie gasped and Cassie understood why. It hit her like a thunderbolt.

"*So maybe Amanda saw the man who triggered the explosion from a distance,*" Cassie said, sweeping her hand and accidentally hitting her cup of wine. Red wine covered the states of North Dakota and Montana like spilled blood.

THEY TALKED FOR ANOTHER HOUR. Leslie tried to punch holes in Cassie's theory and Cassie tried to thwart them.

"The biggest problem with your narrative," Leslie said, "is something I unfortunately see all too often with our own officers."

"What's that?"

"You want so badly to have your conclusion justified that you blindly use everything you find out to build a road map that will get you there. You want to think Kyle and Raheem are still out there and you blame it on the man you've come to hate the most in the world. In your theory the Lizard King is still on the road. Therefore, you plug in every crime and incident that occurred that day to make it all fit together."

Cassie was taken aback.

Before she could argue back, Leslie said, "If you brought me this theory I'd give it right back to you and tell you to find hard evidence to support it. And you know that."

Cassie's shoulders slumped. "You're right."

"I am," Leslie said while she sipped. "But you've also got my brain revved up. I think you really might be on to something. I don't want to discourage you from following it through."

Cassie poured the last of her wine into the cup. She'd need a new atlas.

"In fact," Leslie said, "my office is underbudget this fiscal year. I think you should send everything you have—the forensics on the body, the video clip, the missing person's reports and arson investigation in Sanish—to my office right away. I'll tell everyone this is high priority and I'll get my techs working on it. I'll oversee the investigation and keep in touch with you. Since you don't have resources of your own you can use ours.

"After all," she said, "we're the ones who let that bastard get away."

"Thank you, Leslie."

"It's the least I can do."

Cassie slumped back in her chair. She was relieved. She stared at a Frederic Remington print of a lone Indian scout leaning tentatively forward on his horse on a snowy bluff to assess a far-off winter camp. It was called *The Scout: Friends or Foes?*

Cassie said, "If my theory pans out it means Raheem was murdered here in Ekalaka in the most horrible way. It might also mean we'll find Kyle's body somewhere else."

Leslie got quiet.

"Or maybe worse," Cassie said, "Kyle is still being held by Pergram somewhere. That kid has already gone through hell. I just can't think about Kyle being around that man. It would be better if he was dead."

"Don't say that," Leslie said. "Kids can be tough, especially Kyle. You told me that yourself."

"Either way I need to find out what happened. Lottie needs to know. Raheem's poor dad needs to know. *I* need to know."

"Look, I'll do what I can on my end," Leslie said. "Tomorrow I'll call your Sheriff Verplank and get in contact with the Montana DCI and the North Dakota BCI to see if they'll cooperate on a joint task force investigation. I might even get the FBI involved. But, as you know, these things take time."

"Too much time," Cassie said. "And who knows if the BCI will play along. That's the agency that shut me down."

"Cassie, please . . ."

"If Kyle is still alive and the Lizard King is out there I have to keep pushing," Cassie said. "I can't wait for a joint task force to get up to speed."

"Don't be careless, Cassie," Leslie cautioned. "I can hear it in your voice. I'm not saying this so I can build a perfect case right now. I'm worried about you."

"Don't be."

Leslie calmed herself down and said, "What you need to do is sit tight and continue to think all this through. You need to find evidence that supports your theory. What you don't need to do is go lone wolf on me. Don't think you're suddenly Cody Hoyt. You know what happened to him."

Cassie didn't respond.

"One other thing," Leslie said. "Nobody knows Ronald Pergram *slash* Dale Spradley *slash* the Lizard King better than you do, right?"

"Right."

"So knowing that, where would he go now that he doesn't have his truck?"

Cassie sat up. She was pressing her phone to her ear so hard it hurt. "He's spent his entire life on the road. He's never really had a home of his own but he's probably driven a million highway miles across the U.S. He knows every inch of this country and where he could hide out."

"So where would he go?" Leslie asked.

Where I'm going tomorrow, Cassie thought but didn't say out loud.

EIGHTEEN

Location Unknown

EARLY IN THE MORNING, before anyone got up, and sometimes in the middle of the night, Kyle found himself reliving what had happened since he'd encountered Ron. Some things were so vivid in his memory they seemed like they were happening again right in front of him.

Especially that day when they were still hooded and trussed and on the open road.

Especially what happened to Raheem.

LATE IN THE EVENING on the day they left the trailer by the river and after two stops—one where Ron bought two dog collars and the second when they stopped so he could fill up the truck with gas—Raheem suddenly said, "Just fuckin' let us go, man."

His voice surprised Kyle. Apparently, Raheem had managed to pull the duct tape off his mouth somehow. His friend was still on the floor of the backseat wedged in next to Tiffany.

Ron continued driving and didn't respond. Kyle was frightened for Raheem but he was proud of him for speaking up.

"I said, pull over and let us go. At least me and Kyle. We didn't do nothing to you and we won't tell anybody what happened."

Ron sighed loudly but didn't slow down.

"Look, sir," Raheem said. "Me 'n Kyle were just going on an adventure. No one knows where we are and no one is looking for us yet. You can let us go now before the cops are pulling everybody over to look for us. We'll grab a ride home and everything will be all cool."

Kyle admired Raheem's logic. He heard Tiffany mewl as if to say *What about me?* But the tape on her mouth was secure.

After a few more miles of driving, Raheem said, "Can you hear me up there, man?"

"I hear you," Ron said. Kyle couldn't detect any anger in his voice.

"If you're thinking someone will pay money to get us back that won't happen. My dad don't have any since he got laid off, and Kyle lives with his old granny. Between them they got nothing."

Silence.

"Please pull over and let us go. We swear to God we won't say nothin'. Hell, we don't even know your name and I guess we were trespassing on your land. But let us out now wherever the hell we are and you can forget about us. We won't do no talking. You don't have to worry about me 'n Kyle. We planned that boat trip for years and we kept our mouths shut about it the the whole time. We can keep our mouths shut about this, man."

Then, as an aside, Raheem said, as if to bolster his argument, "Shit, nobody can understand anything Kyle says anyway."

Kyle thought that was mean but true. And if it worked he was fine with it.

Kyle noticed that the vehicle had slowed down significantly but it didn't stop. He guessed they were passing through a small town.

"Tell you what," Raheem said, "how about after you let us go me 'n Kyle will get jobs somewhere. When we earn money we'll send it to you. We'll keep sending it until we're all square. You can name the price but don't get crazy. It's not like we'll ever make a million dollars or anything like that. How does that sound to you?"

"Stupid," Ron said.

"Man, I'm running out of ideas so you tell me. Tell me what we gotta do to get out of this damn truck. Kyle, if you got any ideas now is the time to chime in."

The tape over Kyle's mouth was tight and all he could manage was "*Mmmff.*"

"You talk a lot," Ron said to Raheem. It was a flat statement.

Raheem apparently didn't know how to respond.

The truck sped back up. Apparently they were back on the highway.

Finally, Ron said, "I was wondering what I was going to do with you anyway."

Kyle's heart lept. Then he wondered if "you" meant them both or just Raheem.

The pickup slowed down and soon Kyle could hear gravel instead of pavement under the tires on the right side. Ron was pulling over.

"You okay, Kyle?" Raheem asked, sotto voce.

"*Mmmff.*"

"Hang in there, bro."

RON DIDN'T REMOVE KYLE'S HOOD, so what he would remember about what came next would stay with him as a series of sounds burned into his memory. Maybe that was why reliving that day seemed so real.

The truck stopped but the engine continued to run. Kyle heard Ron shove the transmission into park and apply the emergency brake with a ratcheting sound. Then he got out and his boots crunched on the gravel on the side of the road. The rear door opened and Kyle felt fresh air on the exposed skin of his hands. He also thought he smelled hay and fresh dirt.

"Get out," Ron said to Raheem.

"I'm trying, man," Raheem said, grunting. He heard Tiffany mewl again as Raheem struggled over her toward the opening.

"Stand still," Ron said.

"All right, I will. But don't forget Kyle."

No response.

Ron said to Amanda, "Take that off. That's right, I'll pull that stud out with these pliers and you reach up and unbuckle it and hand it to me."

"Are you sure it won't go off?" she asked. Her voice trembled.

"Do what I tell you," Ron said.

A moment later, Raheem said, "What you puttin' around my neck?"

Silence.

"Hey, don't pull it so tight."

Kyle felt his whole body go cold. He could remember Ron unbuckling the dog collar from Tiffany before he taped her up and put the hood on her. Kyle was afraid Ron was fastening it around Raheem's neck.

"That ain't that damned collar is it?" Raheem's voice was high. He was scared.

"Take off your clothes," Ron said.

"*What?*"

"Take 'em off. Everything except your underwear."

"That's messed up, man."

"Do it."

"How can I do it with my hands and legs all taped up?"

"I'll cut you free."

Kyle heard sharp *zips* that sent chills through his bowels.

After a beat, Kyle heard Raheem say, "Well, shit," as if resigned.

Apparently, though, the zips were from a sharp blade cutting through tape.

"Your shoes, too." Ron said.

"Okay, okay."

Kyle was supercharged with energy. He tried to pull his hands apart. The tape bit into his skin. He rolled his head manically from side to side, trying to catch an edge of the tape to the fabric on the inside of his hood so it would peel back. He would beg for Raheem's life.

"Hey, settle down in there," Ron said, apparently to Kyle. Then to Raheem: "Your friend has got this figured out."

What? Kyle thought. *He's got what figured out?*

To Raheem: "You want to go? Then go."

"I can't see nothing."

There was an unfurling sound of cloth snapping free.

"Now you can," Ron said. "Now run. Run toward that haystack out there. I'll bet you can run pretty fast."

"Where in the hell are we? We're in the middle of nowhere."

"Like I said, you talk a lot."

"You're gonna use that collar thing on me." Raheem's voice was reedy. "You're gonna use that thing on *me.*"

"Hey, it may not work. It probably depends on the distance. There may not be enough of an electrical charge in the detonator to set off the C-4 if you get out of range." Ron sounded calm like he was puzzling out a science problem.

"Look," Raheem said, "Put that hood back on. I'll get dressed again and I'll get back inside the truck and I'll keep my mouth shut and you won't ever hear another goddamn word out of me. I swear it. Just let me back in the truck."

After a long pause, Ron said, "Nah. I don't know what I'm going to do with you anyway. You're sort of a wild card and you've got a mouth on you."

"I'll be good, man," Raheem begged. "I sit in class and I don't say nothing. I sit there for hours. I can do that here."

Kyle had never heard that sad tone in Raheem's voice before. It ripped his heart out.

"I said 'go.'"

"I don't want to. Please don't make me."

"At least this way you'll have a chance. Otherwise, I'll just put a bullet in your head and leave you here on the side of the road."

"Please, man . . ."

"Go."

The last words Raheem ever uttered were "Fuck it."

Kyle heard Raheem start running. Bare feet thumped the ground until the sound of footfalls faded away.

A second passed, then two. Then five.

BOOM.

Amanda screamed in the front seat.

Kyle tried to cry out but his voice was muffled and he sounded to himself like a wounded cat.

Ron climbed back in the front of the truck, closed the door, and said, "That worked better than I thought it would." Pride in his voice.

Before he put the truck into gear he said, "Relax, back there. It was a just a matter of time anyway."

Amanda's sobbing was muffled as if she'd buried her head into the floorboard.

"Everybody relax," Ron said. "We've got a long way to go."

Through his anger and tears, Kyle smelled something sharp and strong: urine. Tiffany had apparently heard what Kyle had heard and she'd voided herself.

Ron smelled it, too, and said, "You people are disgusting."

PART FOUR

PARADISE VALLEY

NINETEEN

CASSIE TURNED OFF U.S. Highway 89 onto a fading two-track road that cut through the sagebrush before she reached Emigrant. She was immediately haunted by a sense of déjà vu from four years before. That was the last time she was there in what was known, ironically to her, as Paradise Valley.

Despite how vast and scenic it was—the snowcapped Crazy Mountains to the north, the Absaroka Range to the east, Yellowstone Park via Yankee Jim Canyon to the south—she could only remember the horror that had occurred there. It seemed to hang like vapor just a few feet above the brush.

The day was cool and overcast, which muted the early fall colors. A small herd of pronghorn antelope flowed across the high-desert steppe in the distance.

There were ghosts here, she thought. Ghosts only she could feel. The ghosts of dozens of women who had been picked up on the highway by the Lizard King and delivered to a bunker that served as a torture chamber just a few miles north of where she was now. Women whose bodies had *still* never been found.

And there was the ghost of Cody Hoyt, her troubled mentor.

He'd left Helena on his own to investigate a report of two missing girls. Both the girls and their car had disappeared between Gardiner and Livingston. It was the last time she saw Cody alive.

Even though she'd identified his body after it had been dug up in a field near the bunker and attended his funeral in Helena, she still had the odd feeling from time to time that any day he could walk through her door, sit at her table, crack open a beer, light a cigarette, and say something outrageous and politically incorrect.

His presence was still with her as well as his advice and admonitions. Especially here.

And now she was back in this valley.

She topped a gradual rise and the wide flat swale opened up before her. There was a black smudge in the small sea of sagebrush and it looked exactly as she remembered it.

The two-track led her there.

UNLIKE THE LAST TIME, when the collapsed pile of black wood was still smoldering, there was no need to watch her step or be wary of disturbing evidence or remains.

Cassie got out of her Escape and pulled her open coat tight across her as if it were a shield. She stepped carefully through the debris. She was a little surprised the site had never been cleaned up. It was as if local law enforcement had simply forgotten about it.

Bits of yellow crime scene tape had blown loose in the howling winds that were ubiquitous to the valley and were snagged within the black tumble of the collapsed house as well as on clumps of sagebrush. There were items in the burned remnants that were recognizable—balls of aluminum foil and even charred newspapers—but no grass or weeds had grown up through the ashes. It was as if, she thought, the place was so cursed and wretched that nothing could ever live there again.

This was where Ronald Charles Pergram had grown up. Although he'd spent nearly all of his adult years on the road as a long-haul trucker, it was the only real address he'd ever had, the only place he'd ever called home. His mother Helen had lived there alone after her husband left.

Cassie saw a thin square that looked like a folder and she bent to retrieve it. It was caught between two burned timbers and she grunted as she shimmied it out. The item was a picture frame. The cracked glass was still largely intact. She spit on the glass and used the edge of her sleeve to wipe away the soot.

The photo behind the glass was the official U.S. Marine induction photo of a young woman. She had clear blue eyes gazing out with a sense of purpose as straight as her jawline.

Cassie recognized the soldier as JoBeth Pergram, Ronald's sister. She'd died in action in Iraq when the Humvee she was piloting was destroyed by an IED.

From questioning neighbors in the area, Cassie later learned that Helen had doted on JoBeth all her life. JoBeth had been a star athlete at Gardiner High School, a straight-A student, and vice president of her class. Helen's kitchen wall was filled with awards and ribbons JoBeth had won.

After JoBeth was killed, Helen became a different person. She withdrew from the community, gained a tremendous amount of weight, and became a hoarder—or "collector" as she called it—to the point that moving through her house was like navigating through tunnels.

The same neighbors had very little to say about Ronald. He was quiet, nonathletic, and a poor student. He didn't hunt or fish, which made him an outlier among his male classmates. He seemed to have virtually no interests anyone could recall. He'd made very little impression on anyone, other than as JoBeth's younger brother.

JoBeth was popular in school and close friends with a pack of other girls. When one of them went missing no one suspected

Ronald at the time. Cassie speculated that JoBeth's friend was his first victim.

Helen's remains had been found in the burned house. The coroner estimated she weighed three hundred fifty pounds. Cassie recalled the coroner saying there was so much fat on the body that it smoldered for more than twenty-four hours.

Everyone suspected that Ronald had started the fire as he left for the last time.

In her face-to-face confrontation with Ronald Pergram in North Carolina, Cassie was getting nowhere until she brought up his relationship with his sister and his mother. It was the only thing she said that got a reaction from him other than contempt.

His response to her needling was to throw himself across the table and try to strangle her in the interrogation room. Officers responded and pulled him off before he could kill her.

CASSIE TOOK THE FRAMED PHOTO of JoBeth back with her to her car, opened the hatchback, and put it inside. She wasn't sure why, but she thought of it as an act of defiance toward the Lizard King—if he was out there.

And he *was* out there, she was sure. She'd spent five and a half hours and four hundred miles of driving from Ekalaka thinking about him.

She leaned back against the squared-off snout of her Escape and slowly took in the panorama of far-off mountains in every direction. The cold breeze teased at her hair.

Ronald Pergram had spent all of his adult life on the road, as she'd told Leslie. He'd been virtually everywhere in the country and possibly Canada and Mexico as well. He was familiar with hundreds of thousands of miles of roadway.

But that life had limited his knowledge as well, which was

something she hadn't thought about when she talked to the North Carolina prosecutor the night before. It had come to her as she drove across I-94 and I-90 through the state.

Cassie had learned from her father, an over-the-road trucker, that driving an 18-wheeler was like piloting a ship on the ocean. The captain of that ship had the entire blue-water sea in front of him and he could go anywhere on it. But when it came to approaching land the captain was handicapped. He couldn't land his ship on the beach or navigate up a river. He had to stay in the deep water.

It was the same situation for a long-haul trucker. The driver was confined to major highways. His life consisted of loading docks and weigh stations. Truck stops were his ports of call. Because of the massive size of his tractor and trailer, he was confined to the highways. If the driver wanted to go into town at night for a meal, he had to walk, hitch a ride, or call a taxi.

So even though Pergram knew every road in the country he likely had very little knowledge of what was beyond the highway. He wouldn't know suburban neighborhoods or downtown streets or unpaved rural roads because he'd *never been there*.

So without his tractor-trailer there was only one place Ronald Pergram had ever called home, one place he was familiar with.

It wasn't right, she thought, that such a stunning landscape had produced a monster like the Lizard King. He was obviously incapable of appreciating the beauty of it.

It made her hate him even more.

CASSIE DROVE AWAY from what was left of the burned down Pergram home. She swept her eyes across the valley and studied the rising foothills and the peaks of the jagged mountains. It was huge country under a massive sky.

If Pergram's first verifiable stop after he'd left North Dakota was Ekalaka he was travelling west toward the Rocky Mountains.

Where was he? And was Kyle with him?

WHEN SHE REACHED the top of the ridge her phone chimed with a message. There had been no cell service in the swale.

It was from Leslie Behaunek and it had been left twenty minutes before.

Cassie pressed the speaker icon on her phone as she bumped along on the two-track through the sagebrush.

Leslie's voice said, "Cassie, I talked to the ME in Montana and he sent me the autopsy photos of the victim. There's no doubt that a two-inch scar is visible on his inside left ankle."

Cassie cursed but kept driving.

"We're putting in a request to the Minneapolis Police Department to obtain items from Mr. Johnson that might contain Raheem's DNA to match it with the victim. If you still have Mr. Johnson's number you might want to give him a call and fill him in and soften the blow. I'd do it but I think it would be better coming from you since you know him. Sorry . . . that's no fun at all. Believe me, I've done it and it tears your heart out.

"I've also talked to Sheriff Verplank—who sounds like a nice guy—and he's FedExing the little electronic parts you-all found in the hayfield to us. Maybe we can figure out where they came from.

"We've got calls in to Montana and North Dakota to set up a conference call about creating that joint task force I told you about. So things are rolling.

"Call me when you get this. Since you didn't pick up I can only assume you're somewhere without a signal or you're busy." Her voice lapsed into her drawl when she said, "I just hope you're on your way home where you can get some sleep. I didn't get any last night thanks to you."

Cassie ended the message and nodded her head. Leslie was pulling out all the stops for her and she appreciated it. She knew Leslie was smart and capable and that her plan to create a joint task force investigation was the best way to proceed long-term.

But it wasn't the fastest way. She'd asked herself, *What if Ben had been taken by the Lizard King?*

If that were the case she'd want the most rapid investigation possible. She'd not want them to waste a minute on phone calls, meetings, or memoranda of understanding.

And she'd want Ronald Pergram in the ground.

WHEN SHE REACHED THE HIGHWAY Cassie paused. Left toward Gardiner and Yellowstone Park or right to Livingston and Bozeman?

Not for the first time in her career, she asked herself, *What would Cody do?*

TWENTY

IN BOZEMAN CASSIE STAYED ON Main Street. There was no reason to go anywhere else.

When she'd left Grimstad for Ekalaka she'd packed an overnight bag and wasn't even sure if that was necessary at the time. But since she'd continued on without going back home she had no fresh clothing and she'd used up the tiny hotel containers of shampoo, lotion, and toothpaste.

She used some of Lottie's cash—she still thought of it as Lottie's and dutifully kept every receipt—to stock up for at least two or three more days on the road. She dreaded breaking the news to Isabel and Ben.

The feel in downtown Bozeman was vastly different than that of downtown Grimstad. In Grimstad, men—and it was mainly men even with the energy downturn—didn't shop so much as resupply. It was all about getting in and getting out with heavy clothing and gear. The outside was icy, flat, and harsh, and it was there to provide these men with a living pumping oil out of the ground.

In Bozeman, with its proximity to Yellowstone, wealthy newcomers, and the local university, the outdoors was showcased as a friendly and spiritual place that everyone *must* appreciate at the risk of being ostracized. It was worshipped like a fetish, she thought. Judging by the shops, the clerks, the items for sale, and the clientele, everyone in Bozeman wore high-tech outdoor clothing as they sipped lattes and wine before cross-country skiing or befriending grizzly bears.

She thought that Grimstad could use a little more Bozeman and Bozeman could use a little more Grimstad.

But she found what she needed: clothing, underwear, and toiletries that she piled in bags into the hatchback of her parked car. Cassie bought area topo maps and guidebooks at the Country Bookshelf and both hiking boots and a good outdoor daypack at Schnee's.

Then she drove east on Main to the Bozeman Public Library.

CODY HOYT HAD TOLD HER the story before he started drinking again. Cody and Cassie had been parked in an unmarked Lewis and Clark County Sheriff's Department Yukon on an overlook near Lincoln. They were keeping an eye on a double-wide trailer set into an alcove of pine trees down a muddy two-track road.

Cody was sure that a meth dealer they were after was using the trailer that belonged at the time to the dealer's cousin. There was an APB out on the dealer but he'd managed to stay out of sight.

If the dealer showed up suddenly they'd have to jump into action and arrest him. But while they waited and hoped, surveillance duty was long and boring and rife with potential annoyances. The two of them were vastly different people and they had no choice but to be cooped up together in the front seat of a vehicle with fast food wrappers and empty Styrofoam coffee cups on the floorboards.

Cassie and Cody had a long-standing dispute about the inside temperature of the Yukon. She wanted it warmer and he wanted it cooler. Their dashboard dance—one of them changing the temperature while the other napped or looked away—went on for hours. They varied between being pleasant to sniping at each other. Cassie and Cody could have a benign conversation that might take a turn and end up an argument about something. Cody was mercurial that way, so Cassie kept her guard up and her opinions as diplomatic as possible.

There were times, though, when Cody told stories or relived experience he'd had that she found wise and instructive. Other "life lessons" weren't helpful. His philosophy about good police work—that the ends justified the means and anything that might have to be done to put dirtbags away was righteous—had horrified her.

On that night outside Lincoln he told her about the horseback trip he'd taken into the most remote wilderness in the Lower 48 states—the Thorofare region of Yellowstone National Park he called "back of beyond." He'd gone there to try and find his son Justin who was on a multi-day expedition with his stepfather and an outfitter based in Bozeman named Jed McCarthy.

After day two in the wilderness, Cody described how miserable he was not only because of the primitive conditions but because he was withdrawing from nicotine and alcohol at the same time. That, and riding a horse ten hours a day.

Eventually Cody found the expedition, and what happened changed his life—for a while.

But although Cody had grown up in the redneck outlaw Hoyt clan that was spread throughout rural Montana, he'd never really been a seasoned outdoorsman. And he knew as little about horses as he possibly could. In fact, he told her, he'd made a point of it.

So how did he locate that expedition in the first place, she wondered?

That's when she first heard the name Bull Mitchell.

Cody had found Bull Mitchell at, of all places, the Bozeman Public Library.

CASSIE GLANCED AT HER WRISTWATCH as she pushed through the double doors. It was ten to five and she hoped most of the staff was still on duty.

A slender young woman with jet-black hair with purple streaks in it looked up from a book she was reading at the information desk. The woman, Cassie thought, had a fresh hipster-outdoorsy look and was likely the target market for many of the downtown shops she'd wandered through that afternoon.

"May I help you?" she asked. She spoke with a flat intonation Cassie had heard described as "vocal fry" that was low, burred, and to Cassie, grating.

"Please," Cassie said, trying to ignore the tone. "I'm from out of town and I hope you can steer me to the right person here. I assume there's someone who is in charge of children's reading programs?"

The outdoor girl glanced behind Cassie and Cassie instinctively turned around to see if there was someone waiting behind her. There wasn't.

"Sorry," the woman said, "I thought you had a little one with you."

"My little one is twelve years old."

"Oh, well, you asked about . . ."

Cassie put on her most pleasant face. She wasn't there to confuse the outdoor girl behind the information desk.

"A friend of mine told me a really charming story a couple of years ago about an older man who read children's stories for a primary-grade group. The audience was all kids except for one senior woman. The older man did it because the older woman was his wife and she had severe Alzheimer's. It was his way to recon-nect with her."

The outdoor girl nodded her head with recognition. "Was his name Mr. Mitchell?"

"Yes. Bull Mitchell."

"He was an awesome dude when he wasn't crabby about some-thing," she said. "He was often pissy about one thing or other. But when he read to his wife"—she shook her head and smiled sadly—"it was awesome."

"Does he still do it?" Cassie asked. "I'd like to meet him."

"When his wife died he stopped coming in," she said. "I haven't seen him in probably a year and a half."

"Oh. Do you have any idea where I could find him?"

The outdoor girl said, "This *is* a library. We can find anything."

"Why do you talk like that?" Cassie asked her.

"Like what?" the outdoor girl said in her fried voice.

EVEN THOUGH THE FRONT DOORS were locked, there were lights on in the second-floor corner of Mitchell/Estrella, Attorneys at Law, in downtown Bozeman. Cassie did a quick search on her phone for the numbers for the law firm and called while she stood on Main Street and looked up. She could faintly hear the phone ring inside.

It rang seven times before diverting to voice mail.

"You've reached the law offices of Angela Mitchell and Jessica Estrella. Our office hours are . . ."

Cassie disconnected, waited a moment, and called again after it went to voice mail.

Then again.

In Cassie's experience most attorneys were under the general impression that they were the smartest people in the room and therefore they were always in control of it. They liked processes to be complicated and stacked in their favor, and they didn't enjoy uncertainty or chaos. Nothing made a prosecutor or defense attorney more uncomfortable than the unknown.

In this instance, the unknown identity of whomever was calling a law office repeatedly after it was closed and not leaving a message? Could it be a client in some kind of trouble?

On the fourth attempt the phone was answered. It was a female and she sounded annoyed.

"This is Rachel Mitchell of Mitchell/Estrella. If you're the one who keeps calling—"

"I am. My name is Cassie Dewell and I'm standing on the street outside your window. I'd like to talk to you about your father."

There was a silent moment. Cassie guessed Rachel Mitchell was weighing whether the call was professional or personal.

"What about my dad?" she asked.

"I need to ask him if he remembers helping out my old boss Cody Hoyt four years ago."

"Now there's a name from the past." She said it in a way that indicated she was likely both as impressed with and annoyed by Cody as Cassie herself used to be.

Cassie looked up to see a slim woman with a full head of auburn hair, peering out the window of the corner office. She had a telephone receiver held up to her ear.

Cassie waved up at her as if to say, *Here I am*.

"Do I know you?" Rachel asked.

"We met once in Helena four years ago," Cassie said. "You came up to see Cody after he came back from Yellowstone. I probably wasn't very memorable at the time."

"What did you say your name was again?" Rachel asked as if to confirm it.

"SO YOU'RE WITH the Sheriff's Department," Rachel said as Cassie entered her office.

Cassie said, "Not anymore. And up until a week ago I was working as the chief investigator for the Bakken County sheriff in North Dakota."

Rachel Mitchell was an attractive, no-nonsense woman. She wore a tailored suit and she had athletic calves. Her manner was cool and professional as she gestured for Cassie to sit down in a chair while she skirted around the desk. Her office was spacious and tasteful, with leather-bound books of Montana Statutes lining the shelves and a collection of family photos on her credenza of good-looking outdoor kids doing outdoor things.

Cassie recalled that she'd felt intimindated by Rachel Mitchell the first time she saw her and she regretted that she still felt that way. When she sat down in the chair Rachel had indicated, she did so in a heavy-bodied way. Especially compared to how Rachel glided into hers.

"If you're not with Helena or Grimstad who are you with?" Rachel asked.

"I'm running an independent investigation."

Rachel shook her head, puzzled. "I don't know what that means."

Where to start? Cassie got the impression she would have twenty seconds to tell her story or she might not get the chance to do it again.

Cassie cleared her throat. "I'm here because I have good reason to believe that a vicious serial killer who grew up in the area might have come back with a captive teenage boy from North Dakota. I think they may be hiding out around here. From what I understand, your father knows the mountains around here better than any man alive—if Cody is to be believed. Cody told me your dad was the best outfitter and guide in the Yellowstone region. I'd like to ask him if he has any idea where I should look."

Rachel sat back in her chair and raised her eyebrows. "My dad isn't in very good health these days. Since my mom died eighteen months ago he's deteriorated. There is absolutely no way he could guide you anywhere."

"I'm not asking him to do that," Cassie said. "What I was wondering is if I could talk to him. He might know something about the family of the man I'm looking for since they were in the area for years when your dad was working."

"Who is it you're looking for?"

"His name is Ronald Pergram," Cassie said.

Rachel flinched at the name but quickly regained her composure. She said, "Also known as the Lizard King. And now I know who you are. You're the cop who shot it out with the trooper. You're the one who almost caught Pergram."

"To be honest, Pergram got away before I knew who he was," Cassie said.

"That was a big story around here. And you've been after him ever since?"

"More or less."

Rachel placed an index finger and painted nail alongside her mouth. "I thought he died someplace in North Dakota a month or so ago? That he blew himself up."

"I was there and I thought the same thing until yesterday. Now I think there might have been another man driving Pergram's truck that day."

"This is a lot," Rachel said while she leaned back as if to distance herself from Cassie's theory.

"It is. I'm aware of that. I can explain how I came to it if you'd like."

Rachel shot a look at her iPhone to check the time. Then she said, "Please do."

Cassie recounted the case from the evening she met with Lottie in the lobby of the Law Enforcement Center to arriving in

Bozeman that afternoon. Rachel eyed her the entire time as if looking for inconsistencies or physical tells.

When Cassie was through, Rachel said, "So you're doing this on your own." It was a statement, not a question.

"I've got that support network in North Carolina I mentioned but yes, I'm basically a civilian."

"Interesting."

Cassie said, "As I told you, Pergram may have killed Raheem. And Kyle Westergaard is more than just a missing person. He's a friend of my son's and we have some personal history together. Kyle has a mild case of fetal alcohol syndrome and when I think the Lizard King might have him it breaks my heart."

Rachel's eyes softened for the first time. "I've got three boys of my own and one very spoiled girl." Then: "And you think my dad might have an idea where Ronald Pergram is?"

"Possibly. I would think he knows the family. They had a place in Paradise Valley that's since burned down."

"Why are you not telling all this to local law enforcement?" Rachel asked.

"Because I know how a sheriff's department works. I hate to say that but it's true. Cops are reactive to live situations, but the process slows way down when it's a complicated case from another jurisdiction that requires serious investigation. Especially when there are local crimes to concentrate on. I can file a report or wait to speak to a deputy and then it's up to them to pursue it, but what I'm telling you consists of a lot of speculation at this point. It could take days or weeks before they follow up, if at all. I can't afford to wait."

Rachel huffed a little laugh. "That sounds like something Cody Hoyt would have said."

Cassie smiled ruefully.

"That kind of thing got him in trouble more than once," Rachel cautioned.

"Don't get me wrong here. I'm not going to try to find where Pergram is and do some kind of citizen's arrest or something. I'm not that brave or foolish. My job as I see it is to build a solid foundational case that he's back in this area. Once I've got solid evidence I'll turn it over to law enforcement and let them take it from there."

The attorney picked up her phone. "Call my cell so I have your contact info," she said, giving Cassie her phone number. "My dad is living with us at home and I'll run this by him. No promises, no guarantees. And he might just refuse to talk to you because he's such a cranky old curmudgeon these days."

"I understand," Cassie said, keying in Rachel's phone number and pressing SEND.

Rachel's phone chimed. She disconnected it after the first ring and dropped it into her purse.

"When it comes to my dad, well, it's hard to predict. He remembers the old days when he was outfitting very clearly. It's the things that happened this morning or yesterday he has trouble with."

"Thank you," Cassie said from the chair and holding out her hand.

Rachel shook it and said, "I'll let you know later tonight. There's no point talking to him until he's had dinner. After dinner—and before he sits down to watch Fox News nonstop—that's the sweet spot to talk to him about anything."

IT WAS FULL DARK when Cassie went outside to her car. She'd need to find a motel in Bozeman and as she scrolled through those available on her phone a text from Leslie Behaunek chimed in.

It said CALL ME.

TWENTY-ONE

"THE MURDERED BOY was Raheem Johnson," Leslie said. "The DNA results are 99.5 percent conclusive."

"Shit," Cassie said.

She'd just pulled off the road and she was parked under the check-in alcove of the Holiday Inn Express on the outskirts of Bozeman. The parking lot was empty except for two other cars. The neighborhood she was in consisted of branded mid-market hotels and fast-food outlets and obviously serviced Interstate 90 that pulsed to the north. Fields of brown grass surrounded the Holiday Inn Express and gave it the feeling of being more isolated than it actually was.

Cassie recalled driving through the area in the height of summer a few years before and seeing full parking lots at every hotel. Tourists on their way to or from Yellowstone. It was different in mid-October. Inside, she could see a male and female behind the check-in counter looking out as if imploring her to come inside to relieve their boredom.

Leslie said, "We've notified the Hennepin County Sheriff's Department to deliver the bad news to Mr. Johnson. He probably won't be shocked by it because he was apparently very cooperative earlier today when he provided Raheem's toothbrush and strands of his hair to the authorities to get DNA.

"So it looks like you might be on the right track after all."

"Still, I would have rather you said it wasn't him," Cassie said.

"Me too."

"I'll call Mr. Johnson as well. Does he know the circumstances of Raheem's murder?"

"Not that I know of but I don't know what the locals will tell him."

"I'll steer clear of that if I can," Cassie said.

"So where are you?"

"Bozeman."

"*Bozeman*? I thought you were going home. I thought we had an agreement." She sounded miffed.

Cassie said, "You made that recommendation and you must have assumed I'd take it. But the more I thought about things this morning, the more I thought I needed to follow the only thread that makes sense to me—that Ronald Pergram finally came back home."

They discussed her theory and Cassie could tell that Leslie was dubious of it for a couple of reasons. The first was that Cassie was flying blind, which Cassie acknowledged. She'd crossed law enforcement jurisdictions and state lines, which was something she never could have done when she worked for the sheriff's department. The second, unspoken, reason was that Leslie wanted her joint task force to succeed.

If Ronald Pergram were to be found and arrested Leslie wanted it to happen so cleanly, to be so procedurally correct, that no defense attorney could touch it. She'd already been burned once by being outmaneuvered in court and she didn't want it to happen again. Cassie understood that. And she understood that Leslie might think Cassie might get too far out in front of the task force and foul up the case by inserting herself into it.

Cassie said, "As I told Rachel Mitchell tonight, I've got no intention of getting in too deep."

"I would say you're already there," Leslie said.

Cassie could tell Leslie was building up a head of steam for a full-blown argument. They'd had a few over the past few years and Leslie, using her prosecutorial skills, usually came out on top.

Then Cassie's phone beeped with another call. She looked at the screen.

"We'll have to talk later," Cassie said to Leslie. "I've got Rachel Mitchell on the other line."

"Look—"

Cassie discontinued Leslie's call and punched in Rachel's.

"Cassie?"

"Yes."

"My dad says there's a guest host he doesn't like on *The O'Reilly Factor* tonight."

"What does that mean?"

"It means come straight over. You've got—and I'll quote him on this—'one hour until *Tucker Carlson Tonight* comes on.' And believe me, he never misses Tucker Carlson."

"I'm on my way," Cassie said as she put her Escape into gear. She could check into the hotel later.

The two clerks inside watched her go with puzzled expressions on their faces.

"What's the address?" she asked Rachel as she roared out of the parking lot.

"HIS CAVE IS in the back," Rachel Mitchell said to Cassie after she let her into her house. "Follow me."

Cassie appreciated that given the time constraint Rachel didn't engage in small talk. The attorney had changed into sweats—she even looked good in sweats, Cassie thought—and led her through her home. It was large and well appointed with overstuffed leather furniture, a flickering fireplace, and original paintings of Montana landscapes on the walls.

As they passed the kitchen Cassie glimpsed a teenage boy doing homework on the table and a man in his mid-forties reading the copy of the *Bozeman Chronicle* that was spread out on a marble kitchen island. The man looked up pleasantly and nodded as they passed.

"My husband, Tucker," Rachel said over her shoulder. Then in a whisper, "He's a *saint*. My dad isn't the easiest guy to live with, you know."

Cassie nodded and they continued down a hallway that seemed to go on forever. She thought the house didn't look big enough from the outside to have such a long passage.

"You'll see why I call it the cave," Rachel said, opening a door and stepping aside for Cassie, who was hit in the face with the uncomfortably loud volume of a TV.

"He won't wear his hearing aids," Rachel said into Cassie's ear. "So prepare to shout."

Cassie stepped into the room as the sound pummeled her. It could have been the inside of a small hunting lodge, she thought. Elk, moose, bear, deer, and antelope heads on the walls, dim light from a deer antler lamp, black-and-white framed photos on the walls at odd angles and heights, at least a half-dozen battered cowboy hats lined crown-down along the top of a bookcase. Wooden pack saddles and battered panniers were mounted on sawhorses, and looped lariats hung from nails in the wall. A glass-fronted cabinet was filled with various long guns.

A large-screen television tuned to Fox News glowed on the far wall and she could see the back of a recliner with two large stockinged feet propped up on the footrest sticking up like rabbit ears.

"Dad," Rachel called out, "she's here."

"*Who's here?*" His voice was a rusty roar.

"Cassie Dewell. The woman I told you about. The private investigator."

Cassie turned to correct her but Rachel winked as if to say, *It's easier this way.*

"Tell her she's got"—he glanced at his wristwatch—"thirty-four minutes," Mitchell said.

"I'll leave you two," Rachel said to Cassie. "I'll hover around outside if you need anything. And to eavesdrop, of course." Rachel stepped back and closed the door with a sympathetic smile.

Cassie had to admit she liked her. She wasn't so sure about *him.*

"Do you mind if we turn that down?" Cassie shouted as she pulled a folding chair over to face Rachel's father.

"*What?*"

Cassie gestured toward the set and repeated herself but louder.

Bull Mitchell was a big man with a white crew cut who filled the recliner. He had a head like a cinder block mounted on broad shoulders. With deep-set eyes and a full mouth drooping down on the corners, he reminded her of some kind of big bottom-dwelling fish.

His hands were huge and scarred and they sat on his thighs as if he didn't know what to do with them. The remote control for the television rested between his legs. He wore faded jeans, a red-checked cowboy shirt with pearl snap buttons, and wide red suspenders.

He squinted as he looked over at her and his mouth curved down even more into a grimace. But he located the remote and brought the sound down to a murmur.

"I feel sorry for you," he said. "This country is going to hell. I'm glad I won't be around to see it burn."

Cassie said, "My mother agrees with you."

"Your mother is a smart woman," he said. "Maybe you won't be a waste of my time."

She didn't say that when Isabel channel-surfed and accidentally found Fox News she would cover her eyes and howl until it was gone. In fact, Isabel had called the local cable service to see if they could remove just that channel so she wouldn't ever have to see even a second of it ever again.

He said, "I remember the day when Republicans and Democrats alike loved America. I had lots of friends and clients who were Democrats. Now they're different. They want to change us into goddamn France or Sweden. And I always thought I was safe from 'em here in Montana.

"But all you have to do is walk around downtown Bozeman to see they've infiltrated here. They always ruin the best places, you know. They move in and set about changing everything to be more like what they left. And I'm not even talkin' about what they've done to Missoula or Whitefish."

She nodded to indicate she heard him but she didn't want to use the short time she had to discuss her mother or politics.

"I've got some questions to ask you if you don't mind," Cassie said.

"Yeah, Rachel told me that. Something about those damned Pergrams down by Emigrant."

Cassie felt her heart lift.

"So you remember them?"

"They were low-rent white trash. Except for the girl. The girl turned out all right."

"How well did you know them?" she asked.

He shrugged. "Well enough, I guess. That valley used to be a whole lot different before all the pinkos and movie stars started buying up ranchettes. I used to run horse pack trips into the park so I'd lease pasture down there, so I got to know just about everybody. That don't mean I palled around with 'em.

"That was back when the park was a national park and not a

candy-assed nature preserve run by Ivy League bureaucrats. It was a whole different world back then," he said, shaking his head.

"Frank Pergram worked for me from time to time."

Cassie looked up. She was interested. Ronald Pergram's father was a mystery to her. She knew very little about him other than he'd deserted Helen and their two children when Ronald was young.

"What was he like?"

"Frank?"

"Yes."

"Frank was a fuck-up. I never would have hired him as a wrangler but it was hard to find people to work back in those days. It wasn't like it is now with people stacked on top of each other around here like it's goddamn New York City."

"I understand," she said, trying to be patient. "But what would you say he was like? Why was he a fuck-up?"

"He just was. He couldn't help it. Having him on the payroll was like having two good men gone. Frank could screw up a two-car funeral, if you know what I mean."

"I don't."

"He was the kind of guy who thought he could impress my female clients by acting like an old-time mysterious cowboy. Like he was Shane or something. When I needed him to picket the horses up in camp he was never where he was supposed to be—he'd be trying to romance some lady from Connecticut. Or he'd be getting into a fight with one of my other wranglers. Or he'd be in charge of the pack horses and he'd forget to bring the panniers. It was always one thing or other with him. He was a malcontent, a goddamn tumor on every expedition."

Bull reached across his body and placed a hand on his armrest so he could lean closer to Cassie. His gaze was intense.

"You probably don't understand how important it was to have a good crew in my line of work. I needed to have men and women

I could depend on because once we set off into the Yellowstone wilderness I was stuck with 'em for days on end. We got clients from all over the country and all over the world who didn't know jack-shit about horses, or packing, or camping in the wilderness. All some of 'em knew about nature was from watching *Bambi*, and the Yellowstone backcountry is raggedy-ass and nothing like *Bambi* at all.

"So we'd take all these people who didn't know each other, who'd never been away from civilization, and put them on horses and take them into wild country. My crew had to be customer-friendly and professional. They needed to be able to overlook the dumb stuff our clients did or said, and I'll be the first to admit some of our clients were real peckerheads. I couldn't have employees who argued with the clients or tried to sneak into their tents at night. That's unprofessional bullshit. Plus, I always had to be aware of the fact that the National Park Service could jerk my license to operate a commercial trip if they got complaints on me. Frank was the kind of guy who clients could complain about.

"I fired him once and he came back and begged me for a second go. Being the soft-heart I am," Bull said with a sarcastic grin, "I let him go on the next trip. But he did the same dumbass things and I fired him as soon as we came back out of the wilderness.

"I can't say we spoke much after that but I'd still see him around. Usually playing cowboy at the First National Bar in Emigrant or here in town at the Crystal. Still trying to impress the ladies with his squinty-eyed mysterious Davy Crockett bullshit."

Cassie asked, "Did he ever talk to you about his family?"

Bull Mitchell was still for a moment. "I know where you're going with this, you know. I ain't stupid. This is about his son Ronald, the no-good murdering pervert, isn't it?"

"Partly," she said. "But I'm trying to learn more about Ronald by finding out about his father. You're the only person around who probably knew him."

He considered that and nodded, apparently satisfied with her answer.

"To Frank Pergram, his family at home was like boils or gout. They were just an irritation that flared up from time to time. He wouldn't even mention them unless somebody asked him."

"What would he say?"

Bull's eyes left hers and seemed to focus on one of the elk heads. "He'd say his wife couldn't even whore around because she was too damned ugly. I know he beat on her but that wasn't so unusual in those days. But I heard he beat on her in front of his kids, and that's not tolerable. He used to say he wished his son had been been stillborn because he was so damned useless to mankind. He made fun of how his kid talked and mocked him in front of other people. There was never any doubt that he was ashamed of them.

"You know," Mitchell said, "I have something to confess here. I actually felt sorry for Ronald back then. The kid was a slug and he was hard to understand—some kind of speech impediment—that's true. He was hard to figure out. But what kind of father is ashamed of his own son? His own family? It wasn't until all this stuff came out about Ronald that I kind of figured Frank might have been right about him all along. But you know what? I don't think Ronald would have been the sick monster he turned out to be if he hadn't have grown up like that."

Cassie was intrigued.

"Did Frank treat his daughter differently?"

"Yeah, he did for as long as he was even around there. He kind of doted on her when she was a baby. But he wasn't there when she turned out to be the good one. Frank was dead by then."

"How did he die?"

"Got drunk and passed out on the railroad tracks in Livingston," Bull said. "Cut into three pieces. Couldn't have happened to a nicer guy."

"Back to the family," Cassie said. "When you were around Frank did he ever mention taking them anywhere? Like a favorite hunting or camping place?"

Bull rubbed his jaw with his big hand. Cassie noticed for the first time that he was missing the tips of two of his fingers. She'd never known a horseman who didn't have missing digits.

"I've got to think about that," he said. "Frank wasn't much of a hunter but he *was* a poacher. He always got his meat whether he had a license or not or whether there was an elk season on."

"Do you know where he hunted?"

"I've got a good idea now that I think back on it," Bull said. "I think he snuck into the park and killed them elk. It was illegal as all hell but that's something Frank didn't have a big problem with. Any peckerhead can kill a docile elk inside the park."

He raised his eyebrows and said, "Hey, you never asked me why they call me Bull?"

She ignored him because she knew the answer. Cody had told her.

"Do you know if he ever took his family with him hunting or camping? Specifically Ronald?"

"I told you I didn't pal around with them."

"But you know, you might have heard something when your wranglers were talking, or Frank bragging in the bar . . ."

Bull closed his eyes and seemed to be searching his memory. Cassie perched on the end of her chair.

Then he opened his eyes and they fixed onto the television screen. She looked over to see Tucker Carlson's opening on *Tucker Carlson Tonight*.

"We're done," Bull said with finality as he pointed the remote at the set and turned up the volume.

"Mr. Mitchell," Cassie pleaded. "I'll only take a few more moments of your time."

He acknowledged her with a nod but gestured toward Tucker Carlson.

"I'm not sure I like her new hairdo," he said, settling back in his chair.

"WELL, THAT WAS FRUSTRATING," Cassie said as Rachel walked her back to the door. "We ran out of time and I have a lot more questions."

"He's a frustrating man," Rachel said. "I've never met anyone as cantankerous as he."

"Yet he read your mother stories at the library."

Rachel looked away but not before Cassie noted the tears in her eyes. "That he did," she said wistfully.

"Can I come back and finish tomorrow?"

"I don't know what to tell you," Rachel said. "I'll ask him, but he kind of fades in and out. Tonight he was particularly loquacious. He liked talking to you—until he didn't. Whether he'll pick up where he left off tomorrow is another matter."

"Other than his age, what are your father's problems?"

Rachel paused and held her hand up. As she spoke she'd raise one finger after another. "Rheumatoid arthritis, gout, high blood pressure, high cholesterol, early Alzheimer's. He's on way too much medication, I think, and the different doctors don't talk to each other. I'm thankful every day that he's still with us, but he does make it tough at times to remember that."

Cassie thanked her for interrupting her evening and was halfway to her Escape when Rachel called after her.

"You know I have a defense practice here in Bozeman, right?"

Cassie turned.

"I didn't know what kind of law you practiced," Cassie said, letting her opinion of defense attorneys show.

"We're not all bad," Rachel said. "Sometimes we defend innocent people who deserve justice."

"And sometimes you get guilty people off."

"We even defend cops who are wrongly accused. They deserve a defense like anyone else."

Cassie instantly regretted where this had gone. She said, "I'm sorry—there's still a lot of cop in me. It's hard to forget preconceived notions."

"I understand," Rachel said tentatively, as if reconsidering whatever it was she had set out to say. Then: "Anyway, my partner and I sometimes need to bring on a private investigator to help with cases. We've not really had much luck hiring a really good one. I've been impressed how dogged you are. Is it something you'd ever consider?"

Cassie was surprised at the question. "I've never really thought about it."

"I'd urge you to think about it, Cassie."

"I live in North Dakota."

"You're *unemployed* in North Dakota," Rachel said. "Montana is your home. I did some research on you. You're not hard to find with a Google search."

Cassie didn't respond.

Rachel said, "You of all people should know what it's like to be railroaded by people in authority. I was just thinking you might be a little more sympathetic to our line of work because of that."

Cassie shrugged and said, "All I can think about now is finding Kyle."

"That's what I'm talking about," Rachel said as she waved good night and closed her front door.

AFTER CHECKING INTO THE HOLIDAY Inn Express and talking a few minutes with Ben—he was ready for her to come back because Isabel's organic cooking was making him sick, he claimed—Cassie drank another plastic cup of wine and called Clyde Johnson. It was an hour later in Minneapolis.

"Mr. Johnson, this is Cassie Dewell. I'm just so sorry to hear about Raheem."

"Yeah, me too," he said. "I was thinking that when they asked me to give them stuff that might have his DNA on it . . ." He was attempting to be stoic but she could sense his sadness.

"I know there's nothing I can really say other than it's a terrible thing. I wish I could have called with good news."

"No shit," he said. "I wish you could have, too. But you didn't. And now I find out he got his damned head blown off and he was left in a field. I can't even . . . I can't wrap my mind around it.

"Tell me," he said, "do you think it was racially motivated? I ask that because Kyle wasn't found with my boy."

"I don't think so, Mr. Johnson."

"Because that would make it worse. That would make it a hate crime: *Let's kill the black one*. And why do you think it wasn't?"

She couldn't think of a good answer.

"Raheem was a knucklehead at times but he was a good boy," he said. "He didn't deserve what happened to him."

"I agree. I'm doing my best to find out who did it."

"When you find them you call me. I'll be there in a heartbeat."

"I'll call," she said. "But not before I get law enforcement involved."

"Great," he said with sarcasm. "The same folks who wouldn't even look for him."

With that he disconnected the call.

CASSIE FELT LIKE she'd been gut-punched, but she forgave Clyde Johnson. She could only imagine how she would react in the same circumstances.

When her phone buzzed she thought it might be him again but the number on her screen was local.

"Cassie Dewell."

"This is Rachel Mitchell. I'm sorry to call so late but my dad insisted I call you *right now this second*." She sounded exasperated. "I'll put him on."

"Cassie," Bull said in a shout so loud Cassie had to move the phone away from her ear, "I blame you for screwing up my enjoyment of Tucker Carlson tonight. All I could think about was that peckerwood Frank Pergram."

"Yes, what about him?"

"There's a section southeast in the mountains where he told me he used to get firewood. It's harder than hell to get to and who knows what the road is like these days. The park border cuts right through it but it ain't like there's a marker or a fence of any kind."

"Can I drive there?" she asked.

"What kind of vehicle do you have?"

"A Ford Escape."

He scoffed. "You'll need more clearance than that just to get close to the trailhead.

"It's probably been twenty-five years since I've even been there. I could draw you a map but unless you've been there before you'd probably get lost."

"Could you take me there?" she asked.

Bull began to shout something but he was interrupted as the phone was pried away. Cassie could hear him say, "*What the hell . . .*"

"Cassie," Rachel said, "my father is in no condition to guide you in the backcountry anymore. I just can't let him do it."

"If he could just take me up there and point—"

"That's not his style, believe me," Rachel said. "He doesn't do anything except with both feet. So I'm very sorry to say that the best we can do is sit down with a map and have him circle where you need to go."

She said it with finality.

"I got some maps today," Cassie said. "I could bring them by in the morning."

"Perfect," Rachel said.

In the background, she could hear Bull saying, *Give me back that phone.*

"Tomorrow," Cassie said.

FIVE MINUTES LATER she got another call. Same number.

"Rachel?"

"Naw. *Bull,*" he whispered. "Rachel's in the other room. She doesn't know I'm calling. You know, she's a good girl but she thinks she's my goddamn nanny. So I waited until she was gone before calling you back."

Cassie raised her eyebrows.

"So you worked with Cody Hoyt?" he asked.

"Yes. He was my mentor. He was tough to get along with at times but I wish he was still here."

"Yeah, I know what you're saying. I wanted to hug him and kill him at the same time when I took him into the park that time. But mainly kill him."

Cassie huffed a laugh.

"Can you ride a horse?"

"It's been a long time."

"Do you have outdoor gear? You know, like a sleeping bag and a rain slicker?"

"No, but I can buy some. Bull, you're not planning to actually go with—"

He cut her off without a response. "Come by the house at ten-thirty after my goddamn nanny has gone to work. We'll take my truck and I'll show you where that peckerwood Frank Pergram used to poach."

TWENTY-TWO

Location Unknown

KYLE'S EYES SHOT OPEN AND he nearly cried out when he received a sharp vibrating pulse on the skin of his throat. He threw off his covers and sat up in bed.

"About time you were getting up," Ron said from his chair at the table. "You're burning daylight, son."

Although Ron usually walked around with the three transmitters hanging on lanyards around his neck, on that particular morning they were lined up one by one on the table. As always, he wore his semiautomatic pistol in a shoulder holster.

Kyle wanted to tell Ron he hadn't slept since he'd had that horrible dream again about what happened to Raheem.

BOOM.

Instead, though, Kyle reached up and slipped his fingers beneath the vinyl collar and rubbed his neck where the two electric prongs were in contact with his skin.

"Just testing," Ron said. The day before he'd placed colored dots on the collars and transmitters that corresponded with each other. Amanda got blue, Tiffany red, Kyle green.

"I'm making sure I got all the colors right," Ron said. "Otherwise,

I might hit the wrong one at the wrong time. We wouldn't want that, would we? Besides, it's time you got up."

Kyle scrambled out of bed and then turned and made it up. Ron was a stickler about neat beds.

THE DAYS THEY'D BEEN at the cabin had started to flesh out into a kind of haunting routine.

It had been difficult for Kyle at first, as it had been for Amanda and Tiffany. Ron somehow expected them to know what he was thinking and act accordingly. When they made a mistake, like sleeping too late or going out of order to the outhouse fifty yards away from the cabin, he would "correct" them, as he called it, with a vibrating pulse on their collars. If they made the same mistake twice or the original transgression was deemed severe, Ron administered an electric pulse.

When they did their twice-a-day outhouse visit, Ron would stand by the window with a transmitter in his hand. He'd watch them go to the outhouse and come back to the cabin. Amanda went first, then Kyle, then Tiffany. As one returned he'd nod at the next in line, grasp the correct transmitter, and watch them the whole way. Color-coding the sets made less guesswork for Ron, Kyle assumed.

When Tiffany spent too much time in the outhouse—in Ron's opinion—he sent a pulse her direction and she screamed inside. Ron had snorted with laughter. It was the first time Kyle had ever seen him laugh.

The next time she spent too long in there Ron bypassed the vibration feature and sent a mild shock that startled Tiffany so badly she fell out of the door with her panties still around her ankles. That had made Ron laugh out loud. He obviously enjoyed humiliating her most of all.

Kyle always did his business in the outhouse as quickly as he could. The structure was small and old and cold wind blew in through the gaps in the planking. He'd never used an outside toilet before and he didn't like it at all. He hated the *plop* sound his excrement made a second after he'd expelled it into the dark cavern below.

KYLE HAD BEEN "corrected" a half-dozen times and each time it happened he froze and closed his eyes.

Once, he'd been clearing away the lunch dishes when the pulse nearly made him drop the plates on the floor. He looked up to see Ron beholding him with distant eyes and a grim expression on his mouth. Kyle didn't know what he'd done to deserve the pulse.

"Clear my dishes first," Ron had said as if Kyle should have known that.

It made Kyle angry when Ron came up with a new rule he'd never used before. When he glared up at Ron he was hit with a mild electric shock that startled him.

Kyle never did *that* again.

He also never opened up to Tiffany or Amanda, even when they were all alone and left in the cabin. He couldn't risk it. He'd observed how Ron played them all against each other. He'd rewarded Amanda with a a smile and a bag of hard candy for telling him that Tiffany had looked into Ron's room while he was away, which was forbidden. Then he punished Tiffany by turning his transmitter up high and bringing her to wailing tears administered by the shock collar.

By the same token, when Tiffany whispered to Ron that Amanda had been stashing food in a cubby near their bed and eating it at night—also forbidden—Ron kissed Tiffany on the top of her head and administered a series of shocks to Amanda that made her sink to her knees and sob.

They were all there to keep watch on each other and tell Ron if any of the others stepped out of line. They were all there to please Ron.

He'd said, "A family is about rewards and punishments. Just like life."

ALL THE MORNINGS were the same. Ron slept in the lone bedroom off the main room. When he woke up, which was before the sun came up, he'd say, "Amanda," and it was her job to spring out of the bed she shared with Tiffany and make coffee. The two of them slept in an iron-framed double bed with their heads on opposite ends with Tiffany closer to the stove and Amanda against the wall. Kyle slept on a single bed four feet away. Both beds were along the back walls of the open room that served as the kichen, dining, and living area.

Breakfast was the same every morning, which was Ron's preference. Bacon, hash browns, two eggs fried in bacon grease. Buttered toast. Amanda received a few corrections the first week while she cooked until she got everything exactly right.

Ron ate first and he did so leisurely. The others ate after Ron pushed his plate away. He made them finish their meals and clean up their plates.

After breakfast, Ron went out. He did most of his work outside close to the ancient log cabin itself but he never mentioned what he was doing or what his plans were each day. They would see him pass by the windows on the side of the wall or over the sink. He chopped wood, repaired the well, cleared brush from the front of the cabin, and he'd often vanish into a small shed for an hour or two.

Other days, they'd hear the pickup start up and drive away. Strangely, Kyle felt more anxious on the days when Ron was gone than when he was just outside, because he never knew when he'd come back or what he'd been out doing. Or what kind of mood he'd be in when he returned.

Twice a week he arrived with groceries, mostly canned goods. He never brought back a newspaper that might let them know where they were and he apparently made a point of discarding the grocery store receipt with the name and location of the store on it so it wouldn't be found in a bag.

When Ron wanted to be alone he marched Amanda, Tiffany, and Kyle outside and into the shed where he'd sunk steel rings into the bare two-by-six framing. He looped a chain around their ankles and secured them to the wall with a large padlock. Then Ron would spend time in the cabin, sometimes for hours.

There was no stove in the shed and even though the days were mostly pleasant it still got cold in there. Tiffany trembled until her teeth clattered together like the sound of a rattlesnake about to strike.

Kyle suspected Ron was watching homemade videotapes on a compact player he'd seen in an open ammo box under Ron's bed. Kyle didn't dare look at them. Ron referred to it as his "Oh Shit" box for some reason.

Ron had warned them all there would be "severe consequences" if any of his personal belongings were moved or touched. He claimed he knew the exact physical location of everything he owned and he marked them with human hairs or finger lines in the dust. He'd *know* if anyone tampered with his stuff, he said.

AMANDA WAITED UNTIL RON WENT back to the cabin and she was alone with Kyle in the shed.

"Kyle?" she whispered.

He turned toward her suspiciously. Kyle was smarter than either Ron or Tiffany gave him credit for, she thought. In these circumstances it made sense to be suspicious.

She said, "I really feel bad for saying this to you because you seem like a nice boy . . ."

He was paying attention.

"I don't want to become close to you and I hope you understand that. I can't risk it and neither can you. If Ron thinks we're close he'll punish us both, but mainly me since I'm the adult. Do you understand what I'm saying?"

The boy simply looked at her. She couldn't tell what he was thinking because his face was still, like it always was. She thought she could see something in his eyes, though. Something very alive.

"I don't like Tiffany," she said. "She's hard to like and I don't think for a second that she wouldn't snitch on either one of us and get us hurt or killed. But you're different, I think.

"It would tear me up inside if we became friends and Ron did to you what he did to Raheem. Like I said, I'm protecting us both. Do you understand what I'm saying?"

It took a few seconds before he nodded almost imperceptibly.

"I'm being selfish," she said, lowering her eyes. "I don't want to get hurt. Please don't let me get close to you."

He nodded again.

ON CERTAIN DAYS RON would have a distant look in his eye at breakfast. On those days he wouldn't talk at all. He seemed angry about something, quick to punish and make corrections, and Kyle kept his distance and he noticed Amanda did, too.

When Ron left in the morning on those days Tiffany reluctantly rose from bed and got ready. Ron had communicated something to her and her alone. She washed herself in a basin and primped in front of a round mirror. There was makeup in a small bag and Tiffany reddened her lips and traced black around her eyes.

Kyle watched her surreptitiously when she cleaned up because he couldn't help himself. She had long legs with barbed-wire tattoos around each upper thigh. There was a sparkly stud of some kind below her belly button and a tattoo of a cat on her lower back. She had no shame when it came to removing her clothing and cleaning up. Tiffany had larger breasts than Kyle thought natural, but he didn't mind seeing them.

Amanda once caught him staring and slugged him hard in the shoulder.

Tiffany had laughed when it happened and said maybe Kyle was normal after all.

But Tiffany quit laughing when Ron came back into the cabin and ordered Kyle and Amanda out to the shed.

Kyle noticed how rough Ron was with his movements on those days when he locked them up. Ron's face was flushed and his breath was shallow.

When Ron went inside the cabin to be with Tiffany it would sometimes take hours for him to come back. When Amanda heard Tiffany's screams she would shut her eyes.

Then Ron would trudge back out to unlock them. His eyes were downcast as if he was ashamed of himself. His movements were more gentle.

Kyle noticed the smell on Ron when he leaned in close to unlock the padlock. It was a musky smell, almost metallic.

When they went back inside, Tiffany would be in her bed covered by blankets. Sometimes she was still. Other times she was trembling.

The days after Ron was with Tiffany, Kyle noticed the abrasions on her face, elbows, and knees. The previous time after Ron had been with her she wouldn't open her mouth until he was gone from the cabin. When she spoke Kyle could see she'd lost a front tooth.

"He's getting tired of me," Tiffany said morosely to Amanda.

"Yesterday, he couldn't be satisfied. I tried everything I could think of. You don't know what it's like to try and keep that man happy."

Amanda looked away and said, "No, honey, I don't know."

"I ain't long for this world," Tiffany moaned.

AFTER LUNCH, RON NODDED at Kyle across the table and said, "Come outside with me."

Kyle felt a chill shoot up his spine and the hair raised on his arms and on the back of his neck.

"Don't look at me like that," Ron said, fingering the transmitter with the green dot.

Kyle looked away. Reluctantly, he pushed his chair back.

RON OPENED THE FRONT door and stepped aside so Kyle could go out first. As Kyle passed Ron in the threshold he glanced at the .380 beneath Ron's jacket in the shoulder holster as well as the transmitter with the green dot hung around his neck by a lanyard.

When Kyle looked over his shoulder Amanda had her head in her hands. Tiffany wouldn't make eye contact.

It wasn't lost on him that in Ron's world, this world or the cabin in a forest, Kyle had no purpose. Amanda was there to cook and clean. Tiffany was there to provide Ron pleasure. Kyle was there . . . for what?

Before Ron sent Raheem off from the pickup, he'd said, "*I was wondering what I was going to do with you anyway.*" Kyle expected to hear the same words at any moment.

Maybe, thought Kyle, Ron wouldn't make him run. Maybe he'd close in behind him and put a bullet in his brain. Kyle preferred a bullet to the exploding collar.

They walked out through the cleared front yard and into the timber. Ron stayed just behind Kyle's shoulder but gave him directions.

"Bear left."

"Cut around that tree."

Kyle liked the way it smelled in the forest. The tall pines were fragrant and the mulch of orange pine needles on the floor of the timber gave out a ripe, musty odor when he stepped on them. Ferns he didn't recognize poked up through the bed of needles. Squirrels chattered to each other down the line as if saying, "Here they come!"

"Climb the hill and be careful of loose rocks," Ron said.

Kyle had to get down on his hands and knees to propel himself up the rocky slope. He could hear Ron struggling behind him and breathing hard.

"Slow down," Ron said.

Kyle suddenly had a thought: what if he could get far enough ahead of Ron to break over the top and run away? He could dislodge some of the rocks under his feet to slow Ron down further and leave the wheezing old man behind him.

Then he remembered the collar.

THE TREES CLEARED near the top of the ridge and Kyle climbed out of them. It was colder than below and if anything the air was even thinner. A cold breeze wafted through his hair.

There was a bald knob on the top of the rim that was rough with granite outcroppings. Kyle stood between two thigh-high boulders and looked out.

He'd never seen a vista like it before. Beyond a tremendous ocean of trees—it looked like an undulating ocean of green had been frozen in place—blue snowcapped mountains jutted into the pale sky.

Kyle had never seen mountains like this before. The closest thing to them were the badlands terrain of the Theodore Roosevelt National Park, where Grandma Lottie had taken him. But those dryland buttes and spires weren't even *close* to what there was out there on the horizon.

The mountains were so high that there were clouds *below* them, stringy clouds pushing through valleys as if they were bony fingers fitting into a glove. And not a single structure, wire, or road anywhere.

What looked like steam wafted above the trees to the south. Kyle smelled something acrid.

"You know what that is, right?" Ron asked between gasps for air. "That smell?"

Kyle shook his head.

"It's sulfur. Kind of smells like rotten eggs, doesn't it?"

When Kyle didn't respond, Ron said, "If you're familiar with that smell you can guess where we are."

Hell, Kyle thought.

"Any ideas?" Ron asked. He stood slightly bent forward with his hands on his hips until he could recover his breath.

Kyle shook his head.

"My guess is you haven't seen much of this country, have you?"

Kyle indicated he hadn't.

"I've seen it all," Ron said. "Coast to coast. North and south. This country is bigger than hell. Parts of it are beautiful, like this. Most of the other parts are nothing more than a human cesspool."

He spat out the last few words. Then: "Day after day I'd wonder why I was spending all my time and labor providing goods to those people out there. Every appliance—every big-screen TV, food, furniture—just about everything they have came to them in my truck and trailer or one just like it. But do you think they ever once said thank you?

"Not a chance. They'd cut me off on the highway. They'd flip me off when my rig was laboring up a hill and they had to pass. At rest stops they'd see me coming and look away like I was human trash.

"But look at me now," Ron said. "I'm on the top of the fucking world."

AFTER A FEW MOMENTS of silence except for the breeze, Ron said, "You don't miss much, do you?"

Kyle looked up to him for more clarification.

Ron said, "You watch everything. You take it all in—all the shit life throws at you—but you don't say anything. You remind me of what I was like when I was a boy."

Kyle hugged himself to try and keep warm. It was exhilarating to see so much wide-open mountain terrain. But it was cold up there and the wind was harsh. He didn't want to admit to himself that he was ready to go back down the mountain to the warmth of the cabin.

And he wanted Ron to shut up. The man seemed to think he was imparting some kind of special insight or wisdom, Kyle thought. But for the first time since they'd left the cabin, Kyle thought that perhaps he'd make it back there alive.

"We know what it's like to be different, don't we?" Ron asked. "I thought about it the first time I saw you when you came off that river. When I saw you I thought to myself, '*He's an other*,' just like me. You and me, we know what it's like to look out at the world from a dark place. And when people see us coming they see something damaged. They see something inferior to them. Right, Kyle?"

He wished Ron would stop talking.

"Some people used to call me the Lizard King and for a while I liked that name," Ron said. "God knows I earned it. But they really used that name because it made me into something less than human. Something twisted. But that ain't me, Kyle. I'm not really like that most of the time.

"You stick with me and you'll learn things," Ron said. "I had to learn everything on my own because I grew up in a house of idiots and morons. Those people had real problems. I'll tell you about my mother some time. She didn't even know what it was like to be happy. She didn't teach me how to be happy. I had to learn it myself. And I'm happy, Kyle.

"Especially now," Ron said. "Now that I finally have what I've always wanted: my own family."

Ron reached out and patted Kyle on his shoulder. "You're like the son I never had," Ron said.

Kyle felt cold and sick.

ON THEIR WAY BACK DOWN the hill, Ron walked side by side with Kyle. When he placed his hand on his shoulder Kyle tried not to recoil from the touch.

"You'll learn things from me, Kyle," Ron said again. "You'll learn that you don't need to take anyone's shit ever again. You'll find out that it doesn't matter how people look at you because you're actually superior to them. You'll have contempt for them but I'll teach you how to hide it and how to use it to your advantage."

He went on along that line and Kyle tuned him out. But Ron's hand stayed on his shoulder.

"WELL, LOOK AT THAT," Ron said. His voice was cold.

They were approaching the cabin and at first Kyle didn't know what Ron was talking about because there were too many trees in the way. But when he stepped to the side a couple of feet, and away from Ron's hand, which fell away, he saw it.

Tiffany's upper body was halfway out of the side window. She was stuck fast and was frantically wriggling her hips in an attempt to get free of the window frame.

Kyle had the strange thought: She looked like a thrashing tongue sticking out of the exterior wall.

"Stupid whore," Ron said in a low tone. "Stupid fucking whore. What is she thinking?"

Ron reached over and instead of placing his hand on Kyle's shoulder he gathered the back collar of his shirt in his hand and pushed, propelling him down the hill.

"Stupid fucking whore—hips too wide to fit out the window," Ron said in a furious whisper.

Kyle had to break into a jog to prevent himself from being run over.

Their footfalls must have made a racket and alarmed her because Kyle saw Tiffany stiffen and look up to see them coming. There was absolute terror in her eyes.

"It was her idea!" she yelled. "Amanda was the one who made me do it."

Kyle felt terrible for Tiffany. She was just stuck there, completely exposed. The glass from the window she'd broken out was in shards in the grass near the foundation of the cabin. He could see long cuts in her arms that were bleeding.

"Stupid, stupid," Ron said as much to himself as Kyle. Then Kyle was heaved aside. He landed on his hands and knees as Ron rushed past.

"Stay!"

As if he were commanding a dog.

Kyle looked up as Ron lumbered toward Tiffany in a half-run. He could see the man fishing inside his jacket with his right hand.

"I'd blow your head off but I don't want to do any more damage to the cabin," Ron said to Tiffany in a roar.

"Please, no," she begged. "It was Amanda's idea. She made me do it, really. She's back in there pushing right now. Please, Ron, no."

He slowed as he got to her. Kyle could see that Ron was flushed and was breathing heavy again from coming so quickly down the mountain.

Tiffany had her hands braced below her under the sill of the window so she could keep her head up. There were tears in her eyes and her mouth was twisted.

Ron raised his pistol and pointed it at her head. The muzzle was several inches away from her temple. She closed her eyes and bit her bottom lip.

Kyle said, *"Ron, no, don't hurt her—"*

There was a sharp loud crack and Tiffany's arms gave out. She flopped forward and her face thumped the log wall of the cabin. Her hands dropped limply and hair streamed straight down. Blood pattered on the broken glass.

Kyle could smell the sharp smell of gunpowder as it drifted to him in the breeze.

Ron shook his head from side to side as he holstered the pistol.

"Stupid cunt," he muttered to himself. Ron roughly unlocked the training collar from her neck. Tiffany's body swayed as he did it. When the collar was free he rammed it into his jacket pocket.

Then he turned angrily to Kyle and started to mock how he'd said *Ron, no, don't hurt her—*Kyle could tell because it had happened so many times before in his life—when Ron seemed to catch himself.

Kyle blinked tears out of his eyes. Ron seemed to be ashamed of what he'd almost done.

"Help me get her out of here, Kyle," Ron said in a soft voice. He turned his back on Kyle and grasped one of Tiffany's arms. Before he pulled, he put the sole of his boot against the cabin for leverage.

Kyle stood up. His feet felt like they were encased in concrete as he trudged slowly to the cabin.

"Come on."

Kyle reluctantly grasped Tiffany's left arm with both hands. Her body was still warm and supple, but there was no resistance.

"Grab it tight," Ron said. "Now on the count of three. One, two, three . . ."

Kyle put his thighs into it. Tiffany's body came out of the window frame much easier than he thought it would. So fast, in fact, that he lost his balance and fell backwards. Tiffany crumpled heavily next to him.

He looked up to see Amanda's horrified face filling the open hole. Her mouth made a perfect *O*.

"Ron, I told her not to do it. I tried to make her stay."

Even Kyle could tell she was trying to lie but wasn't good at it.

Ron narrowed his eyes and thrust his face toward the open window. "Amanda, don't think you're gonna lie your way out of this."

Amanda filled the *O* with the heel of her hand and retreated.

"WELL, THIS WASN'T how I thought this day would go," Ron said after nearly a minute. His breath had returned to normal. Kyle could hear Amanda crying to herself inside and it wrenched at his heart. He wasn't used to grown women crying around him.

Ron bent down and touched the tips of his fingers to Tiffany's neck.

"Dead."

Kyle stepped back.

"Where are you going?"

Kyle shrugged.

"Go in the shed and grab one of those blue plastic tarps. We'll wrap her up in it, then I'll show you where the bodies are buried."

WHEN KYLE WENT into the cabin for his coat Amanda looked up at him with red eyes. She was seated in a chair facing the corner where Ron had ordered her to sit until he came back.

She said, "I don't want what happened to Tiffany to happen to you, either," she whispered. "Or me."

PART FIVE

YELLOWSTONE NATIONAL PARK

TWENTY-THREE

WITH THE BUNDLE of topo maps on the passenger seat of her car and her outdoor gear piled in the hatchback, Cassie swung around the corner of Rachel Mitchell's street to see a three-quarter-ton pickup—it looked like something out of a World War II museum—with a four-horse stock trailer parked out front.

The juxtaposition of the battered four-wheel drive and peeling trailer in front of Rachel Mitchell's magnificent brick house, as well as the other million-dollar homes in the subdivision, was striking. It was like seeing a hitching post in front of an Apple Store, she thought.

Bull Mitchell, wearing a wide-brimmed cowboy hat and lace-up outfitter boots, was struggling under the weight of a pack saddle he carried across the lawn from the house toward the trailer. Two piles of horse manure steamed on the clean black asphalt of the street.

It was a crisp and sunny fall morning. The sky was cloudless and the mountains on the southern horizon were so clear that it almost hurt her eyes to look at them.

Because it was dark the night before, Cassie hadn't realized the big brick home backed up to a pasture. Or that Bull—and possibly Rachel—had horses as well as a barn within walking distance of their back door.

She parked parallel to the street and climbed out. Bull acknowledged her with a curt nod of his head. It was obvious there were animals in the trailer by the way it rocked from side to side.

"What's going on here?" she asked.

Bull grunted as he hoisted the pack saddle into the bed of the pickup. He was breathing hard, but to Cassie the man appeared twenty years younger than he had the night before. He had a full barrel chest on top of his big belly and he looked stout and strong.

"I've loaded up my best three horses," Bull said. "Gipper, Rummy, and Dickie. Gipper and Rummy to ride and Dickie as our pack horse if we need him. I think I'll start you up on Gipper. That's the horse Cody Hoyt rode. There's no way you're a worse rider than him."

Cassie was taken aback. "Gipper?"

Bull winked. "Named after the greatest president of the twentieth century. Rummy's full name is Rumsfeld and Dickie is named for Dick Cheney. They're all damn fine horses."

"This is exactly what Rachel didn't want to happen."

Bull grinned before turning back to the open garage for more gear.

"Bull? I thought you were going to take me up there and point the way. That was the deal I had with Rachel."

Mitchell gathered up saddle pads between his arms and walked toward his truck and trailer. His heavy boots made loud *clunks* on the pavement.

"Do you want to honor your deal with my nanny," he said after swinging the pads over the bed wall into the back, "or do you want to find that boy?"

Cassie took a long time to find the right words to respond.

"Don't worry," he said, "I left her a note. She'll get over it."

"I'm not so sure," Cassie said.

He paused and grinned. It was almost boyish. There was no doubt, Cassie thought, that he was back in his element.

"There's plenty of room in the back of the truck for your gear. Maybe instead of just standing there you can start loading."

BULL'S PICKUP AND TRAILER rumbled through the outskirts of Bozeman onto Interstate 90 with all of the subtlety of a slow-motion train wreck. The exhaust belched black smoke and the inside of the cab shook as if trembling. Cassie held on to a worn leather strap that hung from above the passenger door. She cranked down her window a few inches for fresh air because the carbon monoxide fumes inside were making her nauseous.

She'd noted the faint hand-painted BULL MITCHELL'S WILDERNESS ADVENTURES logo on the door as she climbed in.

"When is the last time you drove this thing?" she asked. Bull ignored her as he built up speed on the interstate after shifting through all four gears. She couldn't remember the last time she saw someone work a clutch. Cars and trucks shot past them and Bull kept the vehicle and trailer on the right shoulder of the road as they approached the canyon out of town.

"I said," Cassie shouted, "when was the last time you drove this thing?"

Bull grinned but didn't look over. He reached out and patted the metal dashboard and answered a question she hadn't asked.

"She's a classic 1948 Dodge Power Wagon, the greatest ranch or mountain vehicle ever made. It's a three-quarter-ton four-by-four perfected in World War Two. After the war all the rural ex-GIs wanted one here like they'd used over there and pretty soon they were on every ranch in Wyoming and Montana. I bought this baby when I opened my company and I never found a reason to get anything else. The original ninety-four horse, 230 cubic-inch flathead six won't win any races but it can grind through the snow and mud, over logs, through the brush and willows. It's as tough as a damn rock. A damn rock! With the big tires and high clearance we could load a ton of cargo on this son of a bitch and still drive around other pickups stuck in a bog."

She nodded.

"Where are we going?" she asked.

"And if we do get stuck—which we might—I've got that direct-drive eight-ton winch on the front to pull us through or over anything."

"Can you hear a single thing I say?"

"We'll need to gas up in Livingston or Gardiner and fill the two five-gallon cans I brought along, just in case we need them. And we probably better grab some food to take along. I've got a couple of bottles of whiskey but I didn't want to run Rachel out of grub. Plus, she eats all healthy and that's not the kind of food we need in the wilderness. We want steaks!"

So, she thought, they were going to take the interstate to Bozeman and turn south at Livingston on US-89 to Gardiner.

"You took your hearing aids out, didn't you?" she asked. "I hope you put them back in at some point."

Bull looked over at her and frowned. He said, "If you're talking to me I can't hear a damn word you're saying. I took my hearing aids out."

"Where are they?"

"We're gonna take a couple of old back roads out of Livingston straight up the mountain," he said, taking one hand off the steering wheel and waggling it from low to high to indicate the turns on the road. "Those were bad roads twenty years ago so I doubt they're any better now. But once we get on top we'll be close to the area where Frank Pergram used to hunt. It's about two hours from town and in really rough country.

"See, Cassie, it used to be that the Park Service wasn't the neo-Nazi organization it is now. Now it's full of true-believer bureaucrats who think their job is to keep people out of the park so the wildlife can frolic on their own. But somebody forgot to tell the wildlife because wildlife doesn't frolic—they eat each other.

"Anyway," he continued, "the Park Service used to tolerate locals and kind of look the other way when someone crossed the boundary a little bit to get their elk meat for the winter. In fact, there were some old cabins up there that were technically inside the park itself. The rangers knew about them but they didn't spend any time kicking people out. They had better things to do with their time than to piss off all the locals. I don't know if those old cabins are still up there or not but I figured it would be a good place to start looking. Frank used to 'borrow' one when he hunted up there. I heard him talk about it."

Cassie said, "Did you take your hearing aids out so you could talk nonstop and not answer my questions?"

"Let me tell you about the other ways the Park Service plays God in Yellowstone . . ." Bull began.

Cassie used the opportunity to turn aside and punch Leslie Behaunek's number on her speed dial.

"WE'RE HEADED THERE NOW," Cassie said after briefing Leslie. Mitchell was still lecturing in the background. "I'm going to ask Bull to stop at the Park County Sheriff's office in Livingston so I can let them know what we're up to."

"Good," Leslie said. "It's about time you involved actual law enforcement."

Cassie let the dig go. She said, "I know the sheriff there from when I was chasing the Lizard King the first time. His name is Bryan Pederson. He's a good guy and we got along well. I think I'll have some credibility with him."

Cassie could sense Leslie's relief.

Leslie said, "We've got a conference call scheduled this afternoon with North Dakota and Montana to get everyone up to speed on this."

"I won't screw it up, I promise. If we locate Ron Pergram or Kyle we'll back off and call in the cavalry."

"I believe you won't *try* to screw it up."

"They might not even be in the area but my guide connects Pergram to the area through his father," Cassie said. "If nothing else we can rule it out."

"Your guide sounds like quite a character."

"Oh, he is. He's crusty and stubborn as hell. And believe it or not he's going to try to get me on a horse."

"Take a photo and text it. This I have to see."

"Doubtful."

"And call in as soon as you can so I can brief the task force."

Cassie agreed and disconnected the call.

Bull said, "Crusty and stubborn as hell, huh?"

"You heard."

"I put my hearing aids in just in time to hear you slander me."

"It isn't slander if it's true."

Bull stifled a smile as they—mercifully, Cassie thought—pulled off the interstate toward Livingston.

They were nearly into town when the pickup shuddered and the motor stopped running. The truck and tailer coasted down the exit ramp until Bull was able to guide it onto the shoulder.

"Well, shit," he said.

"THESE OLD POWER WAGONS are mighty vehicles," the mechanic said to Bull and Cassie as he wiped coal-black grease off his hands with a dark red rag, "but no matter how reliable they are they still need to be maintained."

The mechanic had a clean-shaven head but a silver-streaked

beard that was so long and full it nearly obscured the name DUB over his coverall's breast pocket.

Bull growled and looked at the top of his outfitter boots in shame.

"The engine is fundamentally sound," Dub said to him, "but you'll need new belts, new air, oil and fuel filters, a thermostat, radiator flush, and a carburator clean-up. Then I think we can get it running again.

"How long has it been since you had it into the shop?"

"A while," Bull grumbled.

"When can it get done?" Cassie asked Dub. She was trying not to let her frustration show—or her anger at Bull.

"Three hours at most to do the work," Dub said.

Cassie looked at her watch. They could get into mountains by late afternoon. She said, "That's not bad."

"If we had the parts," Dub explained. "It's not like we have parts for a sixty-nine-year-old pickup in stock. Luckily, I know a guy in Billings who can get me what I need. He's kind of a Power Wagon aficionado and he knows somebody headed this way later today who can deliver the parts."

"So it'll be ready tonight?" she asked.

"Make it tomorrow morning," Dub said. Then: "Make yourself at home here in Livingston. Just don't let the damned wind knock you over. It blows like a mother sometimes."

She looked over at Bull. "*It's as tough as a damned rock*," she mocked.

He said, "You sound like Rachel. No wonder you two get along."

While Bull and Dub worked out the logistics of fetching the horse trailer that was still back on the exit ramp with the tow truck, and where the nearest horse-friendly motel was located, Cassie took a deep breath and stepped outside the auto repair shop. Bringing the horses had complicated matters. And driving that old Power Wagon had complicated matters even further.

The mountains of Yellowstone dominated the southern horizon. She felt helpless. She was *so close* but had no practical way to get there. And she certainly didn't know the backcountry where Bull wanted to take her. She was his prisoner in a sense.

Cassie pulled out her iPhone and queried the address for the Park County Sheriff's Department. The map showed it was five blocks away.

Nobody walked anywhere in Montana, she knew. But the walk would do her good and calm her down.

SHERIFF BRYAN PEDERSON WASN'T in his office at the moment, according to the receptionist who spoke to Cassie through a slot in the thick Plexiglas. The receptionist was in her sixties and had short-cropped silver hair and cat's-eye glasses that were so old they were back in fashion. Her nameplate said MARGARET.

"He should be back within the hour," the receptionist said. "You can come back then."

"I'll wait here. Can you please tell him I'm here to see him?"

"And your name again?"

"Cassie Dewell."

Margaret paused as she scrawled out the message. She gave Cassie a long second look. "Do I know you?"

"Maybe. I used to work up in Lewis and Clark County."

Realization filled Margaret's eyes.

"You're *that* Cassie Dewell?"

"Yes."

"The one who got in that shoot-out with the state trooper a few years ago?"

"Yes."

A steel door next to where the receptionist sat required a key code to enter. Margaret noted Cassie looking at it.

"I'd buzz you right through if it were up to me," Margaret said. Then she gestured toward the cheap plastic chairs that lined the long narrow lobby. "I wish I could do better."

"It's fine," Cassie assured her. One of them was occupied by an American Indian man in a Carhartt jacket clutching a fistful of pink traffic tickets. Cassie sat down in one of the chairs across from him.

"Not comfortable chairs," he said. He had dark eyes and a pockmarked face. He brandished the violation slips in the air. "I'm waiting for my sister to show up with cash from the ATM. They only take cash. Who takes just cash anymore?"

"I don't know," Cassie said. It felt strange to be on the other side of the Plexiglas and the steel door.

"About time they entered the twenty-first century and took credit cards," the man said.

Cassie used the wait time to text Leslie to report that they'd been held up for the day. She also sent a text to Ben telling him that she loved him and that she'd be home as soon as she could.

WHAT CASSIE RECALLED about Sheriff Pederson was how kind he'd been to her in the immediate aftermath of the shoot-out. Rather than question her story or motives like the agents from DCI had, or insert himself into the situation in order to take credit for the outcome like her own boss had done, Pederson had gently guided her through her statement. He knew what she was feeling, he'd assured her.

He'd said, *No matter how tough you are or how justified the circumstances, it's devastating to take another person's life.*

And when they discovered Cody Hoyt's body buried in that field by the Lizard King and the dirty state trooper, Pederson had held her and let her cry. He'd said very little at the time, but the gesture still meant something to her.

Oddly, though, she couldn't remember his face other than it was attractive in a raw-boned, cowboy kind of way. He had a thick mustache. She remembered he was tall and thin and he wore a wedding band. She distinctly remembered that wedding band.

FORTY-FIVE MINUTES LATER, Cassie saw him stick his head into the receptionist office from a door in the back and mouth, *I'm back.* Then his eyes drifted up and slid off the Indian and found hers. He smiled and mouthed, *I'll be damned.*

A few seconds later he opened the steel door.

"Cassie—I thought it was you."

"It's me. Do you have a few minutes?"

"Let's go get a cup of coffee," he said while holding the door open.

When the man got up as well Pederson said, "Not you, Norman. You stay here until you pay your fines."

The man sat down with a sigh.

IN THE SMALL DOWNTOWN DINER across the alley from the sheriff's department she realized he no longer wore the ring. She tried not to stare.

For the last hour she'd brought Bryan Pederson up to speed regarding the Lizard King and his possible kidnap victim. Pederson was vaguely aware of the formation of the joint task force Leslie Behaunek had created because he'd read a memo about it from DCI just that morning.

"If he's up there no one has reported anything unusual," Pederson said.

"That isn't surprising," she said. "The Lizard King is supposed to be dead so nobody is looking for him. Plus, we know that he changed his appearance. I doubt anyone who knew Ronald Pergram back then would even recognize him now."

Pederson nodded. He had more gray in his mustache and temples than she recalled. He'd also lost weight. He looked borderline cadaverous, she thought. She wondered if he'd been sick.

"I can't believe Bull Mitchell himself is taking you up there," Pederson said. "He's a legend around here. Everybody has a story about him. Did you ever hear about the time he took a chain saw and cut a truck in half to settle up with a former business partner? Or about the time a grizzly bear chased him up a tree but the branches broke and Bull fell down on top of the bear and scared him off?"

"No, but now I have one," she said. "About the time we were going into Yellowstone and made it as far as Livingston before his truck broke down."

Pederson smiled at that.

"He's going to meet us here, right?" he asked.

She shrugged. "That's what he said when I called him but his hearing is . . . selective. He said something about going to picket the horses behind the motel and make his way over here. So he'll be here any minute, I'd guess."

"I want to go with you tomorrow."

She nodded that she'd heard him.

"I've got horses of my own. I'm going to ask Bull if I can bring a couple of deputies along with us."

"It's your county," she said, "but it's his expedition. You know how he can be."

"It'll help if you're in favor of the idea," he said.

"My opinion means very little to him."

"He's here, isn't he?" Pederson asked, raising his eyebrows. "He dusted off all his old outfitter gear and fired up that relic of a truck. He loaded his horses up and here he is. I don't think he'd do that if your opinion meant nothing."

"You're right. I need to cut him some slack. It's just that when I think about Kyle I get anxious. If he's actually up there with Pergram every minute counts."

"I understand," Pederson said. "But you're dealing with vehicles, horses, and a mountain search and rescue operation. Time isn't the same up there as it is here in the big city. Everything slows down the closer you get to Yellowstone."

She nodded. "I'm sorry to ask you this but will involving you and your guys slow us down even more?"

"A little. But my guys will be gung ho to go. The tourist season is over and there isn't a lot going on right now. The opportunity to get Pergram is something no one in law enforcement around here could pass up.

"Besides," Pederson said, "if the Lizard King really is up there somewhere you can use more firepower. We don't want him getting away from us again."

"Thank you for saying 'us' and not 'me.'"

"I'll let my office know I won't be there tomorrow," he said. "Tonight I'll call two of my horse-savvy guys. They'll jump at the chance to come along, believe me. And I'll compare notes with Bull to coordinate everything. I'll let him call the shots."

She didn't want to ask him about his missing ring. But he didn't seem like the kind of man who would say anything about it unless prompted.

Before she could think of a way to bring it up, the door opened and its frame was filled with Bull Mitchell.

"Can a man get a beer around here?" he boomed.

BULL WAS ON HIS fifth Coors Original and Pederson his third when Cassie's phone lit up.

She looked at the screen, then at Bull. "It's Rachel."

"Don't answer," Bull said. "She'll try to talk you into going back.

Besides, she doesn't know where we are—whether we're in cell phone range or not."

"I don't feel very good about that," Cassie said as the call transferred to her voice mail.

"It's for her own good," Bull said with finality.

He turned to Pederson. "Do you know why they call me Bull?"

"No."

"Cause he's hung like one," Cassie said.

"You've heard!" Bull laughed, slapping the table with his big hands.

"Cody said you'd explained it to him," she confessed.

THEY AGREED TO ALL MEET in the parking lot of the Tomahawk Motel the next morning as soon as Pederson's men had caught their horses, loaded them into trailers, and geared up.

By then, Cassie hoped, Bull's truck would be ready to get back on the road.

She left Pederson and Bull inside to talk logistics and order another round.

Outside on the sidewalk she turned toward the south. The mountains could be made out only because they blocked out the night sky and stars. It was twenty degrees colder than when they'd crossed the alley to enter the diner.

"Maybe tomorrow, Kyle," she whispered. "Stay strong, little man."

TWENTY-FOUR

EARLIER THAT EVENING and fifty-four miles away, as they approached the small National Park Service building at the north entrance in the Ford pickup, Ron said to Kyle, "We're just a dad and his son visiting Yellowstone National Park. Can you do that, Kyle?"

"Yeah."

He was starting to understand the boy's odd speech pattern.

It was five-thirty in the evening. Tiffany's body, which had been rolled up in the blue plastic tarp, was on the floorboards in back. It was covered by two dark blankets as well.

Ron thought: *I'm still the Lizard King.*

HE'D LEFT AMANDA with her arms and ankles duct-taped to a chair facing a corner in the cabin. She'd been bawling her eyes out even after he'd smacked her and told her to stop it, so he'd double-taped her mouth shut. Before they left he made the conscious decision not to feed the dying fire in the woodstove.

She'd spend hours sitting in that corner in the dark, feeling it get colder inside the cabin because of the open window, really thinking about the stupid thing she'd tried to do.

Thinking about how she got Tiffany killed.

HE'D MADE THREE STOPS in Gardiner on their way into the park. Gardiner was hard on the border of the park itself. The Roosevelt arch proclaiming FOR THE BENEFIT AND ENJOYMENT OF THE PEOPLE was within sight of town.

The first stop was on a side street in an unincorporated subdivision that led to a transient trailer park filled with camper trailers and single-wides. He'd explained to Kyle that the camp was used primarily by seasonal concession workers who couldn't find housing inside the park during the summer months. Because the season was over, many of the lots had been freshly abandoned.

The transients had left black plastic bags of garbage and things they didn't want to take with them, as well as a few vehicles that no longer ran.

Ron pulled up behind a battered 1982 Dodge pickup mounted on blocks and swapped out the North Dakota plates on the Ford for the Montana plates on the Dodge.

The second stop was at the hardware store and he asked Kyle to come inside with him.

He'd said to Kyle, "Remember: You're a kid spending time with your dad. Stick close and keep your mouth shut even though that doesn't seem to be a big issue with you. Oh, and pull your hood up. I don't want anyone seeing that collar."

Kyle did as he was told.

The boy followed him inside and kept his head down as Ron bought an aluminum-framed window to replace the broken one back at the cabin.

At the third stop, the Gardiner Market on Scott Street, Kyle played his part extremely well, Ron thought. The boy shadowed him as he pushed his cart down the narrow aisles and acted as bored and sullen as any other teenager. When asked if he wanted thick-cut bacon or regular bacon, Kyle had shrugged.

Ron wasn't worried about standing out in this small town. It was a tourist town, after all. Only in the deep winter did residents notice strangers.

Kyle's only transgression was when he mishandled a jar of olives and dropped it on the floor where it broke. The boy's face turned bright red as he bent to gather up the shards of glass. The odor from the spill was strong and Kyle was so upset by what he'd done he accidentally kicked a few dozen individual olives across the floor trying to gather them up.

"Just leave it," Ron said. "They'll clean it up."

I'm sorry, Kyle said. *Nime sore-ee.*

"Forget it, son."

Then Ron realized Kyle had sliced his finger open from the glass. It was bleeding small droplets into the olive juice on the floor.

"Christ," Ron said. "Now you've cut yourself."

Kyle clasped his cut finger with his other hand. *It's okay.*

"No—go clean it up. The bathroom is in the back."

Ron had glared at him to show his displeasure but he followed Kyle to the back of the store where the restrooms were. He waited just outside the door with his cart until he heard the flush inside, then he rapped with his knuckles to indicate that Kyle hurry.

The boy came out looking sheepish. He'd wrapped a wad of toilet paper around his finger.

Ron had leaned inside the bathroom to make sure Kyle hadn't left anything. He hadn't.

Ron bought a box of Band-Aids. In the truck he said, "Let me see that finger."

Kyle held it out. The cut was long but not deep—a bleeder but not bad enough to require stitches. Ron fastened two strips around it. Kyle watched him carefully as he did it, and the moment seemed to bring them closer together, Ron thought.

They continued through town on the way to the north entrance. They met only three vehicles coming out, all three with out-of-state plates. In the height of summer, Ron knew, the traffic was bumper-to-bumper in the evening.

THEY CRUISED THROUGH the Ranger Station without stopping.

Ron saw the puzzled look on Kyle's face and explained.

"These are federal employees who work at the entry stations here. They start slacking off in the fall when very few people come into the park this late in the evening. It's the same way early in the morning, believe me."

Kyle nodded slightly.

"You know what I used to say? I used to say that as long as I entered the park before eight or after five, America's first national park belonged to the Lizard King. What do you think about that?"

"I don't know." *Ah non't no.*

"You've never been to Yellowstone before, have you?"

"No." *Nuh.*

"I figured that. Well open your eyes and look around. It's quite a place."

Kyle nodded dutifully.

"How's your finger?"

The boy held his hand up. The Band-Aid was stained with blood but his cut was no longer bleeding.

BEFORE RON NEARED the Gardiner River and the narrow switchbacks that would take them up through the canyon and on to Mammoth Hot Springs, he said, "Tiffany didn't realize how good she had it. That's the trouble with most of them. You feed 'em, you give them clothes and a warm place to sleep and they turn on you anyway. It's something you need to learn, Kyle: Whether it's women in general or your own family—they'll always turn on you because you're different. Always."

Kyle looked away.

He was a hard kid to figure out, Ron thought. He kept his own counsel. But he *might* be coming around.

If only, Ron thought, *he'd* had a guy like him around at Kyle's age.

He'd have conquered the fucking world.

AS HE DROVE he kept a wary eye out in front and behind him. There was always the chance, although remote, that an over-eager park ranger would pull him over for speeding or simply note his presence in the park if questioned later. But like the entrance booth personnel, traffic rangers seemed to vanish from exis-tence once the hotels and visitor amenities inside the park closed for the season.

So Ron kept right at the forty-five-mile-an-hour speed limit even though he was driving the only vehicle on the mountain road.

On the climb out of Mammoth Village toward the steaming terraced springs themselves, he said, "Recognize that sulfur smell, Kyle?"

The boy nodded.

"Yeah," Ron said.

AS HE'D DONE dozens of times before, Ron drove right by the small battered sign on the side of the road that read POISON SPRINGS TRAILHEAD. The sign had deteriorated even since the last time he was there. It was leaning to the side and obscured in shadow from the close walls of lodgepole pine on both sides of the road.

He slowed the truck and Kyle looked over, puzzled.

"There's a little parking area up here," Ron said. "Or at least there used to be."

It was still there. Ron turned off the two-lane onto a gravel road that cut into the pine trees. It went a hundred feet before doglegging to the right and leading them to a single concrete picnic table.

"It's still here," Ron said.

A dark squirrel sat on its haunches on the top of the table eating something between its tiny paws. When Ron stopped and pulled on the emergency brake the rodent ran off.

"Okay, we can get out here."

He heard the tinkle of a tiny runoff creek through the trees in front of him, and there was a low rush of cold wind in the crowns of the lodgepole pines, enough to rock the trees back and forth slightly.

Slamming the door shut, Ron peered through the cab to make sure Kyle was coming. The boy was, but tentatively. That was okay, Ron thought. Better than Kyle thinking he might run away.

"Let's just stand here for a few minutes and listen," Ron said, gesturing with his chin toward the tops of the trees. "We need to make sure there's nobody around and no cars coming."

Kyle just stared at him over the hood of the truck.

There was no road traffic. There had been no cars parked alongside the road so it was doubtful any hikers would startle them coming out of the forest that late in the evening. Plus, Ron knew, this area was not among the highly trafficked trails that existed in other places in the park.

"Okay, come around on my side and help me pull it out."

Kyle came around the front of the truck and stood with his hands in the pockets of his hoodie.

Ron opened the rear door of the cab and grasped the edge of the plastic tarp. It slid out of the truck and landed heavily on the ground.

"Close the door and pick up the other side," Ron said. "We don't have to carry it. We can slide it along the ground."

Kyle shook his head.

"Come on, Kyle," Ron said.

Kyle closed his eyes briefly but shut the truck door and bent over to grasp the plastic.

"Follow my lead," Ron said, turning so he could pull the weight behind him instead of backpedaling. "It's about two hundred yards."

"What is two hundred yards?" *Wha iz too-hunert yahds?*

Ron again resisted the urge to mock Kyle's speech defect. The boy wouldn't be any help if he was crying. Plus, Ron knew what it felt like to be mocked. He was still ashamed at how quickly he'd fallen into that behavior pattern back at the cabin. It was as if mocking a boy had been hardwired into him at an early age.

There was no doubt where *that* had come from.

"It's called Poisoned Springs for a reason," Ron said. "I've been here many, many times."

FIVE MINUTES INTO THE FOREST the trees began to look different. Instead of supple trunks with green needles the trees became stiff white posts. The dead branches above them opened up the sky.

Ron let go of the tarp and paused to get his breath back.

"Look," Ron said to Kyle, rapping a white trunk with his knuckles, "This tree has turned to stone. Like it's petrified. You can blame all the minerals just below the surface for that."

Kyle was obviously intrigued. He stepped over to one of the stiff white trees and knocked on the trunk.

"Crazy things happen in this park," Ron said. "Ninety-nine percent of the people who come here never get off the figure-eight road system. They don't know there are petrified trees just out of sight or that there are natural hot springs filled with sulphuric acid."

He bent to grasp a handful of the plastic tarp to pull the body the rest of the way. "Now be careful when we get close. The crust of the earth is really thin here. If you don't watch where you step you could break right through it and scald your foot."

The sulfur smell was strong as they closed in on Poisoned Springs. The spring itself was kidney shaped, twelve feet by twenty feet, and it was filled with clear sapphire-colored water that licked gently at the crusty edge of the opening. Wisps of steam curled from the surface of the hot water.

"Looks like you might want to take a bath in it, doesn't it?" Ron asked. "Well, don't. That acid will eat the flesh right off your bones."

Ron inched closer to the opening. The brittle crust on the edge overhung the pool itself and it was difficult to see how far it extended into the water. He stopped several feet short of the edge and stood on the balls of his feet so he could see better into the cavern beneath the surface.

"There used to be a femur bone caught on a ledge on the side of it," he said to Kyle. "Doesn't look like it's there anymore, which is good. I guess it finally dissolved away."

"*How many bodies are in there?*" Kyle asked in his mush-mouthed way. It was a clinical question. Ron was pleased that he even understood the boy.

"Dozens."

Kyle looked at him blankly.

"Don't think about it. It's just nature doing what nature does.

Instead, think about helping me unwrap this thing. Then help me find a long pole. We'll push it in with that. No way I'm gonna get any closer to the edge of that spring than I am now."

Kyle's face blanched with horror.

"KYLE, YOU LOOK PALE."

Actually, the boy's face in the diffuse light from the dashboard of the pickup looked pale green.

They were coming down the switchback road from Mammoth Hot Springs toward the north exit. Ron drove slowly and deliberately because there were no overhead highway lights in the park and animals could be anywhere.

"Are you all right?"

Kyle pulled his hood up tighter and looked out the passenger window.

Ron said, "Quit thinking of her as a real person. That wasn't Tiffany we rolled into that spring. Tiffany is gone. Once a person is dead all that's left is bones and meat just like any animal. Think of it that way. Plus, people like her aren't like us. They're losers. They wouldn't even exist if the world weren't so cushy.

"If it wasn't me it would be somebody else. Or she'd have done it to herself with drugs or alcohol. We actually did her a favor."

Kyle didn't react.

As they drove through Gardiner, Ron sighed and said, "We need to get a new one with even bigger hips so we don't have to worry about her trying to crawl out a window. But not you, Kyle. You're obviously not ready yet. Maybe down the road but not now.

"I'm going to take you back to the cabin and fix that window. You and Amanda will be on your own tonight."

Ron paused as he drove past a small lighted football field next to the school where a high school game was in progress. The Gardiner Tigers were playing. He could see teams on the field, knots of students in the stands, cheerleaders on the sidelines, and dozens of parked vehicles in the lot outside the stands.

"Because I'm going hunting."

TWENTY-FIVE

BEFORE DAWN THE NEXT MORNING Cassie heard movement and heavy sounds outside the Tomahawk Motel. She slipped out of the bed and walked to the window with bare feet and parted the curtains.

Under the blue glow of a pole light, Bull Mitchell led his horses one by one from where they'd been picketed in the field behind the motel the night before into his horse trailer. He looked fit and purposeful as he did it, and she noticed he wore a holster with a long revolver on his hip. His breath condensed in the freezing air and haloed around his head.

She thought: *He's in his element.* This is what he did for decades—rose long before the sun came up or his clients arose to break camp. He was doing what he was meant to do and she'd provided the conduit.

She prayed Bull would return to Bozeman and Rachel as healthy and safe when the expedition was over as he appeared at that moment. If he didn't, Rachel would never forgive Cassie and she wouldn't blame her one bit.

Cassie let the curtains close and stepped away to make coffee in the small plastic brewer in the room. She'd barely slept herself;

prey to a combination of a worn-out bed, a room that smelled of Lysol, and nerves. Instead, she'd removed the tags off her newly purchased outdoor clothing and cleaned and oiled her Glock.

She started to write a letter to Ben to tell him how much she loved him in case something happened in the mountains and she didn't return. But she couldn't put what she wanted to say into words and the very act of writing the letter felt like creating a self-fulfilling prophesy. So she abandoned the effort.

At one point during the night she'd considered not going into the mountains herself. Bull knew where he was going and Sheriff Pederson and his "horse-savvy" deputies could likely handle any situation they came across.

But she'd talked herself out of it. She owed it to Lottie, to Ralph Johnson, to Raheem, and to Kyle to see it through. It was because of her the expedition was coming together.

Cassie had lived with the Lizard King in the back of her brain for years. So long that he'd become almost a part of her being.

She wanted to be rid of him forever.

SHERIFF PEDERSON AND HIS TWO deputies pulled into the motel parking lot at seven-thirty that morning. The deputies drove a pickup with a horse trailer behind it and Pederson arrived in his SUV.

Cassie emerged from her room as the sheriff began introductions all around.

"This is Cassie Dewell," he began. "She used to be with the Lewis and Clark Sheriff's Department and was most recently Chief Investigator for Bakken County in North Dakota."

"Pleased to see you again," Mike Pompy said, removing his hat with his left hand and extending his right. His eyes lingered on her after they shook hands. It took a moment for her to recall that he'd been at Paradise Valley when they were digging up Cody Hoyt's body.

"You worked with Cody Hoyt," Jim Thomsen said with a sly smile. "Anybody who worked with that guy has to be tough."

Mike Pompy was in his early forties, short-legged with a barrel chest and a calm disposition. Thomsen was rangy with a cropped ginger beard and light blue eyes. He bounced on the balls of his feet as he talked. He was ready to go. Both were dressed in jeans and wore cowboy boots and tactical vests. Pompy had a semiautomatic holstered under his left arm and Thomsen wore his sidearm on his hip. Combat shotguns and AR-15s with extended tube magazines were clustered muzzle-down between the front seats of the pickup.

"And this is Bull Mitchell," Pederson said, stepping back.

Bull leaned against the front bumper of his Power Wagon with his thumbs hooked into the front pockets of his jeans. He looked over both deputies as if he were looking for good colts at a horse sale.

"Bull will be leading the expedition," Pederson told his men. "He's got a lot of experience in these mountains and he knows this country like nobody else. When it comes to the ride in, listen to him. If we get into a law enforcement situation, listen to me. Got that?"

Pompy and Thomsen nodded in agreement.

"Okay," Pederson said, "when can we get going?"

Bull said, "Twenty minutes. I just talked to Dub and my truck is almost ready."

Cassie was pleased.

"First, let's do an inventory on the gear you all brought," Bull said. "We're going to be traveling light with only one animal other than the horses you're riding. Meaning I don't want to take four of anything except weapons. No more than twenty pounds per man of clothing, gear, and all that electronic bullshit you people think is essential."

"*Twenty pounds?*" Thomsen said.

"Not unless you brought your own packhorse. So start going through your duffel bags, boys, and throwing stuff out."

Pompy and Thomsen looked to Pederson for backup but didn't get it. Thomsen sighed as he turned for his bag to start winnowing out weight.

Bull carefully oversaw the deputies as they consolidated their belongings.

"How many GPS machines and satellite phones do you people need?" Bull barked. "One will do."

Pompy and Thomsen exchanged looks again. Bull, they conceded, had a point.

"The heavier we ride the slower we go," Bull said. "I remember one time . . ."

And the stories began, Cassie thought. Testosterone hung in the air like wood smoke, she thought. In a matter of minutes the two deputies and Bull were exchanging experiences on horseback in the mountains. All three were obviously excited to mount up. She wished she could share in the unbridled anticipation but there was a knot in her stomach and she felt a little sick from the metallic motel room coffee.

"I'm going to delay us a little longer than twenty minutes," Pederson said to Bull. "We got a call last night that I need to follow up."

"What kind of call?" Cassie asked.

"High school girl. She said a 'creepy guy' tried to pick her up last night after the game."

Cassie felt a chill run down the back of her spine.

"Did she get a good look at him?"

Pederson shrugged. "There wasn't much in the report. That's why I need to talk with her in person."

"Can I ride along?" Cassie asked. "There's not much I can do here."

She gestured at Thomsen, Pompy, and Bull, who were in animated conversation about past elk hunts. Bull handed over his long-barrelled .44 magnum revolver for them to admire.

Pederson shrugged and said, "Sure, come on along."

"Let me get my notepad," Cassie said, turning on her heel to go back to her room.

Bull told Pederson, "Meet us at the Gardiner Market down the road. You can leave your Yukon there and ride the rest of the way with us. We need to get some big steaks, don't we guys?" he asked Thomsen and Pompy.

"Damn right we do," Thomsen hooted.

"Cassie," Bull said, "throw your stuff in my truck before you go."

"IT'S LIKE THEY'RE boys going on a camping trip," Cassie said sourly from the passenger seat.

"I'll be honest with you," Pederson said. "I'm kind of feeling that way myself."

"Oh, great."

The sheriff smiled. "This is a lot more exciting than working car crashes on I-90."

"So tell me about this high school girl."

"Her name is Joanne Vinson. She's seventeen. I know her parents, Art and Pat. Art works for the railroad. They're good folks and Jo isn't the type of girl who would file a false report. Or at least I don't *think* she is."

"What were the circumstances last night?"

"Well," Pederson said, "if you can wait five minutes we'll both find out. We're almost there."

THE VINSON HOME was a dark gray one-story bungalow on West Callendar Street. The morning breeze rattled dead cottonwood leaves that still hung in the single tree. There was a small yard and two older vehicles in front: a Dodge minivan and a GMC pickup. The windows were filled with Halloween decorations and there were two jack-o'-lanterns on the porch.

Joanne Vinson sat bent over in the middle of a worn couch underneath an elk head that looked frozen in mid-bugle. She had a cherubic face framed by lank brown hair, and she clasped her hands nervously on her lap. She had large brown eyes that darted between her mother, who stood in the threshold of the kitchen, and Sheriff Pederson.

"Tell the sheriff what you told me and the deputy last night, Jo," Pat Vinson said.

"Nothing really happened," Joanne said with a roll of her eyes. She seemed embarrassed, Cassie thought.

"But it could have," Pat said.

Pederson settled into a lounge chair directly across from Joanne and leaned forward toward her in a comforting manner. Cassie stood to the side behind him.

"Just tell me what happened, Jo."

Cassie observed carefully as Joanne reached up and gently clawed her fingers through her hair. The girl was heavyset but not obese. She was *almost* pretty and she went too heavy with eyeliner. She was uncomfortable being the center of attention. Cassie felt a kinship with her right away.

"Well, I went to the game last night."

"In the minivan," Pat interrupted. "Without asking."

Joanne rolled her eyes and ignored her mother. "I was supposed to go with some friends but they didn't pick me up. I think they forgot so I drove there myself."

Pat said, "Art was working and I was at my bridge club."

Pederson took a deep breath and also ignored Pat.

"So you drove to the game. Did you meet your friends there?"

She shot a glance at her mother and said, "They were there."

"Tell him," Pat said.

"It was kind of a big party night," Joanne said. "I didn't want to have more than a couple of beers so I decided to come home before the game got over. The minivan was on the far end of the parking lot since I got there late. So it was a long walk."

"You were by yourself?" Pederson asked.

Jo looked down at her hands. "Yes."

Cassie wanted to walk across the floor and hug her. There was nothing worse at that age than admitting you were alone on a Friday night.

"So what happened next?"

"I got in the van and it wouldn't start. I turned the key and nothing happened."

"Uh-oh," he said.

"No kidding. I don't know anything about cars and dad wasn't home."

"I don't know anything about them either," Pat said from the threshold.

"Okay," Pederson said to Joanne, "What did you do?"

"Well, I thought maybe I'd walk back to the stadium and find somebody who could help me get it started or give me a ride home. I didn't want to call mom because I didn't want her yelling at me."

"*Like I'd yell at you*," Pat said, nearly shouting.

"Please, Pat," Pederson said.

Pat folded her arms across her breasts and huffed.

"When I got out of the van I saw a man," Joanne said. Cassie shifted her weight.

"What was he doing?"

"Nothing, really, I guess. He was sort of walking through all the parked cars. But he was kind of headed my way."

"Kind of headed your way or headed your way?"

"He was coming toward me but he had to keep walking around parked cars."

"Did you recognize him?"

"No."

"What was he wearing?"

She frowned. "It was kind of weird. He had on like a pair of coveralls. They were all one color. Like my dad wears on the railroad."

"Were they white?" Cassie asked.

Joanne looked up and Pederson looked over his shoulder at her. Both were apparently surprised Cassie had spoken.

"Yeah, light colored. How did you know that?"

"I was just guessing," Cassie said. To Pederson: "Sorry."

"Okay," he said. "Did the man speak to you?"

"Yeah. He saw me there next to the van and he asked me if I needed some help."

"What did you tell him?"

"You know," Joanne said, "I normally would have said 'Sure!' But there was something about him—I don't know. He was sort of creepy. I mean, he seemed nice and everything. He wasn't growling at me or staring or anything. But the way he just sort of showed up right then . . . I don't know."

"So what did you say?"

"I lied and told him I was waiting for my friends to show up."

"Then what?"

"He didn't leave. He just kind of stood there."

"What did he look like?"

"He looked like a normal man, I guess. An old guy just standing there like he didn't know what to do. I was afraid I insulted him."

"When you say old guy . . ."

"He was in his fifties, maybe sixties. He was kind of square built if you know what I mean. Fat, but not really humongous. He had a big head but I couldn't see his face because it was dark. He wore a cap like everybody does."

"White guy?" Pederson asked.

"I'm sure."

"So what happened next?"

"Well, I wasn't sure what to do because he just stood there kind of blocking my way back to the stadium. I thought about getting back in the van and locking the doors, but I was still afraid of being rude, you know?"

"Did he say anything else?"

"He said he was a mechanic or he knew something about cars. Something like that. I can't tell you his exact words because I was trying to figure out what I was going to do. He said I should open the hood so he could take a look at the engine. I told him I didn't know how. And he said *he* did."

"Then he came after you," Pat prompted from the kitchen.

"No, mom," Joanne said with disdain. "He didn't come after me. He just kind of took a few steps closer before I knew it. He didn't *run* at me."

"Did he have anything in his hands?" Cassie asked.

Joanne looked up and said, "I couldn't see. He had one hand behind his back when I think about it."

"His right hand?"

She paused and closed her eyes as if conjuring up the image. Then: "Yeah, his right hand."

"So what happened next?" Pederson asked.

"I heard shouting," she said. "It was a bunch of kids coming out of the stadium to the parking lot to get more beer. They were *loud*. I told the guy, *Here they come now*. He kind of looked over his shoulder at them and then back at me like he couldn't decide what to do. Then he just vanished."

"Vanished?"

"I looked away and when I looked back he wasn't there."

"Did you see him get into a car?"

"No, but I heard one start up outside in that field that's next to the parking lot."

"Did you get a description of the vehicle?"

"No. He didn't turn his lights on. I thought that was weird."

"Tell him about the van," Pat urged from the kitchen.

"My friend Toby looked under the hood," Joanne said. "He said the battery cable or something was loose like somebody had used a wrench and taken it off."

Cassie expelled a long breath.

"Then Toby put the cable or whatever back on the battery and I started it up and came home," Joanne said brightly. "End of story."

"But her mother was home by then and made her call your office," Pat said sternly.

"I'm glad you did," Pederson said.

Cassie stood off to the side while the sheriff talked with Joanne and Pat. He told Joanne that if she saw the man again she should call 911, and she shouldn't borrow the van again without her mother or dad knowing where she went. Joanne still acted a little embarrassed about it all.

As Pederson clamped on his hat, Cassie said to Joanne: "Thank God you're still here."

Joanne's face froze.

"That was kind of a scary thing to say to her," Pat said to Cassie. "Are you trying to give her nightmares?"

"Yes."

IN THE SUV, Cassie said quickly, "It's classic Lizard King: preying on a lone female at night. When he kidnapped the Sullivan sisters they said he wore a white one-piece Tyvek jumpsuit. I'll bet you anything he had a syringe filled with Rohypnol in his right hand behind his back. And he knows his way around cars enough to disable them."

Pederson looked over as he drove. He said, "That kind of thing doesn't happen around here. Not in my county."

"It almost did," Cassie said. She was shaking.

"It pisses me off to no end."

"That was Ronald Pergram," she said. "He's here, all right. He was here last night. *Right here.*"

"There's no proof it was him, Cassie."

"Then let's go prove it."

PARADISE VALLEY FLEW PAST on both sides and the mountains began to close in on them. It felt to Cassie like they were entering some kind of geographical chute that would suck them up and fling them to Gardiner and Yellowstone Park. The terrain got rougher, wilder, and more vertical with each mile. Bison straying from the protected confines of Yellowstone grazed in hay meadows, and Pederson had to slow down to let a herd of mule deer does and fawns cross Highway 89 in front of them.

The V of Yankee Jim Canyon could be seen several miles ahead. Cassie knew there was going to be a signal outage for her cell phone within the canyon so she quickly pulled out her phone and speed-dialed the first number on the list.

"I think we're getting close," Cassie said to Leslie Behaunek. She related the story of Joanne Vinson's near miss.

"Does she know how lucky she was?" Leslie asked.

"I don't think so."

"And this happened last night?"

"Yes. While we were a few minutes away at the time."

"My God."

Leslie said she'd drive to her office and start making calls.

"It's Saturday morning so it might be difficult to get a hold of everyone on the joint task force," she said.

"Don't worry about the North Dakota folks," Cassie said. "Concentrate on the Montana people. Light a fire under them and tell them to be prepared to scramble at any minute."

Pederson, who had overheard Cassie's side of the conversation said, "Ask her to see about any available aircraft. Bozeman has access to a helicopter and the Montana Highway Patrol has fixed-wing aircraft and a helo, too."

Cassie relayed the message and could hear Leslie keying it into her computer.

"Make sure," Pederson said, emphasizing what he was about to say by pausing between each word, "make sure they don't start flying over the top of us until we're ready for them. If one of those pilots finds Pergram before we get to him it could spook the guy and make him run. Or he could kill his hostage. We need to get there first."

Cassie nodded, related what he'd said, and told Leslie, "There'll be five of us. We're well-armed. We'll have GPS equipment and a satellite phone along with us. If we find Pergram we'll call in the coordinates."

"If you locate him don't try to take him by yourself," Leslie cautioned.

"Of course not," Cassie lied. Then: "We're entering a canyon now and I'm about to lose you . . ."

She disconnected the call and dropped the phone into her lap. The mouth of Yankee Jim Canyon was still a mile ahead.

"Clever," Pederson said.

AS THEY ENTERED the tiny community of Gardiner there was very little traffic on the street. Cassie felt suddenly haunted and she glanced up the side of the mountain instinctively and saw the closed-up building that had once been Yellowstone Quilting. It was at Sally Legerski's shop that she'd first connected Sally's ex-husband—a rogue state trooper—and the Lizard King four years before.

That moment, when Cassie viewed images on a crude DVD of women being tortured and raped by Pergram and Ed Legerski was still as shocking to her as if it had occurred that morning.

Cassie's lower lip trembled and she turned away.

BULL'S POWER WAGON with the trailer attached and the deputies' rig were parked side by side off the highway in the parking lot of the grocery store. There were less than a half-dozen civilian vehicles in the lot.

"It'll take me a few minutes to transfer my gear," Pederson said, "and then we can get going."

"*Finally*," Cassie said with a sigh, although mentally she was still in Yellowstone Quilting.

Pederson wheeled his SUV into the lot and parked it behind the sheriff's department horse trailer. Cassie bailed out of the other side and strode up to Bull Mitchell who was standing next to his truck making a show of looking at his wristwatch.

"We're burnin' daylight," he said.

"I know, I know," she said to him. "We're late. But the delay was worth it."

She told him about Joanne Vinson's likely enounter with the Lizard King while Pederson transferred his weapons and gear into Bull's truck.

"So you were right all along. Pergram is here somewhere. We may not be wasting our time after all," Bull said. His tone was more serious than Cassie had yet heard from him. His words drove the point home: *They were hunting the Lizard King.*

He looked over Cassie's head at the other vehicle and said, "Are we all here?"

Thomsen leaned out of the driver's window and chinned toward the grocery store. "Waiting on Mike but he should be here any minute."

"Let's leave him," Bull growled.

At that moment, Mike Pompy emerged from the store clutching a plastic bag of snacks for the trail. He had a look of concern on his face and he marched straight toward the sheriff.

"Bryan, there's something you need to see in here."

The sheriff said, "What is it?"

"You have to see it for yourself."

With that, Pompy turned around and went back inside.

"What the hell?" Pederson asked no one in particular. He looked to Thomsen who shrugged in response. Pederson shoved his hands in his front pockets and started for the store.

Cassie followed and ignored Bull's grousing.

When they were inside Pompy greeted them and said, "You have to see this. The maintenance people were about to clean it up this morning but I told them to hold off."

Pompy strode down the food aisles toward the back of the store. Three lone shoppers and two check-out clerks craned their necks to see what was going on.

The deputy led them to the men's bathroom. A Hispanic man with a silver mustache stood outside the door waiting for them to let him get back to work. Pompy shouldered past him and pushed open the door while motioning the sheriff and Cassie to follow him inside. The bathroom was tiled with polished brick. The janitor's abandoned mop bucket on wheels was near the toilet.

"What?" Pederson asked, looking around.

"Look," Pompy said as he bent forward and flipped the toilet seat up.

On the face of the white underside of the seat, written in smeared dried blood, it read:

IM KYLE W. FRoM ND
IM KIDNAPED
HELP!

Cassie had to reach out and steady herself against the wall so her knees wouldn't buckle beneath her.

TWENTY-SIX

RON WAS IN A DANGEROUSLY black mood at breakfast so Kyle kept his mouth shut and tried not to make eye contact with him. Although his head was bare and his hair uncombed, Ron seemed to be hooded. He hadn't said a single word all morning. He sat there at the head of the table with his legs splayed out beneath it and his big hands resting on top. His eyes were open and unfocused as if he were watching a movie in the middle distance no one else could see.

Amanda, unfortunately, seemed oblivious to Ron's state. She hummed "Santa Claus Is Comin' to Town" while she fried the bacon and cracked the eggs. She'd tied brightly colored ribbons to her dog collar as if trying to make it look like a necklace. Her collar was open to show it off. It was as if she was fishing for a compliment for her ingenuity.

She wore an oversized chamois shirt over her own shirt because it was cold inside the cabin. Ron had shoved the new window into the hole in the wall but hadn't sealed it. A cool breeze blew through the interior.

Kyle glanced over at Ron, who had turned his head to Amanda. The man glared at Amanda and her humming. His eyes were murderous. Kyle wished he could catch her attention and warn her to please be quiet for her own sake.

That's when she began to sing softly.

You better watch out,
You better not cry . . .

Ron fumbled for her transmitter on his chest and Kyle winced.

But Ron changed his mind before he punished her electronically. Instead, he stood up from the table so suddenly his chair fell over behind him. Before Amanda could react to the crash Ron cocked his fist and hit her hard in the small of her back.

Amanda made an *ooof* sound as if all of the air had been crushed out of her and she collapsed in front of the stove.

Ron stood over her glowering and brandishing both fists.

When she moaned and rolled to her side away from him he kicked her in the buttocks hard enough to slide her a foot across the floor.

She squeaked—she was trying to get enough breath to cry.

Kyle said, *Please stop, Ron. Please stop.*

Ron looked up at Kyle. His face was a red mask of anger. Kyle braced himself for a beating.

Then the hood seemed to come partially off and Ron's face softened.

He said to Kyle, "Maybe you're right. Who's going to cook us breakfast?"

Amanda got enough air to weep quietly.

Ron said to her, "All I ask is to eat breakfast in fucking peace. If I let you up can you finish it and keep your mouth shut?"

She nodded vigorously. Her voice was weak when she said, "Yes."

"Good," he said. "Get up."

Amanda rolled to her hands and knees and wheezed for breath. It bothered Kyle to see her that way, to see an adult woman in that position. Finally, she reached out and grasped the handle of the oven and clumsily pulled herself up.

Ron watched her without extending his hand to help. Then he backed up and sat down heavily in his chair.

Kyle briefly closed his eyes, praying that it was over.

When he opened them he heard Ron grumble, "You people don't fuckin' deserve a man like me."

KYLE HAD HEARD Ron come back the night before. It was well after midnight and freezing cold inside the cabin. He and Amanda had added Tiffany's sheets and blankets to their own to try and keep warm.

He'd awakened when a sweep of headlights from Ron's truck raked across the walls through the open window. When Ron came in he pretended he was still sleeping. He'd know in seconds if Ron found out about the message he'd written in blood under the toilet seat. Kyle tried not to tremble.

He listened as the man sighed and paced and talked to himself in a low but angry tone. Kyle couldn't hear the words except for when Ron said, *"Here's your goddamn window,"* as he shoved the new frame into the opening.

Then it got quiet, and the quiet bothered Kyle more than the mumbling had.

After nearly an hour, Kyle opened one eye slightly.

Ron had been sitting in his chair at the table staring at nothing at all. He wore white coveralls over his clothes. Kyle hadn't seen him wear the coveralls before. Ron looked as if he were tortured and was fighting back tears.

Kyle closed his eye before he started to feel sorry for the man for being so sad.

AS AMANDA MOVED the breakfast dishes to the sink with a painful-looking limp, she knew Ron was watching her carefully. When her back was to him and Ron stood up again she didn't know what to expect.

But Ron stepped over to her and gently wrapped his arms around her shoulders from behind. She stiffened at his touch and she was glad he couldn't see her face at that moment.

Ron bent over and pressed his mouth into her hair. "I'm sorry I hit you, Amanda. You didn't have it coming. You cooked a real nice breakfast and I hope you're feeling okay."

After a moment, Amanda said, "Thank you. I think I'll be all right."

"Your collar looks real nice with those ribbons on it," he said. "I meant to tell you that."

"Thank you, Ron."

He said to her, "You're shaking like a leaf. There's no need for that. Nothing is going to happen. Okay, Amanda?"

"Okay. I won't sing no more."

"Best not," he said with a grin that made her stomach clench.

"No more singing!" she said emphatically. Then: "Is humming okay, though?"

"Maybe at times. But if I were you I'd do it while I'm away."

"Okay." She sounded eager to please him.

"Are you sure you're all right?"

"I think so. I really do."

"And we're good?"

"Yes."

"That's what I wanted to hear," he said. He released his hug and kneaded her shoulders for a moment. "What do you have planned for lunch and dinner? You saw all that food I bought yesterday."

She nodded. "I was thinking French dip sandwiches for lunch and fried chicken and mashed potatoes for dinner."

"That sounds wonderful, Amanda."

She turned around and smiled at him, genuinely relieved.

Ron left her and grabbed his jacket from the peg on the side of the door. He said to Kyle, "Come on. We're going out."

Kyle exchanged a glance with her before he went outside. He was assessing her, she thought, trying to gauge if she had changed.

She thought to herself: *I have.*

"GRAB THE TOOLBOX and follow me," Ron said. It was a cool but sunny morning. Sunlight from the east streamed through the pine trees to the forest floor. Kyle noticed that it was taking longer each morning for the sun to warm things up.

Where is the toolbox?

"In the shed."

As Kyle walked toward the shed Ron said, "See? I'm starting to understand the way you talk."

Kyle nodded and opened the door. The rusty toolbox was on a workbench inside and he grasped the handle and lifted it down. He noticed that the workbench was covered with debris from Ron's projects. There were lengths of copper wire, electrical tape, thin cable, and square 4.5 volt batteries.

The toolbox was heavy and the weight of it made him lean to the side as he followed Ron down a rough two-track road into the trees. He switched hands often.

Ron said, "Sometimes you just have to tell women things even if you don't really mean it. I think they know you're bullshitting them but at the same time it seems to cheer them up. I mean, seriously, tying little ribbons to a shock collar? Fucking *Christmas songs*? I'll never understand those creatures.

"Maybe next time I go to town I'll buy her some ice cream. That ought to keep her happy for a while."

Kyle was lagging behind carrying the toolbox. Ron paused to

wait for him. He didn't offer to take the toolbox, just as he hadn't offered to help Amanda off the floor.

"Try to keep up," he said.

When Ron started marching again Kyle mouthed, *Fuck you, Ron* to his back.

The old road wound through the pine trees and soon Kyle could no longer see the cabin. He wondered why they even needed the stupid toolbox.

After another turn Ron paused and bent over and reached for something in the road. It was a length of wire that was partially coiled on the ground.

"I drove through it last night," Ron said. "I wasn't thinking straight and I forgot to take it down."

Kyle had no idea what Ron was talking about. He lowered the toolbox and flexed his hand to get the circulation in it going again.

Ron wound the wire around his wrist and followed it off the road through some heavy brush and into the trees.

"Bring me more wire," he ordered. "The pliers, too."

Kyle opened the toolbox and found a heavy coil of it. He slid the pliers into the back of his jeans. He watched as Ron tied the end of the fresh wire to a loose assemblage of empty tin cans, then fed the wire over a branch and handed the coil to Kyle. He recalled Ron collecting the cans one by one after they'd eaten the contents. He made Amanda scrub out the inside before he took them.

"Back up and stretch that tight across the road about a foot high. I'll hold the cans in the air on this end until you're far enough."

Kyle did as he was told. When he'd crossed to the other side of the road Ron said, "That's good. Just stand there and keep the wire tight. Don't let the cans fall."

Ron emerged from the brush and took the coil from Kyle's

hands. He pulled more of it free and wrapped it around the trunk of a tree.

"Pliers," he said to Kyle.

Ron cut the wire and twisted it around itself. When he was done, he twanged the taut line with the heel of his hand and the empty cans clattered from the other side of the road.

So no one will sneak up on us, Kyle said.

"You got it," Ron said. "We'll hear 'em coming long before they get to the cabin."

He stood up and pointed vaguely through the trees indicating somewhere down the mountain. "I've got the rest of my C-4 down there rigged to trip wires and 4.5 volt batteries. Anybody coming up the road will get a hell of a surprise. But I used up all my inventory of explosives, so the best we can do now this close to the cabin are these old-fashioned empty cans. They work, though," he said while demonstrating the setup again with a tug on the wire.

Kyle tried not to show his disappointment.

"Come on," Ron said, "we're going to rig up a couple more of these on some side trails."

Ron dug into his jacket pocket and pulled out a fistful of objects: clear plastic packages along with the collar he'd taken off Tiffany the day before. He separated the collar and shoved it back into his pocket while he shook the packages with his other hand. They rang musically.

"Bear bells," Ron said. "Hikers use them in Yellowstone Park. Supposedly, the bells let bears know people are coming. In our case they'll let us know the same thing."

KYLE LUGGED THE TOOLBOX through the trees for the rest of the morning. He assisted as Ron strung up four more trip wires across game trails close to the cabin in all four directions. Kyle wondered if Ron was anticipating a visit of some kind.

As Ron did the work he seemed to have returned to his hooded self of that morning. Obviously, something was on his mind.

When he bent over to secure the last wire to a tree, Kyle shot a glance into the toolbox at his feet. There were several screwdrivers in there as well as a heavy pipe wrench. He didn't look at them as tools but as weapons.

But before Kyle could act, Ron stood up and turned around to face him. He said, "I knew what I had to do last night—what I've done a hundred times—and I fucked up. I'm losing my drive. I'm getting up there in years and the drive I need just doesn't seem to be there like it used to be."

Doing what? Kyle asked.

"Well, you probably noticed we don't have a replacement for Tiffany. *You did notice that, didn't you?*" Ron asked with a sneer. He was suddenly angry again.

Yeah.

"I found her, all right. Nice big hips. Young. But I fucked up. I didn't take action with authority. You can't hesitate when you set out to do something like that, Kyle. You have to . . . *pounce.*"

When Ron said the word *pounce* he lunged at Kyle, and Kyle stepped back and threw his arms across his face. But nothing happened.

It had been a bluff.

"Like that," Ron said.

Kyle felt his heart pound in his chest. He wished he'd grabbed a screwdriver when Ron's back was turned.

"My days out on the road are over, Kyle," he said. "I can't get it up like I used to. It's hard to explain. I don't feel it inside like I used to when I'm on the hunt. I guess I have better things to do now, better things to think about and work on. But that doesn't mean I've forgotten anything," he said with a wink. "I know how to stay ten steps ahead and above it all. That's why I've lasted this long.

"I told you you'd learn things if you stuck with me," Ron said. "You will if you want to. I'll teach you. Now grab that toolbox—it's time for lunch."

As they walked back toward the cabin from above Kyle asked, *What will we do if we hear the bells or the cans?*

Ron paused and looked over his shoulder at Kyle with a serious set to his face.

"What will you do?" he asked, patting his holstered .380. "You'll die. Both of you. I'm not taking you fucking people with me."

Kyle felt his mouth go dry.

Then Ron broke out into a grin. He reached out and tousled Kyle's hair and said, "Had you going for a second there, didn't I? Ha! You both mean a lot to me, especially you, Kyle. You're the only family I've got."

TWENTY-SEVEN

BULL MITCHELL'S ANCIENT Power Wagon ground up the rocky rise high above Gardiner to the east like a slow-motion mountain goat. Cassie held tight to the leather strap above the door with one hand and the dashboard with the other. Sheriff Pederson stuck both of his hands straight up and pressed against the underside of the roof so he could steady himself in the middle seat and not get pitched to the right or left as Bull maneuvered over football-sized boulders.

The mountainside was bare of trees and what little grass there was on it clung to the terrain as if for dear life. When Cassie looked out through the windshield she could see mainly blue sky.

"You say there's a road here?" Cassie asked Bull.

"Used to be," he responded.

"'Used to be' isn't the best answer."

"It's the best one I've got," Bull shrugged.

She looked over her shoulder at the sheriff's department pickup behind them. It was then that she realized the angle she was peering down was as close to vertical as she'd ever experienced in a vehicle before. She could see the loose grid of streets far below in Gardiner as well as the Yellowstone River that looked like a rumpled grey ribbon. If the Power Wagon's tires lost traction or Bull missed a gear as he climbed they could roll dangerously backward down the mountain and take out the deputies' rig.

"Is there a better way up?" she called out. As she did she felt her phone vibrate with an incoming call in her pocket. She ignored it.

"Maybe," Bull said.

"Then why don't we try it?"

"We're committed now," he said with a rakish grin. "Once you start on a grade like this there's no way to turn around. Is there, sheriff?"

"I'm staying out of this," Pederson said.

Cassie didn't know whether she should close her eyes and pray or keep them open so she could see firsthand when the Power Wagon stalled out and rolled down the hill. The thing that kept her in her seat was a single word: *Kidnaped*.

That Kyle misspelled it in his own blood made her heart ache more for him.

AT LAST THE FRONT TIRES clawed over the edge of the rim and the pickup and trailer leveled out. Cassie found that she could breathe again and she settled back in her seat.

They were on a rocky plateau and in front of them was an even bigger tree-covered mountain in the distance. But between where they were and the incline was a massive expanse of dead trees that were laid out flat on the ground like they'd all been clear-cut. When she looked closer, though, she could see splintered trunks still embedded in the ground. The trees hadn't been cut—they'd been snapped off. The dead trees all pointed to the south.

On the far end of the dead trees a small herd of elk grazed on a mountain meadow. As one, they raised their heads and stared at the interlopers.

"What in the hell happened here?" Pederson asked Bull.

"Microburst. It happened after I was here last."

"What's a microburst?" Cassie asked.

"Kind of a small contained tornado," Bull said. "It drops down from the sky and just lays all the trees over. They break like matchsticks. Sometimes they fall in a concentric circle and sometimes it looks like this. Like I told Cody Hoyt once, Yellowstone seems to manufacture its own weather. You never know what the hell you're going to get into—snow in July, a heat wave in January, or a microburst on the top of a mountain that knocks all the damned trees over. I've seen the results of dozens of 'em in the park. But this is a problem," he said with a nod toward the mess in front of them, "because the road I wanted to take goes right through the middle of it. Even cutting some of that timber with a chain saw and using the winch won't get us through it."

Cassie refrained from asking again where the road had been in the first place.

Bull pulled ahead far enough for the sheriff's department pickup to join him on the flat. He kept the motor running while he rubbed his chin and looked at the result of the microburst.

Cassie glanced over to Pompy who drove the other pickup. The man's face was white with fear from the drive up and he shook his head from side to side as if he couldn't believe what they'd just done.

Pompy rolled down his window and asked Bull, "So, what's our plan?"

"Plan B," Bull said.

"What's Plan B?"

"Haven't figured it out yet."

"What are our options?" Pederson asked. He had a way, Cassie thought, of making everything he said sound perfectly calm and reasonable. It was a gift she wished she shared.

"I'm thinkin'," Bull said.

Cassie's phone went off again and this time she drew it out and looked at the screen. Leslie had called three times in ten minutes. Cassie hadn't even noticed the first one because she was scared for her life at the time.

"Well," Bull said as he gestured toward the mountainside in the distance, "I wanted to check out the other side of that big hill. My plan was to drive to the top and maybe get the horses out and ride 'em down to where the old cabins are. If Pergram is up there and we come in on horses he won't hear us coming. But it doesn't look like we can drive the trailers to where I wanted to start."

"No, it doesn't," Cassie said.

Bull shot her a look and she figured she probably deserved it.

Pederson said, "Obviously, if Pergram is somewhere up here he must drive to it. He can't go this way, so how does he get up there?"

"Good question," Bull said. "The fact is there are a shitload of old roads all over these mountains—even inside the park. The park service bermed some of the more popular roads to keep people out which is why I was trying this back way. But if Pergram was up here poaching with his peckerwood father he must have learned some other routes.

"We can work our way back down and drive thirty miles to the north and then back this direction to try to find his access," Bull said while gesturing with his hand in a circle, "or we can mount up here and cut straight through that timber toward the other side of the mountain where the cabins were."

Pompy shook his head yes in the other truck. "I don't want to try another hill like the one we were just on with this horse trailer."

"Me either," Thomsen said.

"So what kind of time frame are we talking about with those two choices?" Pederson asked.

Bull said, "If we drive around it might take all the rest of the day and there's no guarantee we'll find the road that takes us to those cabins. But if we saddle up here and start riding we should get to the top by nightfall. The risk is that we'll be traveling light and more exposed if something bad happens."

Pederson nodded while he thought it over.

"Your call," Bull said to Pederson. "You're the sheriff."

Pederson looked to Cassie. "You've got to make the decision."

Before she could reply her phone went off again. Leslie again.

Cassie said, "Give me a moment to take this. If Leslie's calling this many times there must be something important to tell me."

There was only one bar of cell service and that would soon be gone. Cassie sighed and punched it up.

"Thank God you answered," Leslie said. The connection was scratchy and faint.

When Bull started to say something to Pederson, Cassie shushed him. Bull rolled his eyes in response.

"Where are you?" Leslie asked.

"Halfway up the mountain. It's hard to hear you."

". . . aren't the only people up there," Leslie said. The first part of the sentence was lost in the ether.

"Come again?" Cassie said.

"I said you aren't the only people up there going after the Lizard King."

Cassie heard it clearly this time but it didn't make sense.

". . . and his special operations team. They landed their plane in Bozeman and they're trying to nail Pergram on their own before you can find him."

"Who landed?" Cassie started to ask but stopped herself. Suddenly it made sense. "Are you saying Special Agent Craig Rhodine and his Critical Incident Response Group are here in Montana?

"Affirmative," Leslie said.

"How would he even know to be here?"

"My fault, I guess," Leslie said. "We kept North Dakota BCI in the loop as part of our task force like we should have. But from what I've been able to find out your old nemesis County Attorney Avery Tibbs has been in contact with the FBI every step of the way . . ."

A full ninety seconds of what Leslie said was garbled by poor reception. Cassie could clearly hear only a few words and phrases:

"Tibbs in cahoots . . .

"ATVs rented out of Bozeman . . .

"On their way . . .

"Get there first . . .

"Clusterfuck."

"I think I understand what you're telling me," Cassie broke in. Kirkbride's late night warning call to her in Ekalaka now made complete sense. "Do you have any idea where the feds and Tibbs are right now?"

"I only got part of that," Leslie said.

"WHERE ARE THEY?"

"On their way up the mountain to wherever you are headed."

Cassie closed her eyes. She said, "I don't care if they get there first. I could care less that they used me to figure it out. But if Kyle gets hurt in the process . . ."

"I'm sorry," Leslie said. "I can't . . ."

"Never mind," Cassie said. "Thank you, Leslie."

Cassie disconnected the call. She looked over to see Pederson and Bull studying her.

"So you got that," Cassie said.

"Kind of," Pederson said.

"An FBI hothead has been monitoring everything I've done to find Kyle and Pergram. My old county attorney has been feeding him everything that's happened with the joint task force. Both of those guys have it out for me because of what happened in Grimstad. And now they're up here somewhere."

"Where?" Pederson asked rhetorically. "They're not behind us and there are no tracks across that microburst."

"I'd guess they're coming up the other side," Bull said. "On those old roads I told you about."

"Will they get there first?" Cassie asked Bull.

"Hard to say. What are they driving?"

"Leslie said something about ATVs."

"Four-wheelers," Bull translated. "I guess it depends when they left and if they can figure out how to get to those cabins. Problem is, the cabins are hard to find and they're not on any maps. And even if they know where they are—like if they've got satellite images of them or something—they're not exactly going to sneak up on anyone inside riding those electric razors on wheels."

Cassie rubbed her eyes and bit her lip. Things were moving fast and she had no idea how to slow them down or regain control. She could visualize Rhodine and Tibbs roaring toward the poacher cabins. She tried not to visualize what Pergram would do if he heard them coming.

"So . . ." Bull said, looking to Pederson and Cassie for guidance.

"Let's go from here," Cassie said. Before Pederson could reason with her about it she was out the door.

"Mount up, boys," Bull said to Deputy Pompy and Deputy Thomsen. "We're burnin' daylight."

AFTER FORTY-FIVE MINUTES in the saddle, the adrenaline wore off and was replaced by an ache in her lower back and stabs of pain from her inner thighs. Gipper high-stepped through the downed trees and took elaborate routes around particularly thick ones. He wasn't blazing the trail but closely following Bull's gelding, and Gipper would patiently pause while Bull's mount negotiated the best way through the blowdown toward the wall of standing trees. Many times the horse had to backtrack and find a better approach. Cassie figured the horse knew better how to negotiate the microburst than she did, so she simply tried to hold on and keep her balance so she wouldn't be pitched out of the saddle by a sudden turn or acceleration.

"Slow goin'," Bull said as once again his horse stepped back when it encountered a tangle of trees too formidable to step over to find a new path around. "It's like two steps forward and one step back. But we're getting there."

She noted that as slow and lumbering as Bull Mitchell was on the ground, he was a different man when he was in the saddle. His movements were calm and economical, and his ability to shift his weight to aid the progress of his horse was subtle but impressive. *He is a man*, she thought, *who should always be on horseback*.

IT TOOK OVER AN HOUR to reach the outer border of the microburst. Gipper finally cleared the downed timber and he hopped forward onto a grassy patch with triumph. Cassie nearly lost her balance with the leap and she inadvertantly dropped both reins as she lunged for the saddlehorn. But once he was on flat mountain meadow, Gipper stood still.

Before she could lean forward along his neck and retrieve the reins Bull turned his horse, gathered them up, and handed them to Cassie.

"Don't lose those," he said with a wry grin. "Makes it hard to steer."

She snatched them back.

THE FIVE-HORSE EXPEDITION WALKED single file across the meadow until it was swallowed by the sea of dark pine. Bull led, followed by Cassie, Sheriff Pederson, Pompy, and Thomsen.

Cassie tried not to be miserable but it had been a long time since she'd been on a horse. And not just a trail horse shambling along nose-to-tail, but a working quarterhorse in mountain terrain. The pain numbed her and she tried not to think about it. Instead, she contemplated the team of Rhodine and Tibbs on the other side of the mountain with the same destination in mind.

She tried not to dwell on the fact that they'd used her the way they had. Not if the end result was taking down Pergram and rescuing Kyle. But the complete lack of respect they'd shown toward her, not even informing her they were tracking her investigation, saddened her. She'd rather have outright enemies than men who took her hard work for granted and exploited her.

It hurt.

THEY WERE HOURS DEEP into the dark timber and always ascending. The only sounds were chattering squirrels and the moan of tall trees that rubbed together in the breeze. The footfalls of the horses provided a soft thumping cadence to the journey.

Cassie learned that when she relaxed and sat back in the saddle, Gipper relaxed as well. She stroked his neck and told him he was a good horse.

As she sat back she was reminded that Gipper *was the horse Cody Hoyt rode into Yellowstone as well*. She wondered if Gipper had horse memories of her boss and mentor, or if he was just another fidgety dude on his back years before.

THE REALLY HARD PART was climbing off Gipper when they finally stopped for the night. Cassie was stiff from riding and she rubbed the hot spots on her inner thighs through her jeans. She gladly handed the reins to Pompy who'd offered to unsaddle Gipper and water him at a narrow mountain stream.

As the sun slid behind the western summits it got remarkably cooler. While the men had no problem simply turning away from her to urinate, Cassie had to make a quest of it. She walked away from the men and the horses into the lodgepole pines and didn't stop until she could no longer hear them. Along the way she tried to work the kinks out of her back and relax her shoulders. The ground felt solid beneath her boots and although she'd grown to appreciate Gipper, she was glad to be off him.

When she returned she noted that Sheriff Pederson had started a fire and Bull was unwrapping the steaks. A fifth of Jim Beam was perched on the top of of a tree trunk and it was already a quarter gone.

"Aren't you worried about him smelling the smoke?" she asked Bull.

"Naw. We're still a long way away. Besides, this is Yellowstone. There are all kinds of smells."

She sniffed and got a whiff of far-off sulfur. Pompy and Thomsen appeared from the pine forest with armfuls of firewood.

"What can I do to help?" she asked.

"You can brush down the horses," Bull said. "Do you know how to do that?"

It wasn't an unkind question. He didn't know she'd spent a lot of time around her grandfather's horses when she was growing up near Helena.

"I can do that," she said.

On the way to where the animals were picketed in a small mountain meadow she took a drink of the bourbon. It teared her eyes but in a good way.

"Do you have your gun?" Pederson asked her.

She shook her head. "In my saddlebag."

"I'd suggest you take it with you," the sheriff said. Then, raising his voice so his deputies could hear as well, he said, "I'd suggest we remain armed at all times from here on out. You never know who we'll run into—or who might run into us."

Cassie returned to where her saddle was draped over a downed tree and clipped her Glock in its holster to her waistband. He was right.

AFTER A DINNER of big steaks and canned pork and beans, Cassie sat on a saddle pad with her back against a tree and watched the fire from between her upraised knees. She'd forgotten how quickly it got cold high in the mountains, or how brilliant the stars were in the sky.

Although it was still early she fought against nodding off. Her sleeping bag was unfurled to her right and her weapon was within reach on top of it. They'd not packed tents because Bull had decided to leave them back at the blowdown to lighten the load as much as possible.

The men sat close to the fire and passed the bourbon back and forth. As she'd predicted, it didn't take long for them to start on elk hunting stories. Also as she'd predicted, Bull had the best ones.

Pederson appeared and sat down on her sleeping bag beside her.

"Why so quiet?" he asked.

"I don't have any hunting stories," she said. "And I'm bone tired."

"Riding all day will do that to you," he said. "Plus, I'd guess you have a lot on your mind."

"Knowing Rhodine and Tibbs are on the other side of the mountain doesn't give me a good feeling. And I keep thinking about Kyle. I can't even imagine what that poor kid is going through."

Pederson shook his head in agreement.

"Tonight is the first time I've not talked to my son Ben," she said. "He has no idea where I am or why I'm not calling."

"How old is he again?"

"Twelve."

There was a long pause. Pederson said, "I know you probably don't want to hear this, but a twelve-year-old boy is probably not pining for his mom as much as his mom is pining for him."

"You're right," she said. "I didn't want to hear that."

Pederson reached over and gently rubbed her shoulder with his hand.

"Try to shut all that off and get some sleep," he said. "We're only going to be here a few hours. Bull wants to be back on the trail by four-thirty at the latest. The idea is to find those old cabins and get into position before it gets light."

She liked the way he touched her and she wished he wouldn't have taken his hand away. Then she thought of Ian and there was a sharp pang of guilt. It got worse when she realized she hadn't thought of Ian in days.

CASSIE SLID INTO HER SLEEPING bag fully clothed. The stars were white and hard through the tree limbs and they seemed to penetrate her closed eyelids. The men were still telling hunting stories, but since the bottle was gone she guessed they wouldn't last much longer.

She couldn't remember the last time she'd gone to sleep without a shower. Her skin felt gritty and her hair greasy. She could smell her own breath inside the bag.

She thought of Ben, of Kyle, of Pergram. She made herself think of Ian but it didn't seem sincere and she wondered if she was a cold woman like some of her colleagues had whispered.

THEN SHE HEARD IT.

A distant, thundering *BOOM*.

She sat up without unzipping her bag.

"What in the hell was that?" Bull asked from somewhere on the other side of the dying fire.

"I heard it," Pompy said.

"Bigger than a gunshot," Thomsen added. "Much bigger."

They all were quiet, waiting for what came next. But the only sound was the echo of the singular explosion that moved through the timber like rolling thunder.

"Maybe we ought to get going sooner than we planned," Pederson said. "Like *now*."

TWENTY-EIGHT

RONALD PERGRAM'S EYES SHOT open at the sound of the explosion. He threw off his quilts and swung his feet out to the floor.

"What was that?" Amanda asked from the dark in the other room. "Ron, what was that sound? Ron, I thought I heard a—"

"*Hush,*" he whispered harshly.

He heard her make a squeaking sound. That's what she did when she forced herself to pinch off a torrent of babble. The woman talked like she didn't even know she was talking. She talked the way men breathed: unconsciously. He'd punished her for it with a vibration warning half a dozen times and several times with a shock. It had helped somewhat, except now when he told her to shut up she ended it with a squeak.

Kyle, bless him, knew to be quiet. If anything, Ron wished that boy would say *more.*

His knees ached and his back popped as he stood up. He pulled on socks, a pair of jeans, an undershirt, and a sweatshirt. He listened for another explosion to come but it didn't.

Amanda remained quiet although he knew it must be killing her.

Ron pulled on his trucker boots and clomped out of his small bedroom to the main room. Kyle was up, all right, and already dressed. He was riffling through the coats hanging on pegs near the door for the parka Ron had given him.

"Where do you think you're going, Kyle?"

The boy stopped and slowly turned around.

"You stay here."

Kyle looked down at his feet. He was obviously disappointed.

Ron watched the boy slink back to his single bed and sit down heavily on it. He felt something tug in his chest, something he had rarely experienced in his life: pride in the act of someone other than himself. That Kyle would wrongly assume he was going along to check out the explosion with him filled Ron with unexpected pride.

"Can I ask what we just heard?" Amanda asked in a low tone. She was so *meek*, Ron thought.

"You heard a shitload of C-4 being detonated," Ron said as he reached for his coat and watch cap from the pegs. "I'm going to find out what set it off. Could be an elk or a bear, I guess. Or it could have been someone coming up here to find us."

"Oh my," Amanda said.

"I doubt there's much of them left, whatever it was," Ron said while he seated a round into the chamber of his .380 and jammed the pistol into the back of his waistband.

Without another word he returned to his bedroom and located a headlamp in his "Oh Shit" box to take along. He paused in the main room and looked at Kyle. The boy refused to look back. Obviously, he'd hurt the kid's feelings.

Ron had no idea how to address it.

So he ignored Kyle and closed the outside door behind him. Then he snapped the padlock closed through the rungs.

It was cold but still. He guessed it was a degree or two above freezing.

He opened the door of the pickup and slid a shotgun out from beneath the front seat. It was a used 20-gauge Mossberg pump he'd bought at a pawn shop in Livingston. It was a dime-a-dozen kind of shotgun but he'd removed the plug from it so it could hold six double-aught shells instead of the three birdshot shells it was used to.

As he stepped back from the door he glanced up to see Kyle's face in the window over the sink. The boy wanted to see what he was doing out there.

Ron waved to Kyle in the light from the dome light.

Kyle waved back and Ron smiled to himself.

He shut the door and the night was black again. He fitted the headlamp over his watch cap and found the dimmest setting.

Then he followed the bouncing pale orb of light down the old two-track to where he'd heard the explosion.

KYLE WATCHED THE SMUDGE of light bob away until it vanished. His insides were in knots and he felt sick to his stomach.

He didn't realize Ron had a shotgun in the truck. The man kept his secrets well.

Kyle hoped the explosion hadn't hurt any well-meaning people who had come to rescue them. Had they seen his message in the grocery store restroom? Was that why they were in the mountains? Had he caused their deaths?

He stepped away from the window and closed his eyes and bent over and placed his hands on his knees and breathed deeply.

He thought about the possibility that the people who triggered the explosion were hurt or maimed. Wouldn't they be likely to tell Ron why they'd come? Wouldn't Ron *make* them tell?

From her bed Amanda said, "Well, I guess he thinks that he put you in your place, didn't he?"

Her tone was spiteful. Kyle didn't respond.

"You think you're his special little buddy now, don't you? But he put you right back in your place."

"I don't want to talk about it," he said.

She took a deep breath and said softly, "Be careful around him, Kyle. He seems to like you. He certainly likes you more than he likes me, anyway. But he's an evil man. Don't fall for it."

Kyle said, "I don't. I thought *you* were falling for it."

She wrung her hands and watched them. She said, "I admit there are times when saving myself and making him happy are the only things I think of. I admit that. I don't think I'd be human if I thought any other way. But I won't turn on you to save myself. I hope you know that and I hope you won't do that to me to gain his favor."

Kyle rose and looked hard at her. They'd been in the same boat for a long time. He wanted to think of her as his friend—as a wise and friendly adult. He wanted to trust her.

He said, "I'd never do that."

"I'm not gonna tell him you were watching his every move when he went outside," she said. "If he knew that he wouldn't be happy about that. He'd expect me to tell him what you're up to, you know."

She looked up. There was desperation in her eyes. "Please don't do anything that I can't tell him about, okay Kyle? It's like we talked about a long time ago. Don't do something that will get either of us hurt."

Kyle said, "Only you talked about that."

After a beat, she asked, "So what *are* you up to?"

CASSIE RODE WITH HER HEAD bent forward so when the branches reached out for her in the dark they wouldn't claw her face. The horses were nose-to-tail now and she'd learned to surrender her trust to both Gipper and Bull to lead them in the right direction.

They'd climbed up the mountain and were exposed briefly above the timberline before plunging back into the forest on the other side. The moon was as thin and pale as a fingernail clipping but the stars were bright and hard. She'd looked around her in the open to confirm that Pompy and Thomsen were right behind her.

They seemed to be on a game trail because they were no longer pushing through downed timber or meandering through the trees. She could see her breath in pale puffs and her fingers were cold.

The men didn't talk at all. Not that they should, but the fact they didn't drove home how serious it had become. She wished she could talk to Leslie and tell her what they were doing. It always felt good to talk things out.

But not now.

When they left the timber and found themselves in a starlit mountain meadow, Bull turned his horse to the side and stopped until everyone was accounted for. In the stark pale light the old man looked *tough*.

"How close are we?" she whispered to him.

"Couple of miles. We're close."

When they were gathered in the meadow and the condensation clouds puffed out and rose from both the men and their horses, Cassie leaned forward in her saddle to address them. She spoke softly.

"Remember, this is the guy who's killed dozens of women and never got caught. He faked his own death and wiped out some good men in my sheriff's department, including my fiancé. When we get close to those cabins we need to keep alert."

"For what?" Pompy asked.

"Booby traps—ambushes. I don't know."

Pederson said, "I think your friends might have already found one."

Cassie nodded.

"I can't see worth shit," Thomsen said.

"None of us can," Bull said. "What you need to do is keep all your senses wide open. Don't get keyed up and distracted. Look around you. Listen. Smell. Remember that he can't see shit either."

A half hour later the game trail merged onto a rough two-track. Pederson dismounted and shined a mini Maglight on the road. Cassie could see fresh tire tread tracks in his beam.

"Somebody's been up here, all right," Pederson said as he climbed back on his horse.

Bull led them right down the middle of the old road. Now that they didn't have to worry about the terrain or overhanging branches, they picked up speed.

RON FOLLOWED THE ORB of his headlamp down a different two-track. It was so dark that his world was only what he could see when he turned his head one way or other.

But he hadn't gone a half mile from the cabin when he gleaned an idea of what he would find further down the road. Acrid smoke—the smell that came from burning fuel and plastic—crept along the ground.

He no longer thought an animal had tripped his wire. No elk, moose, or bear would smell like that. He knew how animals smelled when they were set on fire because as a teenager he'd observed them. Animals smelled of burnt hair and fat, like grease. No, this smell was from burning vehicles.

Then the pleasant smell of pine. The kind of smell that came when a tree was split or felled. Or blown to pieces.

Ron rounded a long oxbow turn in the road and orange light

emerged through the trees in front of him. He reached up and choked his headlamp off. The light from the fire up ahead would be enough to see.

He paused and reached back to touch the grip of his pistol to assure himself it was there. Then he checked the loads in his shotgun and thumbed the safety off.

Then he cautiously walked ahead.

He was the Lizard King.

It was carnage. Mangled ATVs were thrown about like toys. Pieces of metal, plastic, and body parts flickered in the light of a gasoline fire from one of the four-wheelers. Lodgepole pines had been blown backwards exposing bright yellow-white fibrous breaks.

There were weapons, satellite phones, and clothing strewn about on the road. A boot with a man's severed foot still in it sat upright like a bowling trophy.

He paused and counted the destroyed ATVs. There were six of them.

Then he heard a grunt.

Ron stepped around a burning four-wheeler and saw a man on the ground crawling toward the dark timber on the side of the road. He was using only his hands in an awkward swimming motion to advance himself. His legs didn't seem to work. Blood glistened in the firelight on the back of his jacket.

Broken spine, Ron guessed.

He looked around to see if there were other survivors. He saw none. The fires crackled.

Then he approached the crawling man and stopped his progress by pinning down the man's boot with his own.

"Hold up there, son."

The wounded man looked back over his shoulder. His face was pale and his eyes were wide and scared. He was wearing outdoor clothing and tactical gear that looked straight out of the box. He had a nice haircut and bright white teeth. Ron checked to see if the man was armed and he appeared not to be.

"Who are you?"

"Nobody," the man said.

That told Ron everything he needed to know. The wounded man was evasive, meaning he was up there to find *him*. Otherwise, he'd have asked for help. Plus, he was scared because he knew who had asked him the question.

Ron kept his boot on the man's leg so he couldn't move and he bent over to fish a wallet out of his cargo pants. He lit up his headlamp and flipped the wallet open.

"Avery Tibbs of Grimstad, North Dakota. You're a long way from home. What is it you do there?"

"Please . . ."

"Please what? I asked you a question."

The man looked over his shoulder and said, "I'm the county attorney."

"Ah."

"Look," Tibbs said, "I have a lot of discretion. I have a lot of power. I won't prosecute you if you let me go. In fact, I'll vouch for your humanitarian instincts if you can get me to a hospital. I can't feel my legs right now."

"Really," Ron said. "All that?"

"I just want to get home. I shouldn't even be here. This agent from the FBI dragged me here despite my better judgment. He's dead now, so we can make a deal."

"You'd make a deal with me?"

"Absolutely. Of course. The only reason I'm here is because of Agent Rhodine and someone named Cassie Dewell. I'm just following up on a local problem. So if we can come to an agreement I can promise you you'll walk. I mean, you aren't responsible for this debacle, are you? We just blindly drove into it."

Ron closed the wallet and stuffed it into his jacket pocket. The pocket was still filled with Tiffany's collar so fitting the wallet in was difficult.

He said, "You lawyers always think you can talk yourself out of everything."

"That's not the right way to look at it," Tibbs said quickly. "Not the right way at all. Look—we can decide who to prosecute and what to ignore. I'm a fucking master at ignoring things. We can spin this so you *rescued* me . . ."

"So you're telling me the law is flexible?" Ron asked.

"Absolutely it is," Tibbs nodded.

"Then that means there is no right or wrong."

"Not in a court of law."

Ron lowered the shotgun and shot Tibbs in the head.

CASSIE SNAPPED AROUND at the sound of the gunshot. It had come from somewhere through the trees to their right.

Pompy whispered, "That sounded pretty close."

She nodded although she doubted she could be seen in the dark.

Gipper slowed to a stop and she realized Bull had halted in front of her. The five horses stacked up.

Bull turned and nodded toward Sheriff Pederson and both men stepped down out of their saddles. Cassie wasn't sure what they were doing.

Bull approached her and put his hand on her knee and she bent toward him.

"Look, we're close to those cabins now so I think we should dismount and go the rest of the way on foot. Let's tie up the horses here."

She nodded and stepped into the left stirrup and swung her right leg over the cantle. It seemed like a long way down to the ground. Bull took Gipper's reins and led the horse away, and she bent and roughly massaged her legs to get feeling back in them.

Pompy and Thomsen soon joined her. She heard the soft *snick-snick* of Thomsen arming his AR-15.

Pederson whispered to the three of them, "Bull and I are going ahead to scout. Stay here until we come back."

"You sure?" Thomsen asked.

"We want to make sure we're in the right place," Pederson said.

It was a long five minutes before they returned, Cassie thought. The cold seeped into her and she tried to ward away a tremble that was half from being chilled and half from being scared.

When she heard the crunch of a footfall in the forest she drew her Glock out of the holster and gripped it with two hands, muzzle down.

"Okay," Pederson whispered from the trees ahead. "We found the cabin. There's a light on inside."

The sheriff stepped closer.

"Spread out and walk real carefully," he said. "There are empty cans tied up by wires across the game trails. I almost walked right into one. So go real slow and watch out for trip wires. Push through the brush and stay away from game trails.

"Now lock and load. And no talking. When you see the cabin get behind cover and wait. Sooner or later someone will come outside and then we can move on them."

It made sense, she thought. There was no reason to announce their presence and create the opportunity for a hostage situation or give Pergram an excuse to execute Kyle.

So she waited until Thomsen and Pompy moved away from her in opposite directions and she slowly stepped forward. As she entered the thick trees she glanced down constantly looking for the glint of wire or string in the starlight.

Although she couldn't yet see the cabin she could pick up indications of it up ahead: the smell of woodsmoke, cooking smells that clung to the brush.

Then a single yellow square in the darkness.

She thumped against a downed pine tree and followed its trunk to the upturned roots and settled in behind it. When she raised up she could see the yellow square of the lighted window through a *V* of the broken roots.

"YOU'RE NOT SUPPOSED to get in there," Amanda said to Kyle with rising alarm. "He'll know. And he'll know I know."

"Amanda, *shhhhh*," Kyle said.

He was retrieving Ron's metal "Oh Shit" box from under his bed.

"I'll have to tell him," Amanda said with panic. "You know I'll have to tell him, Kyle."

"*Shhhhh.*"

"Don't shush me!"

She went on but Kyle ignored her. He worked the clasp and the metal lid hinged back. Like he suspected there were no weapons, just an old-fashioned videodisc player and dozens of DVDs in plastic jewel cases. Ron's collection of Ron doing things to women back in the day.

Then he found what he was looking for.

Kyle drew out the remote control device with the red dot on it. It corresponded with Tiffany's collar. Kyle turned it on and hung it around his neck.

Amanda's face turned mean. "What have you got there? Kyle— what the hell are you doing? You're going to get us both killed."

RON THOUGHT HE HEARD a horse snort somewhere up ahead of him in the trees. He stopped and listened but he didn't hear it again. He wondered if it could have been an elk or moose.

Surely Tibbs and his gang hadn't sent others up the mountain as well?

It didn't make sense.

But there was no doubt he likely had just a few hours to pack up and get off the mountain for good. They'd found him and they'd send more men once it was daylight.

It was over.

Sorry, Amanda. She was too much baggage to take along. His second family had been much better than his first—but still not good enough. It was possible they could become what he wanted but there wasn't enough time to make it happen anymore.

Although he did like how Kyle had shown eagerness to go with him an hour before. He found himself getting attached to that boy but he couldn't trust him completely yet.

Maybe he *should* have let Kyle come along? The kid could have put down that lawyer. Then Ron would know for sure if Kyle would develop into who he wanted him to be.

KYLE SAW THE HEADLAMP strobing through the trees in the direction Ron had gone.

"Here he comes," he said.

"I'm going to tell him, Kyle," Amanda said with her hands on her hips. "He's gonna see that thing around your neck."

"Amanda, please."

"I'm gonna . . ."

Kyle said, "I turned on Tiffany's collar."

Amanda stared at him, uncomprehending.

"When I went to grab my parka I reached into the pocket of his coat and turned on her collar."

"Oh my God," she said. He couldn't tell if she was scared or relieved.

CASSIE HEARD FOOTFALLS and saw a splash of light on the trunks of the trees to the right of the cabin.

Then a dark form with a headlamp.

Was it him?

She raised her weapon and rested it in the crux of the *V.* She could barely see the fluorescent dots on the front and back sights but she lined them up and aimed them center mass.

Should she let the man just walk up to the cabin and go inside? Could the others see him?

Then a horse whinnied back in the trees.

RON STOPPED TWENTY FEET from the front door of the cabin.

That time, it was a goddamned horse for sure.

He reached up and turned off his headlamp.

Then he was bathed in the bright white beam of a flashlight. It came from the trees to his left.

He broke into a run toward the cabin door.

A woman's voice shouted, "Facedown in the dirt, you son of a bitch! Facedown!"

KYLE HEARD A SHOUT from outside. He looked out the window and saw Ron coming.

He raised the remote and pressed vibrate.

Ron froze a few feet from the door and looked down at his coat pocket.

Kyle said, "That's right."

CASSIE LEANED OVER THE UPROOTED pine tree with her Glock aimed at Pergram. She hesitated to fire because she didn't want stray rounds to penetrate the wall and hit someone inside. And he'd stopped. He was just standing there looking down at his waist.

"Get down on the ground," Pederson yelled from the dark. It had been his flashlight.

Cassie could see Pergram's face in quarter profile. He'd raised his eyes toward the cabin, toward a face in the window.

Kyle.

Pergram slowly shook his head like he'd been betrayed.

But instead of raising his hands or dropping down, he turned toward Cassie. The muzzle of his shotgun swung up.

BANG.

The shotgun dropped out of his hands and Pergram staggered to his left. His coat was blown open into shards and his entrails tumbled out like a nest of uncoiled snakes.

He fell to his knees and toppled over, but not before turning his head one more time toward Kyle in the window.

KYLE HAD NEVER SEEN THAT expression on Ron's face before. It was half surprise and half bitter resignation that he'd been betrayed yet *again*. When the man slumped to the ground out of view his after-image remained as well as his *what-have-you-done-to-me* eyes.

"What you did to Raheem," Kyle answered. "And Tiffany."

He looked up to see several men emerge from the forest with their long guns aimed at Ron's body. With them was a woman he recognized instantly.

CASSIE DUCKWALKED TOWARD PERGRAM with her arms outstretched, gripping and pointing the gun in her hands. She couldn't see if Pergram had another weapon but she sensed movement from him. She had no idea what had happened to him.

Had he tried, once again, to blow himself up? Did he just detonate some kind of suicide belt?

When Pergram grunted and attempted to rise she stopped ten feet away. He reached for a grip on the log wall to try and pull himself up.

That's when he looked over and saw her for the first time. His eyes met hers and widened with recognition and then revulsion.

She said, "*It's me,*" and she fired. The muzzle flash lit him up orange and she glimpsed his face. He was enraged. He'd thought he'd killed her in Grimstad and here she was.

She didn't stop pulling the trigger until the slide locked back on her Glock because the magazine was empty. She'd fired all ten rounds.

Pergram's body lay still. She could smell blood, viscera, and gunpowder. Her ears rang from the multiple concussions of her weapon.

She felt a firm hand on her shoulder. Pederson.

"He moved. I thought he was going for his gun."

"I saw it," Pederson said. "It was a righteous shooting."

She didn't believe he'd seen anything but it was good enough.

"Damn, Cassie," Bull said with undisguised amazement from the dark. "*Damn.*"

TWENTY-NINE

LOTTIE WAS THE LAST PASSENGER from the plane to appear at the top of the escalator in the Bozeman Yellowstone airport. She looked tiny, frail, and confused. She hesitated to take the first step to descend.

Ben was right behind her with Isabel and when he saw Cassie at the foot of the stairs he waved frantically. Isabel looked annoyed about something, as she so often did.

Cassie's heart filled at the sight of her son and when he descended she hugged him until he was struggling to get free.

"IT JUST DIDN'T make any sense," Lottie said from the backseat of Cassie's Escape. "We flew the wrong way at first to Minneapolis, then we had to get on another plane and fly back across North Dakota to get to Montana. It just doesn't seem like a very efficient way to run an airline to me."

Cassie smiled into the rearview mirror. "First time on a plane?"

"Yes."

"Me too," Ben said. "But I thought it was great. The mountains looked so cool when we came in to land."

Isabel said, "I'm missing the closing on our homeless shelter."

"Really?" Cassie said, impressed.

"Where do you think your determination to get things done comes from?" Isabel asked, her eyes fierce.

AS CASSIE DROVE east on I-90 toward town Ben said, "You got him." He was beaming.

"We got him," Cassie echoed. She still had trouble wrapping her mind around it. Ronald Pergram was a monster but he'd died like a dog. If she could kill him again, she thought, she would.

And as if to remind her that the Lizard King had spent so many years free and on the highway, a black eighteen-wheel tractor-trailer with a Peterbilt cab roared past them in the left lane.

"I heard the sheriff got his job back," Isabel said to Cassie.

"He did. The commissioners offered it back to him to finish out his term."

She didn't say that Kirkbride had called with congratulations on rescuing Kyle and Amanda and taking the Lizard King down once and for all. He'd said, "You did it, Cassie. You got him. You've been exonerated!"

Then he asked her to come back and resume her career as chief investigator in the department and, he hoped, take over when he retired officially.

She told him thank you but she'd have to think about it.

"AND KYLE'S OKAY?" Lottie asked.

"He's being evaluated in the hospital." After a beat, she said, "Physically, he seems okay."

"I can't wait to see him and hear all about it," Ben said.

"He might not want to talk about it right away," Cassie said. "Kyle has seen things. Ben, he might not be the Kyle you remember."

"He'll be Kyle," Ben said as if he knew something she didn't.

Which maybe he did, Cassie thought.

"I still don't know why you didn't just bring him back," Isabel said to Cassie.

"I told you," Cassie said. "Kyle needs to be evaluated and give a sworn statement. I'm scheduled to give more statements to Montana law enforcement myself to wrap things up. So I thought it would be better for you to come here until we're done and so Lottie could see Kyle with her own eyes."

"Still . . ." Isabel grumbled.

SHERIFF PEDERSON WAS WAITING for them in the lobby of the hospital with Rachel Mitchell and Bull. Cassie introduced them to Lottie, Isabel, and Ben.

"So you're Ben," Pederson said to him. "How do you like Montana so far?"

"I like it," Ben said. Then he looked carefully from Pederson to Rachel to Cassie. He'd picked up something in the interaction between Cassie and Pederson that obviously intrigued him.

"I think we might be here a while," she said.

Ben grinned. He liked the idea.

Isabel looked around and said, "Maybe they could use me around here," meaning either Bozeman or all of Montana itself, Cassie wasn't sure.

"Follow me," Cassie said. "Let's go see Kyle."

As she led them through the lobby she looked over to see Amanda Lee Hackl and her husband Harold eating lunch alone at a table in the cafeteria. Amanda wore a robe and fuzzy slippers and she seemed to be staring at something over the top of Harold's head. Harold was busy attacking a plate of fried fish.

She looked lost. He looked hungry.

WHEN KYLE HEARD the elevator chime at the end of the hall he looked up from what he was doing. Voices—Grandma Lottie, Sheriff Pederson—filled the silence. Footsteps—a lot of them—echoed on the tile.

He was excited to see Grandma Lottie again and he was sorry for what he'd put her through. Cassie was always great to see.

He glanced quickly at the list he'd been working on. He could write it from memory.

Sleeping bag
Food
Fishing poles and tackle
Rain coat
Binoculars
Pistol or rifle
Journal for writing

He quickly closed the notebook cover and slid it behind him under his pillow.

As far as Kyle was concerned evil was all around and he'd experienced too much of it. It would be easy to go that route, like slipping off a log. But good was all around as well. It was harder but he knew now that was the direction he wanted to go. It helped that the people coming down the hallway were good and they cared about him.

Theodore Roosevelt had done it after his adventure on the river. So would *he*.

Kyle would finish the list when his visitors were gone. And he'd talk to Ben about joining him this time. He knew Ben also wanted to see America.

They'd name their boat *Raheem*.

ACKNOWLEDGMENTS

The author would like to sincerely thank Sheriff Scott Busching of Williams County, North Dakota, for his previous assistance, experience, wisdom, and expertise. Thanks also to Dallas Carlson and Fred Walker for their sharp North Dakota insight. The author would like to once again thank Butch and Dana Preston of Montana, two wonderful long-haul truck drivers, for technical assistance.

My invaluable first readers were Laurie Box, Becky Reif, Molly Donnell, and Roxanne Woods. Thanks again.

Kudos to Molly and Prairie Sage Creative for cjbox.net, Jennifer Fonnesbeck for social media expertise and merchandise sales, and Becky Reif for legal advice and terminology.

It's a sincere pleasure to work with the professionals at St. Martin's Minotaur, including the fantastic Jennifer Enderlin, Andy Martin, Hector DeJean, and the incomparable Sally Richardson.

Ann Rittenberg, thanks for always being in our corner.

**Beyond roads, beyond streetlights, beyond backup...
Welcome to Joe Pickett's beat**

'Exhilarating' *Sunday Times*

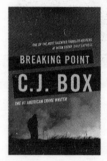

Joe Pickett – 13

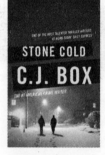

Joe Pickett – 14

Joe Pickett – 15

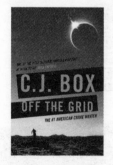

Joe Pickett – 16

Joe Pickett – 17

Cassie Dewell – 1   Cassie Dewell – 2   Cassie Dewell – 3

Cassie Dewell tracks a killer

'Heart-stoppingly good' *Daily Mail*

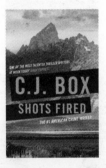

Short stories from Joe Pickett country

'Solid-gold A-list must-read' LEE CHILD